D1560124

The Alpha's
TEMPORARY MATE

a *Fated Match* novel

VICTORIA DAVIES

Entangled Publishing, LLC
2614 South Timberline Road
Suite 109
Fort Collins, CO 80525
Visit our website at www.entangledpublishing.com.

Covet is an imprint of Entangled Publishing, LLC.

Edited by Candace Havens
Cover design by Louisa Maggio
Cover art from iStock

Manufactured in the United States of America

First Edition November 2015

To my wonderful sister who is always willing to help me brainstorm ideas or proofread scenes. Thank you for all your love and support.

Chapter One

"Not a chance."

The man before her arched one dark brow. "I believe you should check with your boss before refusing my offer."

"I don't need to. Despite whatever misconceptions you harbor about this agency, we are in the business of finding *true* love, not the kind you can rent by the hour."

Anger curled through Chloe as she watched a slow smile cross the werewolf's face. Obviously he was not a man well acquainted with refusal.

Every now and then, men of his ilk crossed the threshold of Fated Match, New York's premier supernatural dating agency. They were on the lookout for a casual encounter that would lead to nothing more serious than an obligatory breakfast. And while she didn't like to judge other people's life choices, she'd spent years working to make this agency a success. That success was grounded in the company's mission to match mates. They strove to find that one person their clients had spent lifetimes waiting for—a fated match that would make eternity far easier to bear.

Chloe was in the business of lasting, permanent love, and she'd seen enough of men to know the wolf before her was more likely to run in the opposite direction of his mate than commit to an eternity with her.

Such a pity. Her boss had been on the hunt for another high profile client, and the werewolf community had been just as hard to crack as the vampire population. With several vamp matches already feathering her cap, Vivian was eager to add a few wolves to her roster. Bringing in a pack alpha like this one would almost guarantee a healthy bonus in Chloe's future.

Though she had to admit, an expanding bank account had not been her first thought when the wolf had entered her office.

She was used to meeting powerful supernaturals, given the nature of her work, but this alpha had seemed to fill the small room. His power had brushed along her skin like a physical caress as he folded his massive frame into the baby-pink chair across from her desk. The juxtaposition had brought a smile to her face that she'd quickly tried to hide. If ever a man had looked out of place in her feminine office, it'd been Kieran Clearwater. The wolf brought visions of ruthless battles and tangled sheets to mind, not the dainty pink and silver accents that decorated all Fated Match offices.

Not that he looked ill at ease. Chloe doubted much rattled him. Folding his hands on her white desk, he leaned forward and fixed his unblinking stare on her.

"You really ought to run this by your boss," he said again, an edge of boredom tingeing the command.

Chloe allowed a tight smile to twist her lips. "Mr. Clearwater, let me see if I understand you correctly. You are not here to register for our services. You have no interest in the usual dating package complete with scheduled introductions and access to our substantial internet database of singles."

"Correct."

"Instead, you'd like me to find you a temporary lover."

A grin flashed over his face, causing her heart to hammer once more. "Perfect."

"No."

"Sweetheart, the Clearwater pack is not without resources. Name your price and I'll write you a check."

Chloe clenched her fists under the table and did her best to exude calm disapproval. "Our clients are members of the supernatural community looking for love. They come to us with the understanding that anyone they meet is just as serious about forever as they are. We are not a procurement agency. If that's what you're looking for I'd recommend trying a one eight-hundred number."

There was no mistaking the mockery that flared in his eyes. "Do I look like I'm in need of such a hotline?"

No. The damn man probably walked into a bar, snapped his fingers, and had women willing to follow him anywhere.

The supernatural community had an advantage over humans when it came to physical beauty. Hell, most of her girlfriends were mated to men that rivaled gods, and the wolf before her was no different. Kieran could easily have walked into any modeling agency in the world and wound up on a magazine cover. His auburn hair curled around his ears, with a cowlick falling across his forehead that her fingers itched to brush away. Equally dark eyes focused on her with a sharp awareness that told her Kieran wasn't a man who missed much.

He had the full lips and high cheekbones many women would envy—not that anything about him was the least bit feminine. Especially not when one's gaze dropped below the breathtaking face.

As a species, wolves tended to be larger and more

muscular than many of the other races, and this alpha was no exception. His black T-shirt stretched across a massive chest she wished she could run her fingers over. Thank God his leather jacket hid a more detailed view or she wouldn't have been able to form a single sentence about work. There was only so much one witch could take, after all.

Long legs encased in dark-washed denim folded beneath her desk, and Chloe had fought the urge more than once to shift her own legs to brush against his. Were they standing, she doubted she'd reach much higher than his shoulder. The thought sent a shiver of awareness down her spine. Given her own height, few men could make her feel small.

But his striking looks only made his request that she set him up with a temporary girlfriend all the more bizarre. Surely a man like Kieran needed no help finding a lover.

"I regret that we are unable to help you, Mr. Clearwater. Now if you please, I have another appointment to get to."

Instead of looking chagrined or taking her hint to leave, Kieran leaned forward. "Do you know much about wolves?"

Chloe blinked. "I'm well versed in all the species we represent."

"Then you know all about the mating moon."

When her hesitation gave her away, his knowing smile widened.

"The mating moon," he instructed, filling in the gaps in her knowledge, "occurs one night a year, when newly coupled wolves go before the clan and make their intentions to one another clear. Once they've made their announcement, pairs are considered mated."

"Like a wolf wedding," she mused.

"Precisely. Some couples are together for years, lifetimes even, but without an announcement on a mating moon they are not recognized as truly mated."

"Interesting custom, but I don't see where Fated Match

fits in."

"This year's mating moon is a month away."

Chloe met his dark gaze. "So?"

"So, my pack is pressuring me to participate."

She shrugged. "Congratulations."

A low growl rumbled from his throat, raising the hairs on the back of her neck. "I have no desire for a mate. Managing one of the largest wolf packs on the East Coast is enough of a hassle without throwing a woman into the mix."

"Then again I say, you are in the wrong building."

"What I need," he continued, ignoring her interruption, "is a decoy. My pack wants to see that I'm committed to someone, that I'm not spinning out into lone wolf territory, which would leave them vulnerable to an enemy clan. Unfortunately, tensions are naturally high around the mating moon, and as pack creatures, that heightened unease has started to cause ripples through my community. I need a woman who will pretend to be my lover to get me through the mating moon so that my pack doesn't start questioning our security or my leadership."

Chloe's jaw dropped.

"As long as she's not a wolf, I can use the excuse of our cultural differences to avoid any announcement," Kieran said. "We'll part ways after the danger is past, a tragic case of insurmountable barriers tearing us apart."

"And you came here because…?"

He shrugged. "I can't use any of the women among my current acquaintances, or the charade would never hold up. I need a stranger who will play a part and then disappear. You are a dating agency. Surely you can find a woman to fit my needs."

"You want to buy a temporary lover."

His sharp eyes flicked to her. "I want to buy a temporary girlfriend. I have no need to pay for sex. Write that into the contract if you wish. Along with an ironclad non-disclosure agreement."

"This is so not happening," she replied. "You need to leave."

Kieran heaved a long sigh. "Then, my apologies, but you've wasted enough of my time." He stood, his chair scraping against the tiled floor.

He crossed to her door and stepped out into the hall.

"Who is in charge of this agency?" he bellowed.

Chloe gasped, surging to her feet.

"You cannot simply roar your way into getting what you want!" she declared, tugging him by the arm back into her office. Glancing down the hall she saw shocked faces looking their way from the agency's waiting room. "Did you misplace your manners along with your sense when you came in here?"

Amusement colored his expression as he stared down at her. "You might be cute, little witch, but I'm a busy man. I need your supervisor immediately."

Chloe's brain was still trying to catch up with the unexpected compliment when Vivian appeared in the doorway.

"I believe someone was trying to get my attention," the siren said.

Her tough as nails boss was not usually a figure that inspired comfort, but at the moment, Chloe didn't think she'd ever been happier to see the slender woman. Like most of her race, she possessed a beauty that would drive men to their doom. Long silver hair cascaded to her waist, though today it was pulled back into a tight braid. As always, Vivian chose clothes of silver and white to cover her lithe form. Designer, of course. The image she presented was as striking as it was ethereal. There was a reason sirens were much sought after.

Of course, desired or not, you still had to be careful about their voices. Chloe had once made the mistake of taking

Vivian to karaoke and she, along with the rest of the bar, had spent the remainder of the night worshiping the ground her boss walked on.

But even though Vivian was driven to succeed no matter the cost, the woman still had some tightly held morals, and Kieran buying a woman would cross all her lines.

"Vivian Sands," she said to Kieran, holding out her hand.

"Kieran Clearwater."

Vivian's eyes widened at the easily recognizable name. Chloe tried not to flinch at the accusation in her blue gaze when it turned her way. A client of Kieran's standing should have been passed along to Vivian herself, but she'd been busy and Chloe had made the call to handle the intake herself.

Not a mistake she'd repeat again.

"I've come to your agency with a unique set of requirements," Kieran said. Before Chloe could jump in, he laid out the same information he'd just finished telling her.

Chloe listened to the story once more, still having a hard time believing he wanted them to find some poor woman to be his beard for the next month.

"I've already told him it's out of the question," Chloe said when he finished.

Vivian nodded. "I'm inclined to agree. This agency has been matching mates since 1704. We have a reputation to uphold, and this sort of request goes against our mission. Now, should you wish to locate your mate for real, we'd be more than happy to assist you."

Instead of looking discouraged, Kieran merely took a piece of paper from the inside pocket of his jacket and handed it to Vivian.

Chloe leaned closer to her boss as she unfolded the offering.

"That's a lot of zeros," she breathed as she stared at the check.

"I am serious when I say I want to avoid being mated to someone of my pack's choosing, and that's the way tensions are headed," Kieran said. "That check represents your agency's payment. On top of that amount, I'm happy to pay whatever the woman you find for me wishes, to compensate her for her time and trouble."

Vivian's eyes had not left the substantial check. Chloe could almost hear her able mind whirling through all the possibilities.

"Not enough?" Kieran asked silkily. "I'm happy to write one for whatever fee you require, if you can ensure absolute secrecy and a top notch candidate."

"Vivian," Chloe hissed.

The siren blinked and glanced her way. "Please excuse us for a moment, Mr. Clearwater, while I confer with my associate." Grabbing her arm, Vivian steered them both down the hall and into her personal office.

Chloe didn't bother to glance at the icy wonderland she'd just entered. The office was easily thrice the size of hers, decorated in silver from the shimmering wallpaper to the massive metal desk to the trimmings on all the colorless furniture.

"You cannot be considering this," Chloe said.

Vivian sighed. "I agree it's an unorthodox request, but this is serious money here." She waved the check.

"We do an excellent business. We don't need his bribery."

"Normally I'd toss him out but you know I've been considering expansion for a while now."

"The West Coast office?" Chloe asked, brightening. If Fated Match expanded to other locations, Vivian would have to move with them to ensure the offices were each started up and managed properly. That would leave their New York agency without a leader, and as the longest-standing employee on record, Chloe would be perfect for the job.

"That caught your interest," Vivian said. "That money could help fund our new office…leaving this one open for new management."

The trap snapped shut around her. The siren was nothing if not ruthless when it came to getting what she wanted, and she saw no problem with dangling people's hopes and dreams before them like carrots to ensure the behavior she desired.

"We'll write up the contract," Vivian continued. "Make it magically binding. You can do that easily enough. All participants will be sworn to silence and there will be no chance of our reputation being tarnished. Plus, once completed, we'll have the capital to grow our business."

"I still think it's a terrible idea."

"Enough to give up your dreams of running this office?"

Chloe hesitated. She didn't like Kieran using his wealth to force them to serve up some woman to him on a platter. But did she object enough to jeopardize her life's goal?

"This city is full of women who will jump at the chance to be a powerful man's arm candy for a few weeks for fair compensation. We can add a no sex clause to the contract if you feel strongly enough about it. Make sure everything is above board and fairly handled," Vivian said. "Think of the opportunity, Chloe."

She was. Oh, how she was.

"If I agree to this," she said, not even believing the words were coming out of her mouth, "you will sign a contract as well, naming me as the acting manager of this office upon the opening of a subsequent Fated Match location. This agency will be mine."

"Under my brand umbrella," Vivian agreed. "We'll have to work out the breakdown of profits and what percentage will be owed to me."

"Agreed."

The siren inclined her head. "You have a deal. Make

Kieran happy and New York is yours."

Chloe arched a brow. "You don't want to oversee this yourself?"

"You'll be just as invested as I, and I need the time to put all the wheels in motion to move on. I hear Seattle might be a good place to set up shop."

She chewed her lip, thinking about the beautiful alpha in her office. All she had to do was find him a gold-digger that met his specification. She already had a few names she could put on the list.

"Fine," she capitulated. "I'll do it."

A cool smile crossed Vivian's face. "Excellent. As long as we do well by Kieran, he'll do well by us. And really, how hard is it to keep one werewolf happy?"

Chapter Two

"You are impossible to please."

Kieran merely grinned as he reached for the file Chloe had tossed onto the desk between them. "I just know what I want," he replied.

The words were true enough. He'd never been one to take second best. He decided on a target and pursued his goal until it reached fruition. The tactic had served him well in both his professional and private life, and he saw no reason to change now.

Not even for the witch fuming before him.

He supposed he should give her credit for doing her best. She had, after all, come up with a handful of potential candidates to introduce him to. They'd made each one sign a non-disclosure agreement before explaining his plan, and much to his matchmaker's obvious annoyance, not one of the women he'd met had been put off by the proposed ruse. And why would they be? In his experience, few women would turn down an all expenses paid girlfriend vacation and a month spent on his arm.

"Hopefully your candidate today will be a more viable option than your previous attempts," he said, flipping open the file to stare at a photo of an icy blonde beauty.

"Your dreamboat quotient takes a serious beating every time we speak," Chloe grumbled.

His lips twitched. Usually he wasn't one to tolerate the slightest disrespect, particularly from those in his employ, but there was something oddly charming about the little witch and her moral outrage.

It probably helped that her disapproval came encased in a sexy bombshell of a body. He'd known the second he'd stepped into her office the first time that she was going to be trouble. She'd been at her desk, dressed in a prim black business suit that did nothing to highlight the fairness of her coloring. Then she'd looked up at him, and he'd fallen into a green gaze that made him think of cool glades and spring forests. Her golden hair had been pulled back into a loose bun that had allowed a few stubborn locks to pull free to frame her heart-shaped face. His fingers had itched to brush those tresses away from her creamy skin.

When she'd stood to come toward him, his wolf had whined in its need to touch her. A firm handshake had been nowhere near enough contact, especially not after she turned back to her desk, giving him a chance to rake his gaze over her curvy body. He'd never understood modern sentiment that said women had to be all skin and bones. Chloe was anything but, and for that he was grateful. He'd far rather roll through the sheets with his hands full of generous curves than be on guard for pointy bones.

"You'll need to be on your best behavior today," she said, oblivious to the salacious trail of his thoughts.

"No promises."

Chloe stopped rifling through her papers and pinned him with an annoyed stare. "The woman you are going to meet is one of the fey. Aoife is perfect for you. She's powerful in her own right and would never consider a mate binding other than the traditional ritual her people use, which plays perfectly into your plan. But one thing sure to have her walking out the door is rudeness. You know how prickly the fey can be."

"So you'd like me to rein myself in and be a charming rogue?"

"I'd prefer a professional gentleman." Her eyes scanned over him before she added, "Or as close as you can get."

His inner wolf let out a yip of pleasure. It had taken a liking to Chloe's personal brand of spunk.

"Let's hope this woman is worth the effort. Not that the last two were."

"They were perfect," she said defensively. "You, on the other hand, are just too choosey."

"The dryad was as flighty as a feather. Could you imagine me taking her into the woods? She'd spend the time talking to trees and sleeping under bushes."

"She was lovely and kind."

"And I need strong and deadly. My people aren't exactly cuddly, Chloe, and the woman I bring into the pack will be tested and scrutinized. They won't want to believe a non-wolf is good enough for their alpha." Whomever he took into the woods needed to be strong enough to handle his overly protective pack. It would take a special woman to make his plan a success.

"That's just narrow-minded prejudice," Chloe said with a wave of her hand.

A grin crossed his face. "Fair enough. But you have to admit, not every species is up to competing with werewolves. We tend to be more…demanding of our lovers."

Pink blossomed high on her cheeks, and with fascination he watched the blush spread. The immortal before him had to be rather young to still be rattled by such talk. Those longer into eternity tended to be far more jaded and worldly.

Her gaze never dropped from his, despite her heated cheeks. "Have you ever stopped to think perhaps the problem is you? With your people's reputation for being rough around the edges, maybe these women are looking for something you just can't offer, no matter how deep your pockets?"

"A woman my checkbook can't sway? Show me such a creature and I'll marry her."

Chloe rolled her eyes, unaware his words were probably the most serious ones he'd ever exchanged with her. In his experience, there was very little in the world money couldn't buy.

"Lucky for you, Aoife is just as cold and practical as you are. I'm sure the two of you will have a lovely future together."

As if summoned by her words, a knock sounded at the door.

Brushing past him, Chloe opened the door to admit the fey beauty waiting on the other side.

"Aoife, so nice of you to come."

The lithe woman, dressed head-to-toe in Dior, smiled as she stepped into the office. "I'd never refuse you anything, Chloe. You know that."

Chloe closed the door as Aoife took her seat beside him. He examined the fey's long blonde hair and pixie-perfect features. She was striking to be sure. Aoife met his gaze with a calm self-assurance that told him she probably had the backbone to do fine with his rough and tumble pack. Still, there was something about the woman that made his wolf whine in complaint.

Taking her seat, Chloe slid the non-disclosure agreement to the other woman. "Before we move forward, you'll need to sign this document I spoke to you about."

"Of course." The fey signed her name with an elegant flourish before tucking a stray lock behind her delicately pointed ears. "Now, want to fill me in on the particulars?"

He stayed quiet as Chloe described the situation, using the time to allow his gaze free rein to take in the woman before him. Stunning, powerful, perfect. What was it he was objecting to?

"I think I understand," Aoife said when Chloe finished. "I have no objections to playing this role, though I do have several questions. My work is my top priority, so I'm sure you can understand if that takes precedence over a fake relationship."

"Of course." Chloe was quick to agree. "We want to impact your life as little as possible. For the next few weeks you'd be in the city and able to conduct your life as usual. All that would change is the need to spend several evening with Kieran in the public eye."

"And to move into my penthouse for the duration," he cut in.

Chloe glanced at him sharply. Even he wondered at the request. It hadn't been his original intention, but now that the words were out, there was no doubt they were necessary.

Aoife turned calm blue eyes to him. "Why?"

"Many of my clan live in the city," he said, voicing his thoughts. "I'll be watched if I step out with a non-wolf on my arm. If I were serious about a woman you can be sure I'd move her into my home at the earliest opportunity. It will be suspicious if we live apart."

Aoife tilted her head as she considered. "I have no problem with that, provided my room comes with a locked door."

"I assure you there is no need, but whatever makes you comfortable will be provided." No need at all. The thought of crawling into the fey's bed was about as appealing as cuddling an icicle.

"You will also understand that I may have to work a

number of late nights. We'd have to arrange our appearances around my schedule," Aoife said.

"Of course." He was happy to agree since the odds of ever needing to work around her schedule were growing increasingly slim.

The silence stretched, and Chloe jumped in once more. "The final week before the full moon will be spent on pack lands which are a few hours outside of the city."

"Camping?" Aoife asked with an arched brow. "I don't do camping."

His inner wolf growled at her flippant tone.

"Cabins will be provided," Chloe said. "You won't be in a tent."

Manicured nails tapped against the desk. "I detest the woods. A week away from work will also hamper some of my projects. Should I agree, I'd expect my sacrifices to be reflected in my payment."

"I'm sure we can incorporate those realities," Chloe agreed.

"You will need to play your part convincingly," he added. "My people are very physical. In public you will need to be comfortable with open displays of affection."

He didn't miss the flash of distaste that crossed Aoife's features, but she inclined her head. "I am aware of your people's…baser instincts. I am a good actress when I wish to be."

"Excellent," Chloe said. "That's exactly what we're looking for."

"I also need to go over the proposed contract before I commit myself," Aoife said. "I'd like to see all clauses involved."

"Of course. I have a copy right here." His matchmaker passed over the papers.

"And you assure me sex is not a requirement of this

pretense?" Aoife said, ruffling through the file. Her voice was bland, as if speaking about the weather and not about trading her body for money. "I trust outside of the public eye you will keep your hands to yourself, wolf?"

"Absolutely," he muttered. On paper this woman might be perfect for him, but both he and his wolf agreed it would never work. No one would believe he was madly in love with her.

They sat in silence while Aoife read.

"Everything looks to be in order," she said finally. "I'll expect a fifty percent deposit of my fee up front with the remainder to be transferred after the successful completion of your plan. Should anything go wrong, I'm happy to forfeit the final payment, but I would keep the initial fee to cover the disruptions to my life."

"Sounds fair," Chloe replied. "We'll talk it over and let you know Kieran's decision before the day is done."

"Excellent." She stood with just a cursory nod in Kieran's direction.

Chloe rushed forward to walk her the short distance to the door. "Thanks for coming in," she said.

"My pleasure. Sounds like an amusing enterprise. While I have you, Chloe, could you go ahead and set up that meeting with the griffin you mentioned in our last conversation? For after this charade is over, of course."

"Yes, not a problem," Chloe replied, her voice betraying a hint of surprise.

Kieran's lips twisted. The fey seemed to be a busy, efficient woman but even he thought it was a little cold to set up another date in front of a man she was considering moving in with.

"Perfect. Ring me with your decision." The fey swept from the room without another word.

Closing the door, Chloe moved back to her desk. "So

what do you think?" she asked. "She's pretty perfect, right?"

"No."

Her long-suffering sigh filled the air. "What's the problem this time? Aoife is incredibly professional. She'll follow your requirements to the letter. Plus she is beautiful and powerful enough to put any wolf in their place. She's perfect for you."

"If that woman is what you think I'm attracted to, you don't know the slightest thing about me."

She leaned forward on the desk. "This isn't about attraction. This is about finding someone to help you avoid an arranged mating."

"Everything is about attraction," he replied, shifting in his chair. "My people will be watching me like hawks, and if they see me touching my supposed mate-to-be without any fire they will know immediately it's a trick."

"So act the part," she snapped. "I can't find a woman to meet all your needs *and* turn you on. Handle that part yourself."

"Aoife is beautiful, to be sure, but I would never willingly touch her. She's too cold, too controlled. She makes my wolf want to bare its teeth and howl."

"Your plan is cold," Chloe said bluntly. "Aoife is exactly what you need. Someone who won't let her emotions enter into the equation."

He pushed away from the desk to prowl her office. One hand ran through his dark curls as he paced the confines of the room.

"I don't understand the problem," Chloe said, rising to her feet. "The dryad was too flighty. The sorceress before her, too clingy. You turned down my wolf candidates based on their heritage, and now Aoife is too cold when she offers you everything you've been looking for. What do you want?"

"I want someone my pack can believe I would love." An impossible task.

Chloe snorted as she moved around the desk. "From what I've seen of you, that woman doesn't exist. You're not exactly the lasting relationship type."

A growl vibrated in his throat as he rounded on the witch. She was not going to dismiss his words so easily once again. Time she learned it was never wise to poke a wolf.

Chloe had only a second to see the ring of gold shining around Kieran's irises before he wrapped a powerful arm around her and swung her back against the wall.

Her breath left her as the wolf crowded closer, pressing his hard body along hers. The gold in his gaze was a sign of his rising wolf. Like vampires, any time a werewolf was gripped by strong emotions like rage, frustration, or lust, their eyes would change to reflect their inner beast creeping toward the surface.

But it wasn't the sight of his slip in control that had her heart racing. She couldn't remember the last time a man had stood so close, a sad fact in itself. Perhaps she needed to take some of the advice she spouted to her clients and put herself back in the game. After all, if she hadn't had such a dry spell, it wouldn't feel so good to be held this close to a werewolf on the edge.

Kieran looked down at her with his glimmering eyes. The hand at her waist seemed to burn through her pencil skirt and imprint on the skin beneath. Werewolves ran warmer than the average human temperature, and Chloe tried to believe that was the only reason her body was on fire. Surely the pounding of her heart was just to do with being this close to a predator, and not to the nearness of a man who could easily play out every single one of her fantasies.

"You know nothing about me," he told her, his voice

rough.

No, she didn't. But at that moment, she wished she knew more, wished she knew why a man capable of looking at a woman the way he was right now would have to stoop to buying a girlfriend.

But when his gaze drifted downward toward her chest, Chloe decided it didn't matter. He was a client, and she wasn't a woman one pushed around with impunity.

Lifting her hand, she released a drop of her magic. Lightning crackled from her fingertips as she waved them in front of his face.

"You don't know me either, wolf, so let me make something clear. You try to intimidate me, and I light you up like a Christmas tree." She met his gaze without flinching. "Take your hands off me."

For a moment he didn't move. Chloe wondered if she'd have to follow through on her threat and blast the alpha across the room, but just when she was about to unleash her attack, Kieran moved.

His hands left her body as he shifted backward, and Chloe told herself she didn't mourn the loss of his touch.

Straightening, she smoothed a hand over her unwrinkled skirt. "Now," she said, back to business, "are you sure Aoife is out of the question?"

"Completely," he replied.

"Then it's back to the drawing board." She stepped around him, intending to search through her files for another viable candidate.

"I disagree."

Chloe turned back to him with an arched brow.

"I know the woman we need."

"Then why did you have me call in woman after woman for your review?" she demanded.

"Because I only put all the pieces together a moment

ago."

Her eyes flicked to the wall where he'd just held her, not liking where this was going.

"You, Chloe. I need you."

A shiver ran down her spine. A secret part of her wished she'd heard those words from a man who meant them in the way she craved. Though she'd been alive close to a century, no one had ever looked at her with the intensity that Kieran did now. No man had ever told her that he needed her.

"I'm sure I misheard you," she said, trying to appear unruffled.

"Think about it," he replied as he stalked toward her. "You understand my situation and requirements, plus you're already invested in this operation running smoothly." He stopped when he was before her. "Considering what just happened, I know you can handle yourself around werewolves without appearing weak."

She crossed her arms and tried to stare him down. "I am your handler, not your date."

He ignored her, taking one step farther into her space. "Most importantly," he continued. "I can kiss you and mean it."

The breath rushed out of her. For a split second, the lonely corner of her soul wondered what it would be like to be in this man's arms, even if it was only for pretend.

"I'll write whatever check you want."

The fantasy she'd been spinning in her head crashed back to earth with the ugly reality of his words.

She pushed past him, trying to ignore the hard planes of his chest under her palm. "Let me make something clear, you arrogant alpha. I am not for sale." She dropped into her chair and crossed her legs, taking comfort in the desk separating them. At least she did until he planted his hands in the center of it and leaned forward to tower over her.

"Everyone has a price."

"Not me," she replied. "I'm not interested in being your squeeze toy."

"You know I have a point. Vivian wants this deal, and she's convinced you to want it as well. With you at the helm, there is no chance of a slip up. Plus, you can be assured of complete privacy, which protects both my interests and your agency's reputation."

The damn man had a point. She'd never been comfortable with the idea of buying another person's silence.

"With your experience matching my kind, you have the knowledge to blend into the pack and the skills to keep yourself safe. Not to mention, witches are thoroughly compatible with wolves."

She rolled her eyes at the one. "I take it you're speaking from personal knowledge."

A grin tugged at his lips. "Your people tend to have a wild streak that appeals to weres."

"Not helping your cause."

The smile widened. "My point is that no one will question me showing up to an event with you on my arm."

"Oh really? Let me go out on a limb here and guess you usually date supermodels or actresses. I am a very ordinary witch with no special skills that would explain why a man like you would end up with me. Hell, we can't even offer a logical reason why we met in the first place."

His smile didn't slip, but an emotion she couldn't name moved behind his eyes. "We've already established you don't know me, witchling. My pack has long understood I go for women with fire, no matter what slice of the supernatural world they come from. You're perfect."

Her heart thumped, even though she knew he hadn't meant the words the way they sounded.

"Give me one good reason why you can't do this."

Chloe opened her mouth before realizing she didn't have anything to say. Vivian would be thrilled at this turn of events and give her the time off to see it through. Chloe would both guarantee the agency's protection and ensure no other woman got in over her head. Plus Kieran had a point—with the time she'd spent researching werewolves for her job, she did already understand the culture and hierarchy of a pack.

She was the right woman for the job, damn the man.

"I want that room with a lock Aoife was talking about."

Triumph gleamed in his expression. "Absolutely."

"And you make sure to stick to all points of the contract."

"Of course." He straightened as he added, "But you should remember the no sex clause was written to ensure no woman felt she had to sleep with me for money."

Chloe arched a questioning brow.

"You turned down my check, sweetheart. There's no money involved between us."

She opened her mouth to argue, only to realize he had a point. The magic she'd woven into the contract was only binding if money exchanged hands. Her deal was with Vivian, not Kieran.

A fact she had little doubt the wolf would use to his advantage.

"Make it two locks on the door," she growled.

Kieran pushed away from the desk with a chuckle. "Pack a bag. I'll come by tomorrow after work to collect you."

As he strode from the room she wished she could come up with a decent excuse for not doing this.

Unfortunately, the infuriating wolf was right. She really was perfect for him.

Chapter Three

"Wow."

There was really nothing else to say.

Chloe stepped through the door of Kieran's home and stopped. Her heels rested on the black and white checkered floor of the entranceway. Ahead of her she saw a black twisting staircase leading to the second floor, and to her left, arched doorways offered teasing views of the elegant living room set up before bright glass windows.

"Welcome home," Kieran purred in her ear as he took her coat.

Leaving her suitcase by the door, Chloe wandered farther into the penthouse where she'd be spending the next few weeks. Art set on marble pedestals lined the entranceway, lit by a sparkling chandelier above.

Several doorways led to various parts of the house, but she moved toward the natural light and stepped into a very masculine living room. The color palette of Kieran's home was based on earthy tones. Brown and black leather couches were arranged around the spectacular view of central park.

She noted a spacious balcony beyond the windows as well. Given the real estate prices of the city, she didn't even want to guess at what a home this size would cost.

Her own investments had been doing well in the past decades, but it would take her lifetimes to accumulate the wealth that older supernaturals enjoyed. It made her wonder whether this was Kieran's money or that of his pack. Wolves had a tendency to share their possessions amongst their clan the way a family would.

"Bedrooms are upstairs," Kieran said from behind her, as she stared out the large windows. "The kitchen is fully stocked if you're hungry."

Unable to help herself, she pushed through the balcony doors and stepped outside.

Wind whipped her hair around her face as she took in the wide patio that extended half the length of the penthouse.

She heard the door opening behind her as she strode to the edge of the balcony. The black iron railing was smooth beneath her hands as she waited for her host to reach her.

"Beautiful view," she murmured.

His hand appeared next to hers as he leaned forward on the rail. "We don't like to be away from the forest. My inner wolf is always clamoring for wide open spaces, which can be hard to come by in this city."

"Wouldn't it be easier to live outside New York then?"

He glanced at her with a grin. "Perhaps. But there is so much life in this place. Many of my pack choose to stay here. Easier for work, for mingling with other supernatural members of the community. But we do organize several retreats throughout the year to give the pack an excuse to leave the city behind and go somewhere every wolf can be itself." He looked out over the view. "You're in for a crash course in werewolves when we head to pack land."

"I can handle it," she replied, rolling her shoulders back.

"Yes," he murmured. "I believe you can."

Chloe glanced at him to find his dark gaze locked on her. A thrill of awareness shivered through her before she ruthlessly tamped it down. This was a game to Kieran, and she had no intention of being the loser.

Drawing her professional persona around her like a shield, she pointedly looked away from the tempting wolf.

"What's our next step?" she asked, looking out over the park.

"I've arranged for us to go to a gallery showing tomorrow. Several of my pack will be in attendance, and once they see us together, word will spread quickly."

She nodded. "That works. Vivian has me on the day shift for the duration of our time together, so my evenings will be free."

"For whatever I need?" His voice was pitched lower, the sound almost a physical caress along her skin.

She leveled her best disapproving look at Kieran and crossed her arms. "So, is this what normally works for you? A dash of charm and all the women trip over themselves to get to you?"

Instead of withering under her stare, Kieran merely curled his lips into an amused smile. "Usually."

"Well, it won't work on me."

Kieran leaned closer, crowding into her space. "It has to, my witch. When my pack is watching, you need to look at me like I'm the only one in the world for you."

"I can be a fine actress, thank you very much. I won't give us away."

He snorted. "I haven't known you long, but even I know you can't lie to save your life."

She blinked at the words. It was true she'd never been very gifted at deception, but that wasn't an insight she'd expected him to have—not based on their limited relationship. Unease tugged at her as she realized Kieran saw more than she intended him to. It was so easy to write him off as a spoiled playboy, she tended to forget he was much more than that.

The man before her ran a powerful, dangerous pack with an iron fist. He'd weathered challenges to his leadership and threats from intruders. If she ripped open his shirt she had no doubt she'd see scars from his many battles marring his golden skin. She needed to remember Kieran wasn't a man to be trifled with.

He was a predator, and she very much wanted to avoid being prey.

"I wouldn't have agreed to this charade if I wasn't confident I could do it," she said, swallowing hard.

Kieran moved, trapping her between his arms as he gripped the railing on either side of her body.

"You can't jump when I touch you," he breathed against her ear. "You can't look at me like a wayward schoolboy in need of a reprimand." He drew back enough to meet her gaze. "We're supposed to be lovers. There wouldn't be a single inch of your skin I wouldn't have run my lips over."

Heat suffused her face.

"There, you see? You blush when I'm close."

"I don't," she denied, lifting her chin.

Kieran snorted. "People will take one look at us and know we're pretending. If we'd really been lovers for months, there's no way you'd still look so goddamn innocent."

"Maybe I'd teach you a thing or two instead. Ever think of that, wolf boy?"

A chuckle rumbled from his wide chest. "Witchling, if you ever want to try and teach me something new in the bedroom, I promise I'll be a most diligent student."

Her cheeks were on fire despite her desire to remain unaffected by Kieran. He was right, damn him, she needed to stop acting like a giddy teen when he touched her.

"I'll work on it," she growled, pushing at him to force him back. "By tomorrow I'll be ready. I just need to wrap my mind around all this." Sidestepping him, she headed back into the apartment.

"I'm going to unpack," she called over her shoulder. "And there'd better be a lock installed on my door."

Another low laugh drifted to her ears. "A promise is a promise."

Kieran ran a hand through his hair as he watched the witch walk away from him. His wolf growled at the sight of her leaving, and he had to strangle the impulse to call her back. Claws ached to spring from his fingertips as the wolf prowled within him. Never before had his other half reacted so strongly to a woman. Though both sides of him loved the chase and enjoyed the numerous females who had tumbled into his bed over the years, none of them had ever lit his blood on fire the way the little witch did.

Purposely turning away from where Chloe had disappeared, he stared down at the trees below. It must be the mating moon messing with his instincts in such a way. All wolves sensed the extra tension this time of year, the heightened realization that a powerful event was drawing nearer. Given they were so tightly tied to the lunar cycles, any fluctuation in those forces could cause mental and emotional disruptions.

Once the moon had passed, his wolf would stop focusing so singularly on Chloe.

It had to.

Shaking his head, he wondered if he should sneak out tonight for a run in his wolf form. He was too contained in his human skin. Maybe a break would help calm his mind.

Because it looked like a run was the only release he'd be getting any time soon. Once his clan saw him with Chloe tomorrow he'd have to be careful to be tied only to her. Wolves did not cheat on those they loved, and for this charade to be successful he'd have to hold to that standard. There'd be no calling any of the women in his Rolodex who'd be happy to help him with a little creative stress release.

He dragged a hand down his face. When he'd come up with this plan, a few weeks of celibacy hadn't seemed like much of a problem.

But being around the tempting witch, with no outlet other than his hand, was going to be a special kind of torture. For all his teasing, he very much doubted Chloe would let him into her bed, and if he were a better man he'd be grateful for the fact. This relationship was supposed to come with clear lines. Once the moon had passed, he wanted to separate from Chloe with no lingering feelings of attachment. They needed to be partners in this enterprise, and she wasn't the type of women to treat sex as casually as his kind tended to do. No, she looked at the world with stars in her eyes. He'd bet anything that she hadn't crossed her first century yet, though he'd come across many supernaturals younger than her with a far more cynical outlook of the world.

Chloe was simply…special. Some people had the power to live through the best and worst the world had to offer without ever giving up their faith in the goodness of others. For all his words to her earlier, Kieran suspected Chloe was the sort of woman who could be in his bed for years without ever losing that air of innocence that clung to her. After the years of battle and death he'd survived, that made her uniquely attractive to his wolf. The damn thing wanted to roll on its back like a puppy any time she was near. Well, either that or strip her down and luxuriate in the skin-to-skin contact he craved.

"Keep your hands to yourself, Clearwater," he muttered. More was at stake than lusting after a pretty witch. He couldn't do anything to jeopardize this plan, or he'd end up trying to hold together a disintegrating pack. Wolves took their cues from their alpha, and a mated leader was more stable than a single one. He'd waited far too long to take a mate. Even if he got through this month he'd need to start seriously focusing on finding someone to help him lead. One way or another, his single days would be ending in the next few years. But even so, he wanted to choose his own partner rather than have the pack select a woman for him. And to earn that necessary time, he had to get past this mating moon.

Which meant keeping his relationship with Chloe professional.

His wolf growled at the thought, not liking that reality at all.

"Just hold on for a while longer," he said to his other half. "Then we'll find some nice wolf that will have you panting for her. Promise."

He just needed to get through the next few weeks in one piece.

Chloe stared at the lock on her door and snorted. The gleaming hook and eye latch screwed into the dark wood would be useful in keeping out exactly zero supernaturals. Which, she supposed, was the point. It didn't matter what sort of lock she put on this door, if a determined werewolf wanted in, nothing was going to stop him.

Well, nothing except her.

"Okay, wolf," she breathed, eyeing the large doorframe. "Two can play this game."

Dropping her purse to the beige carpet, she stepped up

to the door. Magic rushed through her body in a comforting caress. Tiny lightning sparks snapped at her fingertips as she rose on her toes and touched her hands to the top of the doorframe. Whispered words tumbled from her lips as she drew her hands apart, running her fingers over the sides of the door and leaving shimmering sky-blue magic behind. She brushed her hands across the threshold on the floor before snapping her fingers. The blue trail encircling the door brightened for a moment before disappearing from view.

Satisfied, she sat back on her heels. Nothing was getting through that entrance without an invitation. Famed werewolf strength or no.

Not that she truly thought she needed such protections. Kieran might play with her, but for all his bluster he held is own set of morals that would keep her safe from him if she ever wanted to turn him away.

Wanted being the operative word.

Chloe licked her lips as she pushed herself from the floor. Just a few more weeks and she'd be far closer to fulfilling her dreams than she'd been before the wolf had entered her office. As long as she kept her eye on the prize she could avoid falling into Kieran's clutches.

Even if a forbidden part of her whispered that wouldn't be a terrible fate.

Shaking her head, she looked around the stately guestroom. The floor to ceiling windows that had lit the open concept living room were continued here. Natural light flooded in from two sides, though a quick inspection revealed blackout curtains that would no doubt come in handy when trying to sleep.

A king bed sat in the middle of the room, its headboard pressed against one wall. The linens were all shades of green and brown, complete with a green comforter shot through with golden threads. Tasteful, yet at the same time she couldn't help noticing there was more than enough room for two people to roll around quite comfortably on the soft covers.

Shaking her head, she grabbed her suitcase and headed for the walk-in closet. Never in her life had she stayed in such a large, decadent room. She tended to be a studio apartment kind of girl. Now she had a gleaming marble en suite, the biggest flat screen she'd ever seen bolted to the wall, and more space than she knew what to do with.

Logically, the layout of the room made sense. Wolves hated to be penned in, and their living spaces were often minimalistic out of necessity rather than aesthetic. When one turned into a large animal frequently, one didn't want breakable furniture that could be bumbled into unintentionally. Though her own apartment looked like the home of a pack rat, she rather enjoyed this change of pace.

Wandering over to the windows she looked down on the city below. "You can do this," she whispered. Kieran might be tempting but she was no stranger to gorgeous supernatural men. She could smile and kiss him for their audience without allowing any of her emotions to become entangled. Pressing her hands to her cheeks, she vowed to crush the humiliating blush that rose every time she was around him. He was just a man, after all. And she was professional enough to handle this assignment for the duration of their contract.

"Still, maybe I should research glamours," she muttered. The simple spell would act as the perfect mask, hiding her rosy blushes from the world.

Staring at her ghostly reflection in the glass, she lifted her chin. She wouldn't let Kieran down, and when this was all over, she'd have both her business, and her heart, safely secured.

"**D**inner."

Chloe glanced at the door as the shout echoed through the house. She'd spent the last two hours unpacking before turning to her laptop for a refresher course in pack culture. Night had fallen over the city and she'd barely noticed.

"Coming," she shouted back. Ignoring her shoes, she raced from the room in her polka-dotted socks. It hadn't taken her very long to change from her formal pencil skirt and gray blazer to her comfiest jeans and a light purple sweater. She was halfway down the stairs when it occurred to her she could have changed into something more stylish for dinner.

Pausing, Chloe eyed the upper landing from whence she'd come. Kieran was no doubt surrounded by impeccably dressed females during his usual life. While she didn't think she looked like a train wreck, she was certain she didn't match her predecessors' elegance. Shrugging, she continued down the stairs. If they were going to live together for weeks he'd better get used to the fact that she was a jeans and a T-shirt sort of girl.

Stepping off the black spiral stairs, she followed her nose through one of the large archways. The kitchen came into view, complete with all the latest stainless steel appliances and what looked like a living wall of herbs.

"Hope you're hungry," Kieran said, glancing at her over his shoulder from his position by the stove.

"Starved," she replied and meant it. Too nervous about how this day would play out, she'd only snacked on a power bar for lunch.

Hopping into one of the high chairs pulled up to the large marble island, she rested her chin in her hand while she watched Kieran shake some spices into a pot of spaghetti sauce.

"I didn't realize you could cook," she said.

"Love it," he replied. "Prepare to be spoiled this month."

"Between the balcony's view, and the way that sauce smells, I think it will be an easy task to accomplish."

"So simply? Where have you been all my life, Chloe?"

She huffed a laugh. "I think I've made my view on your usual type of women pretty clear. You've just been dating the wrong people."

He looked away from his sauce to pin his dark gaze on her. "Perhaps."

A shiver ran down her spine, and she reached for the plate of sliced baguette on the island to give herself something to do.

"So where did you learn to cook," she asked, trying to change the track of the conversation.

"I did quite a lot of traveling in my younger years," he replied. "My pasta skills come from the time I spent in a small Italian village south of Rome."

"Wow," she breathed.

"I can also whip up a red curry so good you'd swear you were sitting in Bangkok."

"That sounds amazing."

He glanced her way as he strained the spaghetti. "Haven't you traveled?"

She shook her head, knowing it was an unusual response for an immortal being. Most supernaturals tended to move around the globe on a whim. For one thing, it was safer never to stay in one place too long. Humans might notice their neighbor never seemed to age. For another, the older a supernatural creature became, the more easily they became bored. Traveling was often a quest for a new experience or flavor to drive away the monotony that developed with age.

"Why not?" Kieran asked, pouring the sauce into the pasta.

She shrugged. "I was born just before the Great Depression. Much of my first decade or two was simply trying to survive."

"I thought witches had covens the way my people have packs?" He brought the pasta over to the table and set it before her before taking the seat to her side.

"Most do," she acknowledged as she spooned some spaghetti onto her plate. "I didn't."

He paused, reaching for the wineglass at his place setting.

She understood why he hesitated. Few supernaturals enjoyed talking about their pasts, especially those who had been originally born human and later turned, like the vampires. Though witches didn't fall into that category, it was a good rule of thumb not to ask about another's past without first being invited.

"Do you want me to change the subject?" he asked.

She thought about it before shrugging. "I'm not touchy about my history. Probably not old enough to care yet. I was in my early twenties when World War II ended. You know as well as I that those years were not ideal for anyone."

"Particularly a young immortal still growing into her powers," he guessed. "Where were your people?"

"Don't know." She took a bite of her food and made appreciative sounds. "I was raised an orphan. Tried to track them when the technological age exploded but never had much luck. Besides, by then I had a good life. I was working with Vivian and loved New York City. I didn't have much reason to go questing off after random witch covens. I always figured if I actually had blood-kin they'd have been looking for me with far more success."

Kieran tipped his head in acknowledgement. It was well known witches tended to take blood bonds very seriously. If she'd had family left, they would not have given up on her easily.

"Still, figuring out everything on my own meant I didn't always have the capabilities to travel."

Because unlike many of their kind, she didn't have anyone looking out for her. Added to her troubles was her species. Some types of supernaturals could live in rivers or go for months without food. Witches, on the other hand, were painfully human in too many ways. Though they could tap into ancient magic, they still needed food, water, and shelter to live, just as any mortal would. During her early years she'd had trouble finding all three.

"I've seen most of North America though," she added. Traveling from town to town in search of work and safety counted, right?

The unexpected feel of his fingers tracing over her cheek made her freeze in her seat. "Incredible," he murmured. "You have not had an easy time of it."

She glanced at him before leaning away from his touch. "Made me into the woman I am today. Wouldn't have it any other way."

"For a were, being cut off from one's pack would be unimaginable."

She nodded, understanding the bonds weres formed, especially wolves. As arguably the strongest of the shifter supernaturals, they were far more susceptible to some of the largest weaknesses. Isolation could be used as physical torture on their kind. Being incredibly tactile creatures they needed constant contact with others. One of the reasons wolves had earned their reputation as playful seducers was their driving need to touch. And it didn't have to be just in a romantic setting. Platonic touch could be just as important to them as a sexual caress.

"Lucky I'm not a wolf then," she said, saluting him with her wineglass.

Still, her flippant words did not erase the pity in his eyes. Taking a large swallow of wine, Chloe decided this was the reason people didn't talk about their pasts. If their stories involved any bumps in the road they were met with unwanted sympathy.

"Keep looking at me like that and I will turn your spaghetti into worms," she warned as she twirled some pasta around her fork.

He hesitated with his fork halfway to his mouth. "You wouldn't."

She leveled a bland stare his way. "Care to try me, big bad wolf?"

That drove the pity from his eyes. Unfortunately it was replaced by a hunger that had nothing to do with food.

"Darling," he purred, "if only you meant those words another way."

She swallowed, looking away from him. "Well, I didn't. So behave."

He gave a mock shudder. "Never."

"Focus. Is there anything I need to know about tomorrow night?" she asked as she shoveled more of the tasty pasta into her mouth.

"We're heading to the Draven gallery," he replied. "I'd expect as least three of my senior pack members to be there."

"Senior?"

He nodded. "Wolves have a hierarchy, and I'm at the top."

"Thanks, but I'm not that much of a simpleton. Did figure out that part on my own."

"Hush," he teased. "Werewolves 101. I'm at the top, then next comes a group of dominant wolves that help me rule, and ensure the stability of the pack. Many of them are older, have more life experience. It is rare that a young wolf would be dominant enough to break into the senior ranks of a pack."

"So in other words, tomorrow I'll be meeting people who have known and worked with you for years."

"Decades."

"Decades," she amended. "And we're supposed to fool

people who know you so well on our first night out?"

He leaned closer. "Yes."

"What if we slip?" she asked, anxiety rising. "What if I do something stupid like flinch or blush or stumble on my words?"

A breathtaking smile curved his lips. "I have to admit, I'm becoming partial to that blush of yours."

Good, because she could feel her cheeks heating. "You know what I mean."

"They'll think you're charming," he breathed. "And what's more, they'll love that you have a good head on your shoulders. I don't tend to date women so…"

She arched a brow. "Normal? Practical? Boring?"

"Wholesome." His fingers trailed over her hand in a light touch.

A shadow flitted over her growing interest. Wholesome. Was that what she brought to a relationship? Simple Chloe. The witch men settled for when they tired of sexy, sophisticated partners.

A deep, secret part of her wished she were the kind of woman who could drive a man mad. Someone who was the opposite of wholesome and predictable. One that Kieran's packmates would look at and think, *here comes trouble*, rather than that their alpha was finally ready to cast aside his wild ways.

But that was obviously not her. Kieran wouldn't have picked her for this assignment if it were.

"Hey," he said. "Why the long face?"

"Nothing," she replied, forcing a smile to her lips. "Nothing at all."

His chocolate-colored eyes held hers for a long minute. "Did you know," he said, "that wolves can detect changes of emotion in your scent? Yours just grew…sad."

For a moment she had the overwhelming urge to tell him.

Secrecy had never been part of her nature. She was more of a speak first, regret later girl. But self-preservation held her back. She didn't want to share with him, bond with him. This was a job, and if nothing else, she'd learned how to be an excellent professional.

"Stop sniffing me," she replied, pulling her cool business facade around her like armor. "You have the right to my presence by your side. Not to my thoughts."

Pointedly looking away from him, she reached for her wineglass and finished the last sip.

"Dinner was wonderful," she complimented as she pushed her empty plate away. "Do you need help with the washing up?"

"No."

"All right. Then I think I'll say good night and head to bed. There are a few cases I need to go over before work tomorrow."

"I understand."

"I'll be back around dinnertime tomorrow, so don't worry about cooking. I'll grab something on my way."

Again he inclined his head.

He's up to something, her instincts whispered. *He's being far too nice about being brushed off.*

Nonsense, the practical side of her replied. *He's merely seeing reason.*

"Good night, Kieran," she said as she hopped down from the chair.

"Just one problem," he said.

She froze, her back to him. Knowing she'd regret the decision, she slowly turned to face him. "And what would that be?"

"Tomorrow, in front of my pack members, I'm going to kiss you."

Fire licked through her veins. Her heartbeat kicked into

high gear, pounding in her ears as she looked at the smugly satisfied smile on her partner's face.

"You've already warned me of my role," she said, unwilling to let him rattle her. "I'll be ready."

He slipped from his own seat with grace, prowling a step toward her. "Yes, but as we established, you are not a born actress. If our first kiss is before prying eyes you will give us away."

She frowned, wishing she could dispute his words but knowing he was probably right. "Then what exactly do you suggest I do?" she snapped. "Visualize our ruse going well?"

A wolfish grin curved his lips, which had nothing to do with his inner animal. Knowing she'd just made a huge tactical error, she waited for the trap to snap shut on her.

"You know as well as I do, darling," he said, leaning in until she felt the heat of his skin against her own. "Practice makes perfect."

Chapter Four

Vivian's nails clicked against the metal top of her desk. "Forgive me, Chloe, but you appear distracted."

"Nothing of the sort," Chloe replied.

"I asked you how things went with Kieran last night."

Chloe shrugged. "This is just a job."

Fingers tangled in her hair, lips pressing against hers, hot and demanding…

"We're both sensible adults able to keep our personal and professional lives separate."

His hands around her hips as he ground her back against the island…

"I have no hesitation whatsoever staying with Kieran."

Amusement shone from her boss's eyes. "So you have no intention of mixing business and pleasure?"

Chloe tried to focus on the question. She really did. But her mind flung her back to the night before. Kieran hadn't listened to any of her protests that practice was unnecessary. No, the wolf had crowded her up against the island until every inch of his hard body had pressed against her.

"I will remain professional at all times," she assured the siren.

Of course, she'd been unable to stop the gasp of pleasure when Kieran had slipped one leg between hers, pulling her up until she'd been riding his firm thigh. The wolf hadn't had any problem taking advantage of her parted lips.

"I only ask because I know how easy it is to get caught up in a game like this," Vivian said. "I don't want you hurt when this ends." Her blue eyes flicked up to Chloe. "And make no mistake, darling, it will end."

"Worked out for Abbey," she said before she could call the revealing words back.

Vivian's eyes narrowed dangerously. Abbey, the only mortal on the Fated Match team, had once received similar advice from their boss about the powerful vampire elder she'd been dating. The elders were the supernatural version of an overseeing council. Representing every key race, the council members were both ancient and powerful.

"You know as well as I do Abbey was a one in a million case," Vivian said. "Who could have predicted the strongest vamp in the city would fall for our little human?"

"I know," Chloe said. "I'm not expecting anything of the sort to happen here. I don't want it to. I was just making the argument."

"Abbey was Lucian's mate," the siren continued. "Bonds like that mean far more than blood or station. But wolves rarely take mates outside of their species."

Just like vampires never fall for humans. She bit back the reply before she could voice it. The last thing she wanted was for Vivian to think she'd let her emotions get entangled with Kieran's plan.

After all, lust didn't really count. Right?

She curled her hands around her black pencil skirt to numb the tactile memory of her palms sliding over his chest.

Even through the dark sweater he'd worn, the heat of his body had enveloped her hands. She'd run them over the rock hard muscles, wondering what he would taste like if she ran her tongue along those same contours.

"Will you be able to carry on your regular duties during this time or shall I pass some of your clients over to Tasha?"

"I can't see why it would be a problem," Chloe replied. "Kieran works much the same hours I do. There'd be no point in me sitting in his apartment twiddling my thumbs."

"Excellent. I've booked you off for the week of the mating moon, of course," Vivian said. "Should anything arise unexpectedly, just call me directly. This enterprise takes priority. If you can't make it in for a day here or there, I'll take over your duties."

Chloe arched a brow. Vivian was always busy, which made the offer unexpectedly generous.

"I appreciate it," she replied. "Though as I said, I don't foresee it being a problem."

Vivian slid over a black debit card. "I've had an expense account set up for you," she said. "Funds are available through that card."

Chloe blinked. "I have money."

"Not like the women dating Kieran usually do. I'm not saying you have to use it, but just in case you need an appropriate wardrobe update or something, it's better to be safe than sorry. This ruse needs to be perfect."

Chloe turned the card over between her fingers. "Will Kieran end up getting the bill for whatever is missing from this account by the end of the contract?"

A cool smile twisted the siren's lips. "I run a business, Chloe," she replied.

Which meant yes.

Chloe tossed the card she'd never use into her purse. "Anything else?"

The smile slipped from Vivian's face as her icy blue eyes grew serious. "A word of warning," she replied. "I know how tempting power can be. It's easy to lose yourself in a fantasy."

Chloe blinked. Vivian never shared personal details about herself.

"Don't let this month go to your head," the siren advised. "Enjoy yourself. Hell, enjoy your wolf if you want to. But protect your heart at all costs."

"I know how this story ends," Chloe said.

A sad smile graced Vivian's face. "Thousands of women have said those words and ended up heartbroken all the same."

Like you? It was the first time she'd ever considered Vivian's life before Fated Match. What had the siren experienced before dedicating her life to finding mates for supernaturals?

"I'll be fine, Vivian."

"Of course you will be," she replied. "Now, I have a troll coming in for an intake interview in ten minutes. You can show yourself out."

Chloe gave her a mock salute before pushing to her feet. That was the boss she knew—brusque, single-minded, and utterly focused on the job.

Leaving the silver wonderland of Vivian's office behind her, Chloe ducked into the washroom next door. She made a beeline for the sink and turned the cold water on.

"Get a hold of yourself," she told her reflection as she splashed some water on her face. She was at work. She needed to focus.

And not to think about how Kieran had threaded his fingers through her hair, unraveling her bun. How he'd twisted the locks and used them to pull her face up to his.

She closed her eyes, her fingers touching her lips.

His mouth had been hot, demanding. A dominant wolf

ready to take advantage of any opportunity she offered.

Her fingertips brushed against her lower lip as she remembered how he'd caught it between his teeth, nibbling gently. His tongue had invaded her mouth, taking utter control as one hand on her lower back had forced her close.

There'd been no escape, no hiding. She couldn't pretend he didn't want her, not when she'd felt his rock hard erection pressing against her body.

If he kissed her like that in public they might set fire to the gallery—and scar any children in the audience for life.

Never before had she experienced such explosive heat. Wrapping her arms around his shoulders to hold him close while she'd rocked against his thigh had seemed like the most natural thing in the world. When his fingers had brushed under her shirt to trace along her naked skin she'd thought she would drag him to the ground and take him right there in the kitchen.

Chloe wasn't a one-night stand girl. She preferred committed relationships where chemistry developed slowly as she grew closer to her partner. Now Kieran was making her rethink her standards. Maybe there was something to be said for animalistic attraction. Once this was all over, perhaps she'd revamp her dating profile to target weres. If the rest of them were anything like Kieran, she'd be one happy girl.

Looking up into the mirror, she remembered Kieran's parting words. He'd run his lips over hers once more before pulling back and allowing her to slip down his body.

"Just like that," he'd whispered in her ear. *"Always react to me just like that."*

She adjusted her bun, smoothing back pieces of hair that didn't need attention. "I'm new," she told herself. "I'm just a change of pace. That's why he pursued me. Tonight it will be out of his system and we'll be able to go to the gallery far more comfortable with one another."

Lies. The idea of being comfortable on Kieran's arm seemed like a fool's dream. All he had to do was enter the room and her body was pulled as taut as a bowstring.

"You're not one in a million," she told herself. "Remember Vivian's warning."

Once the mating moon was over, Kieran would be gone so fast her head would spin.

And he wasn't taking any piece, no matter how small, of her heart with him.

Chloe was ready to get back to a day filled with work, but fate had other plans. When she entered her office, she saw a woman waiting for her with an expression that was anything but welcoming.

"You've got some explaining to do."

Sighing, Chloe closed the door and crossed over to her desk. "Who told you, Jessica?"

"I was trying to locate you yesterday when Vivian told me you'd probably be at your boyfriend's place. Boyfriend, Chloe? Since when are you dating? And more importantly, since when are you dating without telling me?"

Chloe drew a very careful breath. So it had begun. Only she and Vivian knew the details of her arrangement with Kieran. To the rest of her coworkers, it would appear like a sudden, and startling, shift in her usual routine. A shift she needed to normalize as soon as possible before tongues wagged.

"I wanted to tell you," she began.

"Yeah?" Jessica arched a brow. "That's because when you make life altering decisions, you want to fill in your best friends. What the hell, Chloe?"

"We had to keep things hush hush," she tried. "I couldn't

tell anyone. Not even you."

Jessica tucked a strand of hair behind her ear. "Why not? You tell me everything."

Chloe flinched at the hurt she read in the succubus's eyes. Jessica had started working at Fated Match a few years ago, but despite the relatively short time frame—to an immortal's view—she'd become a fast friend. For the first time Chloe forced herself to consider the toll this ruse would take on her own relationships. She'd only ever thought of this game as lies told to Kieran's people, not her own.

"He's not my usual sort of guy," she started. "And because of his position, we had to keep things quiet until we were sure we had a future."

"But you never even hinted that you were seeing someone. How did you guys keep it so completely secret? You usually blurt out whatever passing thought crosses your mind."

"Thanks," she drawled.

Jessica shrugged. "You know I'm right."

"Look, we were able to keep it so quiet because"—*I didn't know Kieran existed*—"I knew this time it mattered. I didn't want to mess this up—unlike my last few failed attempts into the dating world."

"You think I'd mess up your chances with Prince Charming?"

"No." She shot forward and gripped her friend's hand. "I trust you to keep a secret. But I also…" She paused, trying to think of something Jessica would believe. "I knew you'd talk me out of it," she said at last. "And just this once, I didn't want to listen to reason."

Jessica's eyes narrowed. "Who, exactly, are you dating?"

"Well," Chloe hedged. "He's a wolf."

"Tasha already told me that," she replied, referring to their werewolf colleague.

"How did she know?" she demanded.

Her friend shrugged. "You know the wolves. Absolutely nothing is secret. But she said he wasn't from her pack so she didn't know much."

"No, he's from the Clearwater pack."

Jessica's brows shot up. "No wonder Vivian's been whistling around the office. A link to a pack that powerful must be like Christmas coming early for her. Is that why you kept things quiet? So she wouldn't badger you to make him sign up all his kin?"

"Partially," she lied.

"Do I get a name?"

"No judging."

Jessica tossed her chocolate-colored hair over one shoulder. "I make no promises."

"Kieran," Chloe said, fighting the urge to hold her breath. "I'm dating Kieran."

The succubus blinked. Silence stretched.

"Jessica?"

"You—sunny, loyal, *monogamous* Chloe Donovan—are dating one of the top playboys in the state?"

"Playboy until he met me," she stressed.

"You are the least materialistic person I know. What could you possibly have in common with someone like Kieran?"

"He's more than his pocket book," she snapped.

"What do you talk about?" Jessica asked. "Or is he not a fan of conversation?" A knowing brow arched in a question.

"You see," Chloe said, pointing at her, "this is why I didn't want to tell you."

She held up her hands in peace. "I'm sorry, he just doesn't seem like your type. The two of you are from different worlds."

A stab of pain she had no business feeling shot through her. "You mean different leagues. As in, he's out of mine."

"No." The word was said softly. Serious blue eyes met hers. "Any man would be blessed to have you. And in terms of morality you're probably way out of *his* league."

"You don't even know him," she said, unsure why she felt such a need to defend Kieran.

It's part of the game, she reasoned. *If he were really my boyfriend, I'd fight tooth and nail for him. This is just keeping in character.*

"Hey, I read those articles in the Magical Times and Witch Weekly just like anyone else. He's never been one to fly under the radar has he?"

"Look, just reserve your judgment until you meet him." The words were out before she could think better of them. Had Kieran been her real lover, she would have wanted her friends to meet him as soon as possible. As it stood, the less he had to do with them the easier it would be when the time came to separate.

"Fine," Jessica said before she could call the offer back. "I can do dinner any time this week."

"This week," she repeated, mentally kicking herself.

"I'll start trying to think up neutral topics of conversation," the succubus said. "Not that an evening talking about playboy antics or brilliant investments doesn't sound like fun."

"Investments?"

Jessica arched a brow. "It's what he does, right? I read he was the go-to investment guru for the supernatural elite. Word on the street says he's able to predict the next big cash cows with uncanny accuracy." She shook her head. "I wonder if he has some oracle in his bloodline. How else would you explain investing in both Apple and Google? Devil's own luck." She leaned forward with a grin. "Think he'll give me some stock tips?"

"I'm sure you can ask," she replied. She'd known Kieran was some sort of whiz with numbers, but it was starting to sound like what she *didn't* know about her would-be lover could fill a book.

"How about I talk to Kieran and get back to you with a date?" Chloe offered. "Right now I really need to find a suitable match for a Minotaur on my client list, and you know how picky they can be."

"Bullheaded men." Jessica sighed. "I'll leave you to it, then. Just give me a call when you have a time, and I'll clear my schedule."

Chloe watched her friend leave the office before waving a hand at the door. It shut and locked with a shimmer of blue magic.

Alone, she quickly pulled up a supernatural search page on her computer and plugged in Kieran's name.

The list of sites it brought up was endless.

"Hell," she breathed as she skimmed through the articles that alternated between financial journals and tabloid pictures. Just as Jessica had said, it seemed Kieran had made his money through strategic investments. He now ran a highly sought after investment agency, which only took clients with multimillion dollar accounts to play with.

She swallowed hard as she read one report on how he'd managed to take a failing pack like the Clearwater group and transform it into one of the leading clans in the country. There was no record of his age online, but references to Kieran leading his people dated as far back as the late 1800s.

Clicking open another link, Chloe hissed at the image of Kieran lounging in a club, surrounded by half-naked women. There was no doubt he was a man who worked hard and played harder, but Jessica was right—no one in her circle would ever believe she'd picked him. Kieran stood for luxury and decadence, whereas she preferred simplicity and restraint.

"Don't borrow trouble," she scolded herself. Maybe her friends would just think she was going through a pretty boy phase. Besides the ever-protective Jessica, no one else would have to meet him. And she could do damage control for one dinner. If anyone was going to unravel their deception it was far more likely to be on his side of things.

Speaking of which. Chloe glanced at her watch. A few more hours and she'd have to call it a day.

"Better get something worthwhile done," she said as she reached for the thick stack of intake files. She had more to think about than one werewolf and his sinful touch.

Kieran stared at the numbers on his screen as if they were symbols he'd never seen before. He loved his job, loved knowing which investments would do well and what to gamble on. His world was one of both order and controlled risk. Here he was utterly confident in the power he wielded over his successful domain. But today he was just going through the motions.

It couldn't be nerves. After all, he was never anxious. Outside the office walls, his life was filled with uncomplicated pleasure and within this room he executed his duties with ruthless efficiency that helped swell the investments of all his clients. Simple. Easy.

Two words that would never be applied to the witch in his home.

He rubbed the bridge of his nose. Tonight would change everything. Either they'd succeed, or his freedom would be a thing of the past.

The problem was timing, he mused. Chloe didn't know him. She wasn't at ease when he walked into a room. Throwing her into a gallery with his packmates was too much too soon. If she made a mistake…

She'll do well tonight. She had to. Besides, he'd picked her, and he never made mistakes.

At least, not anymore.

Chloe would be the woman he needed. There had to be another reason he was distracted.

The shrill of his telephone cut through his thoughts.

"Clearwater," he answered, bringing the receiver to his ear.

"You'll be at the gallery opening, correct?" a male voice replied, not bothering with a greeting.

"Hello to you, too, Niall." He sat back in his chair, a smile on his face. Niall had been a friend since childhood. Hundreds of years as packmates had made the other man the closest thing Kieran had to a sibling.

"I just wanted to confirm. If you're skipping out on me there's a gorgeous swimsuit model I'm going to take to dinner."

"I'll be there." And bringing a plus one — though he kept that information to himself.

A sigh carried through the phone. "I was rather hoping you'd ditch me."

"By all means, go to dinner instead." Though introducing Chloe to Niall would be a surefire way to spread news of her existence around the pack, a brief delay might not be the end of the world.

"No, no. It's been forever since we had a night out. Besides, there are pack issues to discuss."

"Everything on track for the retreat?"

"It'll be the largest turn out in years," Niall confirmed.

"All right. If we're going to be a full house, I'll drive out there this weekend and make sure all the cabins are in decent shape."

"No," Niall countered. "I'll drive out this weekend and check. You were going to try and delegate more, remember?"

He rubbed the bridge of his nose, not liking the idea of giving important tasks to others, even those he trusted implicitly. "I'll leave it to you, then." He forced out the words.

"Good man."

"Care to comment on why we're having such large numbers this year?"

There was nothing but silence on the other end of the phone.

"Dammit, Niall."

"Not my fault," the other man denied. "Take it up with the other senior pack members. Apparently word on the street is that you're looking for a mate."

He groaned into the receiver.

"I happened to glance at the RSVP list, and let me assure you, every wolf you've even smiled at in the past century is coming this year. No doubt to try and win your frozen heart."

"You're lucky you're not close enough to strangle."

"Why do you think I'm telling you over the phone?"

Kieran pushed out of his seat, taking the cordless with him. "The pack can't expect me to just select some random woman to tie my life to."

"Hardly random when you've known most of the candidates since you were a cub."

Niall might have a point, but he was certain his fated mate was not among his own pack. Crossing the length of his office, he rested an arm against the wide windows and looked down at the bustling Manhattan streets.

"You know I won't pick one of them."

Niall was silent. Never a good sign when it came to the gregarious wolf.

"Niall."

"You need to pick someone," he replied. "And you know it. The pack needs the stability. The younger wolves are picking up on the tension. It's not a good situation."

"I'm working on it."

"Are you?" The doubt in Niall's voice was palpable. "Since when?"

"You might be surprised," he growled.

"I hope I am. Look, I've got a meeting in a few minutes. Want to grab some beers before the opening tonight?"

"Can't," he replied. "Busy."

"All right. I'll find you there then." The call disconnected without any farewell.

Kieran's arm dropped to his side. He was used to fending off the attention of many of the single women in the pack but it sounded like this year would be an extra level of hell. It might also be more than Chloe signed on for. Not only would she have to deal with prejudiced wolves taking issue with her witch blood, but she'd also be faced with women envious of her position as his lover.

"She can handle herself," he said aloud. She was his employee not a true girlfriend. What did he care if her time at the retreat was uncomfortable? All that mattered was success.

Besides, if their charade was discovered tonight then worrying about the retreat would be a moot point anyway.

Returning the phone to its cradle, he grabbed his suit jacket and headed out of the office.

"Going to lunch," he told his secretary. Maybe a change of scenery would do him good.

At the very least it should help get a certain blonde-haired witch off his mind.

Chapter Five

It was dark when she entered the penthouse. A last minute client interview had carried her later into the evening than she'd anticipated. Now she'd have to rush to get ready. Thank God she had a little magic on her side.

"I was starting to think you weren't going to make it."

Drawn by the silken voice, Chloe stepped into the sprawling living room to find Kieran relaxing on his sofa. His arms were draped over the back of the couch as he watched her.

"Work ran late," she replied.

"Some lovelorn swain having issues?"

"No," she said, stepping farther into the room. "I had a client interested in our platinum package."

He arched a questioning brow.

"The platinum package includes a decade of access to our online database of potential matches. Thirty hand-picked dates over the course of the access period, managed by yours truly, and relationship coaching as needed. Plus their profile gets pushed to the top of the search page. All things you would know had you come to the agency looking for your mate rather than a lie."

"So far the lie has been a hell of a lot more fun," he replied, his voice decadent.

"How long do I have to get ready?" she demanded.

He glanced at his watch. "Is an hour long enough?"

"Works for me. I'll go get started."

"Chloe." His voice froze her on her way out of the room. "I left a little something in your room. I hope you like it."

As she glanced back at the man in the shadowed room, an awareness tingled through her, which she wished she could ignore.

Without replying, she left Kieran and ran up the stairs two at a time.

Focus on the job, she chided herself, trying not to remember the feeling of his mouth on hers. Whatever he left for her could surely be ignored as easily as her wayward desires.

Except once she stepped into her room, her resolve cracked.

There, lying across her bed, was a breathtakingly beautiful dress. With a worshipful hand, she reached for the ribbon and lace concoction—so light it felt like a dream in her hands. Catching sight of the designer tag caused a ripple of vertigo to flow through her. No doubt this single item cost more than most of her wardrobe put together.

Unable to stop herself, she tugged her dress shirt over her head and stepped out of the pencil skirt before reaching for the little black dress. It floated around her body, fitting her to perfection. She wondered where he'd found a designer dress large enough for a real woman and not a slender model. Then again, a man like him probably had little trouble finding exactly what he wanted, when he wanted it.

Gliding before the full-length mirror, she couldn't help

spinning on her toes. The creation was undeniably sexy. Though much of her skin was hidden, the lace allowed for peek-a-boo moments when she walked. It was a dress for a beautiful, confident woman.

Chloe met her own reflection in the mirror as her smile slipped. It was a gown for any one of Kieran's nameless lovers. He was treating her as he'd done all the rest. He threw money at his girlfriends, and they fawned at his feet.

A woman my checkbook can't sway? Show me such a creature and I'll marry her.

His words from one of their first meetings swirled through her mind. He might touch her and tease her but she was nothing special to him. Just another woman drifting through his life, who would leave with a few hot memories and some new clothes when he was done with her.

Reverently, she ran her hand down the perfect dress before pulling it over her head. Even if she wanted to let herself fall into the fairytale, she wasn't a woman who could do such a dress justice. Kieran might want her dressed up like a doll on his arm, but not even for Fated Match could she act like someone she wasn't.

Hanging up the dress, she turned her attention to the clothes she'd brought with her. Though nothing was as expensive as the black dress she'd rejected, Vivian had insisted she top up her wardrobe when her work duties had evolved to wooing high profile clients. If she was going to go after the crème de la crème of New York's supernatural society, she had to look the part.

A grin curved her lips as her fingers touched red silk. Though she'd bought it years ago she'd never had a chance to test it out. The color was a touch too bright for a work event, even an after-hours one. But tonight Kieran wanted all eyes on her.

And in this dress she could definitely comply.

Wardrobe decided, she rushed through her shower and toiletry routine. Usually she preferred to pull her blonde hair back into some semblance of a bun, but tonight she ran her fingers through her hair, leaving instant, magical curls behind. As a bonus, the bouncing locks would stay soft and perfect without the aid of any hairspray. Turning to her makeup, she made it a little more dramatic than her standard neutrals, knowing she'd need to balance out the brightness of her dress. Chloe blew a kiss to her reflection through scarlet red lips.

Standing in her towel she glanced at herself with a critical eye. She needed to match the image of the type of woman the Clearwater pack would expect Kieran to date, but she also needed to look like herself. She ran a hand over her full hips before staring at her breasts with a sigh. Even if she duct taped the girls down she worried they'd be too large to compliment to the classy look she was trying to effect. Not that there was much she could do about that. She hoped Kieran had thrown a few curvier women into his parade of model lovers, or his pack would have questions she didn't want them asking.

Tossing the red dress over her head, she let it fall into place around her body. A black belt helped define her waist before the silk fell into a slightly fuller skirt that brushed just above her knees. The deep V of the dress added some sex appeal to the otherwise demure creation.

Twirling before the mirror in a pair of black pumps, she grinned at her reflection. Kieran's dress was more stunning, but she didn't think she cleaned up too badly when left to her own devices.

"And I look like me," she whispered to herself. And that was the most important outcome.

Grabbing her clutch, she headed for the door, all the while steeling herself for Kieran's rejection. The wolf didn't strike her as a man who cared to have his plans upset.

She lifted her chin. Too bad she wasn't a woman who

followed orders easily.

Kieran stared out over the darkening city, a tumbler of whiskey in his hand. Tonight it'd begin. Once he took Chloe to the gallery there was no going back. They had to be convincing, or it was his head on the chopping block.

For a man who didn't believe in nerves, his had continued to make an annoying appearance throughout the day. Not for the first time, he wondered if he'd let his cock make decisions his brain should have had utter control over. The fey woman he'd met would have had no problem rubbing elbows with the pack's elite. Chloe, however, was a far less predictable animal. While that made his wolf snarl in approval, the man dreaded what failure would mean to them all.

The click of heels on the stairs reached his ears, and he downed the last of his drink. Setting the glass on the bar cart, he went to meet her. Tugging his black cuff into place, he strode into the entrance hall.

And forgot how to breathe.

That was definitely not the dress he'd so carefully selected. Usually he farmed out such tasks to an assistant, but this time he'd spent his lunch break perusing women's fashion until he'd found a dress he thought would do her justice. An outside observer might make the mistake of thinking the action was uncharacteristically sentimental, but he preferred to think of it as being prepared. Every detail of this night needed to be perfectly planned, including every inch of his date. He'd tried to give her a color that would help her avoid the spotlight, knowing she was nervous enough about this outing as it was. Every decision about that dress had been made to help her blend into her surroundings without stealing the show.

But Chloe wasn't a woman for the sidelines.

There would be no missing her in the fire-engine-red gown she'd selected. Nor would anyone who saw her doubt why he'd pursued her. Not with silk accentuating every curve until all he could think of was blowing off the show and taking her to bed. He'd peel the red silk away from her delicious body, running his lips over every inch of creamy skin he uncovered. Those soft curls would be tangled around her face as she writhed beneath him, her luscious red lipstick smeared as she begged him for one more kiss.

And those sky-high black heels? Hell, they could stay. He bit back a growl as he imagined them digging into his skin as she locked her legs around his hips.

She stepped off the stairs and glided toward him. Kieran couldn't help his smile when he noted her raised chin. His lovely fake lover was ready to fight.

Chloe stopped before him, looking up, even in her heels.

Knowing she was waiting for his judgment, Kieran took his time allowing his eyes to rake down her body then slowly back up to her face. Not what he'd planned, perhaps, but definitely worth the detour.

"I'm going to have to fight off challengers tonight," he said finally.

She blinked, as if expecting far different words. "Why?"

He reached out to wrap an arm around her waist and pulled her closer. "Because, sweetheart, every man there will want you for his own."

Her sharp inhale when her body collided with his pacified the wolf pacing within him. It whined in pleasure when he stroked his fingers down her bare arm.

"Be serious," she huffed, trying to appear unaffected even as a telling shiver gripped her body.

"Trust me, Chloe. I am."

Was she trying to drown him, he wondered, as he looked down into her wide green eyes. A secret pleasure lurked there that she couldn't hide. Not that Chloe was very adept at hiding much. The woman was an open book to any who cared to read her.

Kieran had a feeling he'd always be paying that extra bit of attention when she was around.

"I can't keep the other dress," she said, trying to step back.

He refused to allow her to retreat. "Why?" he asked. "I'd love to see it on you. Didn't you like it?"

"It was beautiful. Perfect."

"Then why?" he breathed, his head moving closer to hers.

"I won't let you buy me, wolf."

He paused, considering her words. Had he been? It's true his past relationships had revolved around a certain give and take, his contributions being mainly monetary. Any other lover would have taken the expensive gift without a second thought. A wolfish grin twisted his lips as he thought of all the ways they'd thanked him for his generosity. Perhaps he'd wanted Chloe in exactly that position.

Defiance filled her eyes as she stared up at him. "You've given Vivian more than enough to ensure our compliance. I'll follow your lead. There's no need to bribe me."

"Did you ever stop to think maybe I was just doing something nice for you?" he asked.

Her eyes slid away from his as she considered his words. "If you want to do something nice for me," she said at last, "buy some boxes of tea. I hate drinking coffee, and that's all you have in your cupboards."

Tea. He'd tried to spend hundreds of dollars on her, and she wanted tea. Kieran stared down at the woman in his arms, aware that his wolf was holding itself very, very still. Watching. Waiting.

She glanced back up at him, and Kieran heard her breath hitch. While her wide eyes locked on his, her body was carefully still in his arms.

He wasn't a man who ever let an opportunity pass. Not when he wanted a woman the way he wanted this one. But Chloe was different. This was different.

Think of the job, he scolded himself. Tonight was about more than a delicious woman. He needed to keep his eye on the prize and off his lovely companion's cleavage. She was an accessory in his plan, nothing more.

When her gaze flicked to his mouth, it was all he could do not to press his lips to hers.

"Kieran," she whispered, before straightening her shoulders. "Aren't we going to be late? Don't want to miss your packmates."

"You're right, of course." His arms, however, refused to release his prize.

She hesitated for a heartbeat before stepping back and away from him. "Then we should get going."

A growl rumbled from his chest before he could bite it back.

The witch glanced at him with a coolly arched eyebrow.

"After you, darling," he replied, gesturing toward the door.

Still, as they left the apartment Kieran couldn't help placing his hand at the small of her back. Though she stiffened at the touch, she didn't shrug it off. Progress.

And tomorrow, he decided, he'd buy all the tea he could carry.

Chapter Six

Chloe couldn't help sneaking sidelong glances at her date. He looked downright dapper in his all-black suit— sophisticated, elegant, just like the businessman he was by day. But every now and then he'd look her way, and the wolf would be staring out of his dark eyes.

Like when she'd come down the stairs.

Her fingers curled tighter on her clutch. She'd been surprised her dress hadn't ignited from the searing heat of his gaze. Crossing the distance of the foyer to him, she'd been prepared for an argument. Instead she'd been faced with absolute approval. Something deep within her coiled more tightly at the knowledge that she—plain old Chloe—had had the power to stun a man as powerful, and as experienced, as Kieran.

Maybe this plan might just work.

"Ready?" Kieran's voice broke through her thoughts as the car pulled to a stop before a brightly lit gallery.

She drew a deep breath and nodded. "We can do this." He'd been very clear about her role tonight. She knew exactly what part to play.

Fingers entwined with hers, drawing her attention back to the man at her side.

"We can do this," he agreed, pressing his lips to her knuckles without ever dropping his gaze.

Chloe stepped out into the cool night air and rubbed her knuckles on her skirt to banish the heat of his mouth. Kieran appeared at her side seconds later to offer his arm.

Together they walked into the gallery already teaming with life.

Sound hit her like a wave when the doors opened. Pounding music filled the air, her first clue that this wasn't any staid, predictable art show.

Though colorful paintings lined the pure white walls, the lighting of the gallery would have fit more easily into a rave than a studio. Chloe's ears were on overload, and she glanced at her date, a creature with senses far more finely tuned than hers.

"What is going on?" she asked.

"That would be Patrick Draven," Kieran said. "He has never been a fan of the expected."

"But doesn't this all seem rather garish?"

"Precisely. If I hazard a guess, I'd say he's trying to keep human critics away. Make them think the viewing is all flash and show without substance."

"Why?" she asked as they moved farther into the packed gallery. "Isn't more interest better for the artists he represents?"

"Not when he wants to give the supernatural community first crack."

With his hand around her waist, Kieran guided her to one of the champagne towers set up along the walls and passed her a glass.

"Is anyone from your pack here?" she asked, using the

flute to cover her lips.

"Several," he replied, a sharp glance raking the other attendees. "I give it two minutes before they descend on us."

She swallowed, the bubbles burning her throat. "Okay," she wheezed. "Then tell me more about Draven."

Not releasing his grip on her, Kieran guided her around the impressive art lining the walls. "Draven is one of a kind. No one really knows where his talents come from, be they magical in origin or merely learned, but either way, he is able to predict artistic genius."

Surprised, she looked more closely at the work lining the walls.

"These artists are unknown," Kieran continued. "Once word gets out of a Draven show, our kind flocks to the gallery in order to snap up the next big masters while the prices are still affordable. For the human artists, they'll do anything to win a space on Draven's docket because once they do, they know their first shows will sell out with inexplicably high prices."

"He can't be right every time," Chloe murmured.

Kieran shrugged. "Word is he was the one who recommended Michelangelo to paint the Sistine Chapel."

"That can't be true," she said.

"Human history has a way of leaving out the supernatural influences that descend on them from time to time. Either way, Draven's personal collection of antiquities would bring many a historian to tears."

"Have you ever seen it?"

He smiled down at her. "Once."

"He won a tour on a hand of cards, if I remember correctly."

Chloe spun at the new voice. Standing behind her was a striking man with ink-black hair shot through with the odd silver thread. Though like many of the attendees he was taking care to appear human, there was a wildness about his presence that her magic immediately picked up.

Wolf. The knowledge whispered through her. The man smiled, the curve of his lips softening the harsh planes of his face, but his sharp green eyes assessed her in a way that was far from friendly.

"Niall," Kieran greeted, holding out his hand. "So you truly gave up that dinner of yours."

The other man shrugged. "Told you I would. Besides, wouldn't do to miss snapping up a painting by the next Van Gogh. I've made that mistake too many times in the past." His eyes had not left her despite his words to Kieran. "I didn't realize you'd be bringing a date tonight."

"Chloe Donovan," she said before Kieran could. "And I'm not here only for the evening."

"Nice to meet you," he nearly purred, claiming her proffered hand in one far larger. "Chloe, you say?"

She hesitated, knowing what she should do. The plan had been simple. All she had to do was pretend they'd been found out by mistake. Chloe was to twirl her hair, act like she didn't have a brain in her head, and smile like any of the other women to have temporarily grace Kieran's arm. That was the plan Kieran had drilled into her head. That was the woman he wanted her to be.

But looking at the keen eyes of the man before her, she realized that plan would never work. He'd see right through her, and Kieran's jig would be up.

Two options. Smile coltishly and feign anger that Kieran had been hiding her away. Or, brass it out and be herself without pretense.

Here's hoping Kieran wouldn't be too angry at her change of plans.

After all, the man did have the power to grow wicked fangs and claws.

"Don't worry," she said, shaking his hand. "None of your pack has heard of me. Doesn't mean I don't know a great deal about you."

Niall's brows arched even as Kieran tensed behind her.

"And why would that be, Ms. Donovan?"

"Because I'm in love with your alpha," she lied. "Have been for months."

Shock flashed across the man's face as his eyes lifted to Kieran. "I feel like I've missed a few steps here," Niall said.

"Enough, Chloe," Kieran growled. "We're leaving."

"So you can hide me away again?" she demanded, rounding on him. "I'm tired of being your guilty secret. It's time you told your pack about us. If you're so ashamed of having a witch on your arm then we've got bigger problems than your family finally knowing the truth."

Understanding flickered in his dark gaze but, unfortunately for her, it was coupled with an emotion that looked a great deal like rage. "You know I'm not ashamed of you," he said, sliding into his role.

"Then you won't have a problem introducing me to your friends. Why else did you think I insisted on coming with you tonight?" She glanced at Niall and shrugged. "I'm not a huge art fan."

"Well, I for one am grateful you showed up," Niall said, taking her hand and threading it through the curve of his arm. "Come, let me show you some of the sights, and we will see if we can inspire an interest in these paintings."

"Niall," Kieran warned with a rumble.

"I'll take excellent care of your lady. Never fear."

With one last look at the thunderous alpha she was leaving behind, Chloe allowed Niall to whisk her away.

On her own, she prayed she'd made the right decision. Without her partner by her side, she stood a great risk of revealing the limited knowledge she actually had of him.

Pasting a smile on her lips, she followed Niall across the gallery to a wall of paintings.

"You've truly never heard my name before?" she murmured as they stopped before a watercolor.

"No," Niall replied.

She nodded, lifting her chin as if the truth hurt. "He warned me we had to keep things quiet. I guess I always hoped I meant enough to him that he'd tell his friends."

"How did the two of you cross paths?"

A sardonic smile twisted her lips. "You mean, what's he doing with a girl like me?"

The large wolf offered her a guilty smile. "His tastes have never been subtle."

"True," she said. "But everyone grows up eventually."

A rough chuckle escaped her escort. "So after hundreds of years you think he's finally ready to settle down?"

Hundreds of years? She lost her step before ensuring none of her shock showed on her face. Kieran was a strong were, and age and power tended to go hand in hand, after all. It shouldn't be a shock that he was far older than her.

Except they were already on such uneven footing. Every time she turned a corner she discovered something else that moved him further and further from her reach.

"I'd like to believe that, yes," she replied.

"You said you've been dating for months?"

"Yes, for a while now. Why?"

"Kieran never stays with a woman that long. Not since… well, you know."

Chloe inclined her head, pretending she understood what he was talking about.

"But if you've managed to heal him, then few of our pack will object to you."

"Even though I'm a witch?"

Niall shrugged. "At this point, I think our people would

accept a gorgon if we thought it would bring Kieran back to life. The pack needs stability."

She snorted. "Even before we met, I'd heard about his exploits. I don't think enjoying life is Kieran's weakness."

"Then you need to look harder."

She glanced up sharply. There was no humor in Niall's eyes. This was dangerous territory. The situation needed to be diffused before she revealed how little she actually knew of Kieran's life.

"You obviously care for him." She leaned closer and whispered conspiratorially, "Since you've known him longer than I, how do you figure I should atone for letting the cat out of the bag tonight?"

He snorted. "How do you usually diffuse his anger?"

Chloe blinked, unsure of what to say.

Luckily, Niall took her startled silence as embarrassment and released a rough laugh. "Yes, that's what I thought. Kieran's always been, shall we say, a passionate man. You might be in for a long night, darling, but he'll forgive you long before the dawn."

Chloe swallowed her horror as Niall pulled her toward another painting. If Kieran's anger was usually soothed by sex, what the hell was she supposed to do about it? Glancing at her wolf out of the corner of her eye, she realized he still watched her with a stormy expression. Somehow she doubted coolly argued logic would sway him once he got her alone in the car.

"Of course if that doesn't work," Niall continued, "Kieran's always had a soft spot for peanut butter cups."

"Really?" she exclaimed.

Her surprise was met with a questioning frown. "Surely you know about his sweet tooth?"

"Of course," she hastily amended. "I think one of the reasons he's kept me around so long is the to-die-for brownies

I make."

Niall's frown smoothed into a smile. "That would keep him happy all right." They paused when they reached an older couple studying one of the smaller sculptures.

"Since you are so determined to emerge from the shadows, Chloe, I figured you should meet a few others tonight. Darrel and Julie are also members of the pack."

"Nice to meet you," she said, holding out her hand. "I'm Chloe, Kieran's girlfriend."

As the couple raked her head to toe, their astonishment obvious, Chloe decided meeting Kieran's family like this would be a humiliating experience if she were a real lover. She might not be Kieran's usual type, but the polite thing to do would be to hide the jaw dropping shock that seemed to overcome his pack members every time they met her.

"Nice to meet you, Chloe," Julie said, no doubt realizing the silence had dragged too long. "Are you the reason our alpha looks ready to bite the poor human artists in half?"

"Unfortunately," she agreed. "I'm sure to get an earful on our way home."

"You are living with Kieran then?" Darrel asked.

She nodded. "For a while now. I wasn't sure at first about moving in so quickly but Kieran convinced me. Sometimes when things are right you just have to jump, you know?"

Julie was smiling but Darrel appeared less than convinced. "You'll be coming to the pack retreat at the end of the month, I take it?"

Chloe opened her mouth, unsure whether she should agree or feign ignorance, when warm hands settled on her shoulders.

"She'll be there," Kieran answered for her.

"I'm looking forward to it," Chloe added, reaching up to lay a hand over his.

"I didn't think I'd ever see the day when you'd willingly

bring a partner to our event," Darrel said.

"I didn't think I'd ever find someone like Chloe," Kieran replied. He dropped a kiss against her cheek and Chloe didn't have to feign the shiver that ran through her.

"You're a lucky man," Niall said, releasing his grip on her as Kieran slid his arms around her waist and pulled her back up against his chest.

"Where did you find your witch?" Darrel asked.

"You've been telling me for years I need to find my mate," Kieran replied. "I listened and went to Fated Match."

"The dating agency?" Julie said. "My, my. I've heard of it, though I never had need of their services myself." She smiled up at her partner.

"Well, when Kieran came in I couldn't bear to match him up with any of our eligible singles," Chloe said, taking up the fake story. "Not when I wanted him for myself."

"And the rest, as they say, is history," Kieran said.

"Are you still working?" Darrel asked.

"Do you not approve?" Chloe replied coolly.

"I'm just wondering how you will manage to find the time to come to our retreat."

"Wouldn't miss it," she said. "I've already booked that time off. As soon as Kieran invited me, I ensured everything would work out."

"How fortunate."

Despite the polite words, Chloe was sure Darrel meant them about as much as she meant her proclamations of love. The older wolf did not like her. Why? Because of her surprise appearance?

Or because she wasn't a wolf?

"Couples should be supportive of each other, shouldn't they, Darrel?" she asked.

"I'm sure your presence will make for…an interesting mating moon," he replied. "Are you two going to be participating?"

Kieran tensed behind her. "Darrel," he said. "That is an incredibly personal question."

The older wolf met Kieran's gaze without flinching. "You know what the pack is hoping to see."

"And I know it's still my decision," he replied.

"We haven't discussed things like that yet," Chloe said to ease the tension. "Witches have a far different view of mating than wolves."

"Yes," Darrel said. "A wolf would understand."

She narrowed her eyes. "What are you implying?"

"Nothing," Julie cut in, elbowing her mate pointedly. "It will be lovely to have you there, Chloe. I'll spread the word that we will be expecting a special guest this year."

"Thank you, Julie. I'm looking forward to the experience. As you can see, Kieran's been very close lipped about his family. I look forward to meeting them all."

"Excellent. We'll see you there, then. For now, I'm going to drag Darrel over to the artist in the corner and see if we can haggle for that rosy watercolor."

"Good luck," she said as the older couple strode away.

Chloe let out a long sigh, conscious of the arms around her.

"Don't worry, Chloe," Niall said. "As long as Kieran is by your side no one will snipe at you openly."

She pinned the large wolf with an icy stare. "Do I look like a woman who appreciates having a man fight my battles?"

A slow smile curved Niall's lips. "I'm beginning to see why Kieran didn't want to let you get away."

"Thanks, I think."

He finished off the last of his champagne and set the glass on a passing waiter's tray. "I'll leave you two lovebirds to it and see if I can find my own company for the night."

Chloe snorted. "If you ever get tired of the single life

feel free to drop by Fated Match. If we could meet Kieran's expectations, I'm sure we could do wonders with you."

Niall tossed her a wink before moving off toward a laughing harpy.

Alone, she cautiously turned in Kieran's arms.

"Not here," he bit off when she went to open her mouth.

"Fine," she replied. "But you know I did good." She kept her voice low, conscious she was in a room with creatures that could hear far better than she could.

A soft rumble vibrated through his chest, but he didn't protest her words.

"How long do we have to stay?" she murmured.

"Not long," he replied, bending so his lips grazed her ear. "But make no mistake. All three of them are still watching us."

"Then I suppose that kiss you were planning will have to be an angry, make up kiss."

His eyes darkened as he drew back. "Looks like."

"Think you can make it convincing?"

The curve to his lips was slight but present nonetheless. "Sweetheart, enraged or blissfully happy, I don't think I'll ever have an issue kissing you convincingly."

Her breath caught as her mind spiraled back to their first attempt in his kitchen. "I might not want to kiss you," she pointed out. "After all, you hid me away for months."

"And you made me pay for it tonight," he replied, waltzing her back against the wall. "Tomorrow my entire pack will know I have a girlfriend calling the shots."

"Poor alpha," she purred. "Can't handle little old me?"

"You might be feeling brave because of our audience, but keep in mind, Chloe, it's only you and me at home." His hands molded over her hips as he stepped closer. "I would love to prove just how thoroughly I can handle you."

"In your dreams, wolf," she whispered as her hands twined

around his neck.

"Every damn night."

His mouth came down on hers, silencing the retort on her lips. Chloe had worried about engaging in PDA with him, but the second he touched her, their audience fell away. It didn't matter that curious eyes were on them. All that mattered was the electric desire burning through her.

His lips slanted over hers as his tongue demanded entrance. Chloe didn't hesitate to allow him the access he sought. With the pounding music filling her ears she was glad for the first time for the unusual environment of the gallery. If she was going to make out with her date with the enthusiasm of a teenager, at least the dim lighting would help hide their activities somewhat.

Her arms tightened around his neck as she pulled him closer, returning the kiss with a fervor she didn't have to fake. His tongue tangled with hers as he deepened this kiss. *A girl could get addicted to a man like this,* her wayward mind whispered.

It was true. Already she felt drunk on the sensations he inspired, and it had nothing to do with the champagne she'd barely touched.

Something about this man turned her libido up to eleven with just a touch.

Wishing they didn't have to stop, she still forced herself to push him back with a hand.

"You are making a scene," she said, as if that hadn't been his intention from the start.

His eyes glowed wolf gold as he looked down at her. "Then let's get out of here."

Were the words for her or the fake girlfriend he'd hired? Shaking herself, she allowed a coy smile to curve her lips as her fingers tangled with his. Stepping away from the wall, she pulled him toward the door.

They wove through the throngs of people between them and the exit. Niall caught her eye before they left and sent her a knowing smile that brought the heat of a blush to her cheeks.

Her heels hit the sidewalk, and she sighed with welcome relief. The normal noise of the New York street was far preferable to the pounding club racket they'd left behind.

But her body refused to relax with the predator at her back.

"Car," he breathed in her ear.

Nodding, she allowed him to steer her toward the town car awaiting them.

He held open the back door for her before following inside.

"Home," he told the driver before snapping up the divider.

Chloe scooted as far from him as she could get, crowding up against the opposite door. "Let's talk through this like rational adults," she tried.

His golden eyes glowed in the dim light. "No."

She swallowed. "Kieran."

"You were bad tonight, Chloe."

The words unleashed a flood of heat that pooled low in her abdomen. "I thought wolves liked bad girls?" As soon as the words left her, she couldn't believe they'd come from her mouth.

Kieran, on the other hand, grinned widely. "Oh sweetheart, they definitely do."

Chapter Seven

The passing streetlamps cast brief blazes of light through the car as they sped down the New York streets. With his wolf's vision, Kieran didn't need the extra illumination to help him see Chloe's wide, worried eyes. The damned minx was right to be nervous.

She'd squeezed herself against the door, angling her body to keep him in her sights.

"Kieran," she warned.

Ignoring her, he crawled closer until one hand rested by her hip, the other braced against the headrest for balance.

"If you'd think for a moment, you'd see I saved us by acting the way I did." Her voice had taken on a breathless quality he very much enjoyed.

"We had a plan," he purred, his eyes fixed on her face. "One I spent time crafting."

His wolf prowled close to the surface, urging him to touch her. He didn't need her swift inhale to know his eyes were transforming from their usual brown to a bright gold.

"It never would have worked," she squeaked.

"And you based this on your depth of knowledge of my kind?"

"No." She stared up at him as if afraid to blink. "Based on my knowledge of me."

His head tilted as he studied her.

"You said I was a bad actor," she continued. "Niall would have seen through me."

He hated that she had a point. "So instead you turned yourself into a lover who wouldn't follow her alpha's orders?"

She swallowed. "You're not my alpha."

A growl broke from his throat, proving to them both that the words she'd uttered were dangerous ones. His wolf bared its teeth, taking the words as a rejection of their claim on her. Not that they had a claim, his human side was quick to point out. But logic did nothing to comfort the animalistic urge to prove to her exactly which one of them was in charge.

His eyes raked down her body and he imagined tearing the bright dress off. Oh, how he'd like to show her just what he could do if given the chance. How she'd beg him to take her. Beg him to dominate her. To be her alpha in a way both the wolf and man craved.

Chloe swallowed twice under his burning gaze. "If you were in a relationship with me—the real me and not the girlfriend you invented—this is exactly what would have gone down. This charade can still work. We just need to…tweak things."

He stifled the urge to rip through her clothing, in order to focus on what she was saying. "I paid for that perfect girlfriend."

Pain slid through those damnable green eyes, slicing him like claws. Though he'd only spoken the truth, he wished he could call the words back.

"I might not be your ideal lover," she agreed, her voice soft, "but I can be a convincing one." When she lifted her chin he could almost see her building up her defenses against him. "A girlfriend your pack will believe you could love."

"Will they?" He leaned closer. How could she be so damnably infuriating and heartbreakingly vulnerable all at once? He was torn between the need to chastise her, putting her in her place, and to hold her close, soothing away that cursed hurt in her expression.

"Didn't tonight work well?"

"Yes." Better than he'd dared hope for all day, which grated like nothing else. He should have anticipated this. Should have crafted a story that fit the woman he'd cast to play this role, rather than those from his past. He might have been able to hide away one of his women who asked little of him, but he'd never have been able to do it with Chloe. If she were his lover in truth, she'd eventually have demanded to be taken out of the shadows. To be treated as an equal.

There was a reason he avoided dating women like her.

"There, you see?" Her hopeful voice brought him back to the present. "No need for anger."

How little she knew of his kind. He adjusted his hand to align with the curve of her hip. "You expect a werewolf's anger to evaporate just like that?"

She tensed. Clearly, she hadn't been paying attention to her lessons on how to handle weres.

"How did Niall advise you to calm me?"

Her eyes grew impossibly wide as she realized his sensitive hearing had picked up her conversation.

"Peanut butter cups," she said, her voice high.

A grin touched his lips. "Liar."

"Sugary confections are all you're getting from me, wolf."

He leaned down until his lips brushed her cheek as he moved toward her ear. "Challenging an alpha?"

She exhaled slowly, the breath caressing his skin.

"It's not in me to be anything but a partner with the men

I'm with," she finally said. "Even if the rest is pretend, that's not going to change."

He smiled against her neck, his inner wolf prowling ever closer to the surface. It was more than pleased with her answer. After all, an alpha wolf needed a partner who wasn't afraid to go toe-to-toe with him every now and then.

Not that he was looking for a partner to keep.

"You, little witch, are far more trouble than you're worth."

She pushed him back with a hand on his chest. "And you don't do trouble," she said, her voice dull. "I told you I was the wrong choice."

The idea of having Aoife in his arms, or any of the other candidates she'd paraded before him, was inconceivable.

"Wrong choice," he mused, the words leaving him before he'd even thought them through. "That is getting less and less true with every hour I spend in your company."

Her jaw dropped at the unexpected praise, and Kieran was ready to take full advantage of her surprise.

His lips crashed down on hers. One hand glided up to her waist, the thin silk a weak barrier at best.

Chloe made no protest as he threaded one leg between hers, angling her until she lay spread across the seat under him.

Another man would have found their positioning too awkward to work smoothly. Not so Kieran. Not once did he release her lips as he pulled her into the exact position he wanted—open and willing beneath him.

Her skirt rode up, caught beneath her so it pulled high on her thighs. Her first thought was she wasn't wearing any hose to smooth out her curves. But when his mouth slanted over hers, the thoughts were jettisoned from her mind. Kieran didn't strike her as a man who'd care about such things with an eager partner lying beneath him.

A gasp escaped her as his fingers brushed the naked skin of her upper thigh. This was too much. Too revealing. Too close to being something she'd never be able to forget.

His tongue lapped against hers as he rocked his hard body against her far softer one.

Bad idea, her inner voice yelled.

But it was hard to remember why with his fingers tracing over her leg, creeping steadily higher.

Chloe kept her eyes tightly closed. She wanted to concentrate on the feelings he inspired, not the logic that demanded she push him away. After all, she had no illusions. This was nothing but a wolf releasing some tension. She'd challenged him, and he wanted a little payback. It was his nature. Really, any other girl could have been here with him and he wouldn't have objected. No doubt he'd had his dates in this exact position more times than she could count.

She wasn't special to him.

When he touched her, it became harder and harder to remember that fact. Because no man had ever inspired such need. She hadn't even known she was capable of the mind numbing lust roiling through her. Certainly none of her past lovers had come close to igniting such a blaze, and they hadn't been slouches in the bedroom.

There was simply something about Kieran. Something that made him different from any other man.

Something that made him special to her.

"Dammit," she swore, pushing him back with both hands. The thought was too real to allow the fantasy to continue. What was she doing? Though she enjoyed sex as much as the next woman, she also had her self-respect. She knew exactly what she was to him and it wasn't much. A body. A willing woman to add one more notch to his bedposts.

He hung over her, allowing her to stop his touch but not giving an inch more. "Did that brain of yours start overanalyzing again?"

She glared up at him. "Move back."

"Make me."

Chloe bared her teeth in a very wolf-like expression and snapped her fingers.

Magic lifted Kieran and folded him back into his own seat. She pushed herself up, smoothing her skirt over her legs and ignoring the crick in her neck. She wanted to repair the barriers he'd tried to tear down, go back into her professional shell. Dammit, she was better than this. She wanted more than a hasty tumble in the backseat of a car. What had gotten into her?

"I keep forgetting the magic." He sighed.

"Dangerous mistake."

"Apparently." But there was humor in his words, not anger.

Looked like Niall had been right about the best ways to calm an irate wolf. Not that the information did anything too cool her own irritation. It didn't help that she only had herself to blame for falling for his no doubt well-practiced seduction.

"That cannot happen again," she said.

Kieran watched her with amused eyes. "I promise I'll do my best to ensure it will."

She swallowed, her body applauding his statement. "We had a deal."

"Yes. But if you are allowed to change the rules so am I."

"That's not fair."

He shrugged. "When you play with wolves, Chloe, there are no guarantees we'll behave."

"There had better be this time." She wasn't at all sure she could push him away again. Her body was protesting her decision. It urged her to forget about her commitments and ethics and give in to the pleasure she hadn't know she was missing.

Kieran merely smiled. "And what will you use to ensure my compliance? We both know you're not walking away from this."

"You're right," she agreed. "But we also know I'm not the woman for you." Truer words had never been spoken, and they both knew it.

A frown touched his brow.

"I don't do casual," she continued, ignoring the fact that he sometimes made her wish she did, "and you wouldn't know monogamy if it hit you in the face. You go down this road with me and it will lead to complications you don't want." She swallowed, wishing she could be like Jessica and just leap at opportunities that presented themselves, without worrying about the future.

"Tell me I'm wrong," she said, knowing he couldn't. Though she might long to hear he was as desperate for her as she'd been for him, she knew it wasn't even close to the truth. This man had a dozen women on speed dial. She was entirely replaceable.

A depressing thought if ever there was one.

Kieran dragged his fingers through his hair as he finally turned away from her. "I'll go insane before this is through."

She hadn't wanted him to argue she meant more to him. Really she hadn't. "Better than getting caught up with a woman who won't disappear with the dawn, right?" She turned her gaze to the window, staring blindly at the streets whizzing by. "Any physical contact we have needs to be restricted to when we have an audience. When we're alone, you keep your hands to yourself."

"It wasn't just me doing the touching."

She closed her eyes. No, it wasn't. Despite her reason and logic, she'd wanted him with a need she didn't want to admit.

She could not want a man who was so clearly wrong for her. Not when she knew exactly what would happen if she gave in. She'd get a few nights of mind- blowing sex, and then he'd be gone. On to the next conquest. He wasn't a man who stayed around, and she wasn't a woman who'd settle for less.

"It won't happen again."

His huffed laughter grated over her nerves. "I wish I had your confidence."

"Just focus on the bigger picture. The only reason you're interested in me is because you can't have anyone else. Once this is over, you can go back to your gorgeous models who won't ask anything from you that your wallet doesn't want to give."

He grabbed her arms and dragged her around to face him. Kieran's eyes glowed gold once more but this time she doubted the small shift was due to lust.

"Is that what you think of me?"

She blinked, surprised by the sudden turn. "Of course," she replied, not giving in to the urge to retreat. "You're a playboy through and through. One woman would never be enough for you."

He uttered a curse that burned her ears. "You know nothing about me," he snapped. "Nothing about what I'm capable of."

"So you've tried commitment?" she mocked. He might be old as the hills, but she'd bet her last dollar he was still a wolf who'd never grown up. At least not in this arena.

"Yes."

Shock rolled through her. "What?"

"And you know what I learned, little witch? That it is far easier to indulge and move on than to fight for a fantasy that can never come true."

The car slowed to a halt before the apartment building, and Kieran was out of the door in a flash.

She followed far less gracefully, her mind still reeling that the man she'd pinned as an eternal bachelor had once been faithful. Who had she been? What kind of woman would have been able to pin Kieran down for longer than a brief fling? Curiosity ate at her.

Her partner stalked into the building without waiting for her. Tripping over her high heels, Chloe did her best to jog after him. Obviously she'd touched a nerve with her questions.

Kieran waited by the open elevator, his expression anything but pleased. Not knowing what to say, she slipped past him into the small space. The wolf followed her in, punching the button for the top floor.

"Who was—"

"I don't want to talk about this with you."

She swallowed, watching the floor numbers climb above the door. "You don't think this information will come up when I'm around your pack? Niall already assumed I knew about…her."

Kieran said nothing. He didn't so much as look at her.

"How long were you together?"

"Forty two years, three months, and ten days." The doors parted and he strode out, keys in hand.

Forty-two years? Shock snaked through her. He'd had a relationship that had lasted practically half her life. Keiran, a man who eschewed any kind of commitment to the point of hiring a lover rather than risk letting one in for real.

Dazed, she followed him into the penthouse apartment. Once inside, though, he'd disappear in seconds if she let him.

"We need to talk about this," she said, reaching out to him.

A snarl rent the air as he grabbed her. Chloe's breath rushed from her as he twirled her back up against the wall, crowding into her space.

She angled her face up toward his as he pinned her body in place with his own. Every inch of his hard form pressed against hers, though she tried to focus on the enraged gaze and not the rock solid erection against her stomach.

"You've pushed me tonight," he told her, his voice rough. "Listen when I say you've dared enough."

"I need to know," she replied. "If you'd stop to think for a moment you'd see I'm right. I'm not asking you to bare your soul, but give me a few details so I can sound convincing when the topic comes up."

"A few facts?" His smile was anything but pleasant. "Retell that disaster like a bedtime story for you?"

The accusation stung. "You know that's not what I'm asking."

He tilted his head as he leaned down closer to her. His lips were a kiss away. All she had to do was angle her head just slightly and—

"I may have enjoyed playing with your body, witch, but despite that, we are virtual strangers. I do not discuss that period of my life with anyone, let alone an employee."

She flinched as the hard words tore through her. She'd wanted a kiss and instead she'd been slammed down to reality. A couple sentences. That was all it took to burst the ridiculous fantasy she'd been caught up in. One where she'd thought her opinion had substance, and that he'd been gripped by the same maddening connection as she. But he'd just reduced her to a paid employee. A woman he was happy to screw but not to trust. As if she could ever be anything else in his mind.

No matter what kind of man he may have been in the past, he wasn't what she needed in the present. She couldn't afford to forget that again. This was a job. Kieran wasn't her boyfriend; he was her meal ticket.

"I see." She forced the words out of her tight throat. It shouldn't hurt that he'd confirmed exactly what she'd always known to be true. She could be any woman for all he cared, as long as the role was played appropriately and her legs opened when he wished. "I want it on record, should this come back and bite us later." She turned to stalk toward the stairs and stopped. "You know what I wonder, *boss*?" she said, her voice caustic. "Why the hell is hiring a pretend lover easier for you than finding a real one?"

Head held high, she swept from the room without another word.

Claws erupted from his fingers, implanting several inches into the wall. Kieran cursed as plaster bits rained down on his shoes. He'd screwed up. Royally.

Ripping his hand from the wall, he strode into the living room and did his best to ignore the *click-clack* of her heels as Chloe walked away from him.

He poured a tumbler of scotch and then doubled the dose before setting the bottle back down on the bar cart.

"Dammit," he said, pushing out onto the balcony.

The brush of New York air hit him like a comforting blanket. His highly attuned ears picked up the sounds of the traffic below and the two taxi drivers arguing on the south street corner. He breathed in scents of the park across the street mixed with the faintly metallic smell of the city itself. If he cared enough to glance over the rail, his eyes would be able to pick out minute details carved into the surrounding buildings, which a human would never see in the dark.

All his superior senses and he'd still not been able to stop the train wreck this night had turned into. Kieran closed his eyes, his hand tightening on the glass. She'd fit so perfectly in his arms. His witch was an intriguing mix of passion and hesitation. As if she weren't quite sure how to act but was willing to throw herself whole-heartedly into the exercise. She'd be an eager lover, ready to learn, ready to give.

He'd taken that desire to want to do her job to the best of her ability and thrown it back in her face.

Why is hiring a pretend lover easier than finding a real one?

The words were repeated again and again in his mind. There was only one answer to her question, though he'd be damned if it was a tale he'd share with anyone. Collapsing onto one of the metal chairs, he stared at the dark sky above. He didn't talk about Lisette if he could help it. Those years had been both the best and worst of all his centuries. When he closed his eyes, he could still picture her bright smile, hear her tinkling laugh. But the good times had never endured.

As a were herself, Lisette had been dominant enough that their wolves never grew comfortable with each other. For every day they were content, there'd been two where they fought and argued endlessly. But that hadn't deterred them. *A passionate relationship*, they'd said. That was all it was. For decades they'd tried to make it work because, while their wolves didn't like each other, their human hearts loved.

"Foolish," he whispered. He should have realized when neither of them felt the urge to declare their relationship under the mating moon that they weren't meant to be. But every time he'd tried to walk away, they'd end up back in bed. The sex had been explosive, but what he missed all these years later was the way she'd turn so trustingly toward him in her sleep. How it had felt to know when he came home at night the house wouldn't be empty. The security that any problem could be overcome with enough effort. He'd always thought their relationship was worth fighting for.

Right up until the night he'd come home to find someone else in his bed.

The glass cracked in his hand, scotch running over the wounds the shards sliced in his palm. Biting back a roar, he shook the mess from his hand before pulling out the lingering glass from his skin.

Lisette had been smarter than him. She'd known they would come to no good, and she'd known he'd never be the one to pull away on his own.

So she gave him a reason to. The only reason he would have accepted.

Though still technically a member of his pack, she'd left right after their relationship ended. He hadn't seen her in the century since.

Like him, she'd never mated in the years they'd been apart. He never learned the identity of her lover, though the man's face was seared into his memory. Not that he mattered. Only his lover's betrayal did.

That had been the start of the one-night stands and the endless parade of women through his life. That was the reason it was easier to hire an actress than to risk trusting another lover the way he had Lisette. Never again would he make the mistakes he'd made with her. He'd been young and foolish in those days, thinking love would solve any problem when all it did was exacerbate them. It wasn't a weakness he would ever allow twice.

Except, for the second time a woman was worming her way into his life.

Chloe had a point, even if he hated to acknowledge it. She would be asked about Lisette eventually, and if he really loved her, he would have confided in her. Her lack of knowledge was a problem.

But the idea of discussing his past made his wolf long to howl. Lisette was not a topic he liked thinking about, let alone sharing.

And because of it he'd hurt yet another woman who's only crime was trying to help him.

"Smooth move, Clearwater," he said, mocking himself. He'd worried about Chloe messing up their charade, but if he couldn't let her in, he'd be the one to doom them to failure.

Chapter Eight

"Anna Samson?" Chloe glanced up from her registration form to run a critical eye over the women crowding Fated Match's waiting room. Every one of them was a werewolf and all had requested that Chloe process their intakes.

Vivian had come to her rescue, informing the mob in no uncertain terms that registration would be done on a first-come, first-serve basis. Chloe practically saw the dollar signs shining out of Vivian's eyes.

The front desk, a role she took from time to time, was being manned by their part timer while all the more experienced staff was huddled in their offices, processing one client after the next. Chloe doubted any of them would get more than a fifteen-minute lunch break today.

"Anna Samson?" she called again.

"I'm here. I'm here." A petite wolf battled through the crowd to stand beaming in front of her.

"Nice to meet you," she said. "I'm—"

"Chloe Donovan," the wolf said. "So nice to meet you."

Kieran had warned her word would spread fast, but still,

she hasn't pictured anything like this.

"Follow me, please," Chloe said to her bouncing client.

Ushering the were into her small office, Chloe shut the door and gestured for Anna to take a seat.

"So you are interested in registering for Fated Match?"

"Absolutely," Anna replied.

"And how did you hear about our agency?"

"The were community is buzzing about how you managed to snag one of our strongest alphas," the smaller woman gushed. "When I heard you worked here I thought I should sign up. If you can meet men like Mr. Clearwater through this company then I'm all for it."

Chloe sighed. It was the same story she'd been hearing all day. No doubt her co-workers were ready to kill her over her so-called relationship.

"Anna," she said, shutting her file. "We are a serious agency set to match like-minded singles in an effort to match mates. There is no guarantee about what kind of men you will be meeting beyond the in-depth screening process that helps us safeguard your security. Do you understand?"

"But didn't one of your colleagues mate with a vampire elder?" Anna asked. "And his ward used your services and ended up with the necromancer leader. Here you are, beloved by the wolf we all thought would never settle down."

Chloe winced. "Those are the high profile stories. We have far more ordinary men and women finding their other halves. Last week I got a save-the-date card from a were-moose couple I introduced. They are down to earth people who teach elementary school in Brooklyn. No shining penthouses or expensive jewels involved in that story."

Anna frowned. "You're right. Maybe you have to work here to be connected. Are there any available positions?"

"I think we're done here," Chloe said, standing.

"No, no, wait. I apologize. Normal is fine with me. Sign

me up."

"You have to be serious about finding your mate."

"Oh I am," Anna replied. "I've been alone for a few centuries now and it's not as fun as it used to be."

Chloe studied the woman, who looked like a college senior. "All right. Then we should go over our package options. They range from basic access to our dating database to hand-picked dates designed to match your preferences and personal dating consultation appointments with one of our match specialists."

"Just the standard access is fine," Anna replied. "I want to see what's out there."

Pulling out the proper paperwork, Chloe set the pages before her client. "You can indicate the contract length here," she said, circling a section of the document. "We sell access by the year. You get discounts if you wish to sign up for longer periods of time."

"Might as well," Anna agreed, reading through the fine print. "Eternity's not getting any shorter."

While her client filled out the forms, Chloe grabbed a registration kit from her desk drawer.

"I'll need to take biological samples from you," she explained as she took out her swabs. "We use a pairing of psychological and scientific assessments to help determine your match rankings. I'll need a mouth and skin swab and a few strands of your hair. Should you produce any sort of venom or toxins I'll need some of those as well."

"I'm just plain were," Anna said, setting down her pen and taking the swab Chloe held out. She popped it into her mouth before dropping the sample in the baggie Chloe held out. Anna repeated the process with the other swabs and wipes until Chloe had all the samples needed.

"The standard processing time is one week," Chloe said as she sealed the swabs into a package ready to be shipped off to the lab. "But you will have access to your online profile immediately."

"Awesome," Anna replied. "I can't wait to get started."

"Here is your access information." Chloe held out a plain white card. "My number is on the back should you need assistance."

"Do you have any tips?" Anna asked, looking in no hurry to leave.

"Smile."

The wolf rolled her eyes. "You know what I mean. How did you attract the Clearwater alpha's attention?"

Necessity and desperation, she wanted to reply. She was such a fraud. Who was she to give dating advice when her last real relationship had been years ago? All these women were looking up to her with stars in their eyes, when really she was just as lonely as they were.

Not lonely, she denied. *Focused on what matters. Fated Match is what's important. Not some emotionally stunted wolf.*

"Just be yourself," she said. "I'm sure your matches will find you irresistible."

Her words were greeted by another sunny smile. "Thanks. I'll let you know if I run into any issues. I can't wait to set up my profile when I get home."

"Good luck." She watched the excited wolf skip out of her office and sighed. Chloe knew full well it was a running joke in the agency that she was usually the starry-eyed optimist. But her fight with Kieran had left her feeling far more hollow than happy. Wolves, both men and women, were flocking to the agency under the belief that they could literally work miracles. If a Fated Match member could snag Kieran Clearwater, then the impossible really could happen for ordinary people. How else could a coven-less witch attract one of the elite of their community?

Sighing, she glanced at the registration package and

snapped her fingers. The plastic-wrapped items blinked out of existence. They'd reappear in the intake box at the processing lab.

Job finished, she left the office and headed for the break room. She could use a few minutes respite before repeating the speech she'd just given to the next client.

As soon as she stepped into the room, she realized she hadn't been the only agent with that plan.

"Coffee?" Jessica asked, waving her over. "I just put on a fresh pot."

She smiled in thanks, nodding to the other two women at the small table. Abbey sat with her head down, resting on folded arms, and Tasha had her feet kicked up on one of the empty chairs. Chloe filled her cup and wondered if it would be better to take her liquid jolt back to her office.

"I know that look," Jessica said. "Sit down."

"Hello to you, too," she replied, taking a seat beside her friend.

"Chloe, girl, you should be paying us extra for today," Tasha said.

"I don't pay you at all."

"Fair point. You should ask Vivian to pay us extra for today."

"You are welcome to try."

Both Tasha and Jessica shuddered. "I'd rather do the rest of the intakes single handed," Jessica replied.

"We only have a couple hours to go," Chloe said. "Not so bad."

"Not even when I started dating Lucian did we get a rush like this," Abbey said, not bothering to lift her head.

"That's because your main squeeze didn't want his vampires joining. Kieran has no control over what other packs do."

The brunette sat up and fixed her with an evil eye. "At

least we all knew what was coming. You didn't even give us a heads up before this mob descended on us."

"How was I to know what would happen? I only met a few members of Kieran's pack last night."

Abbey rolled her eyes. "Internet, cell phones, emails. You know wolves can't keep a secret."

"Hey," Tasha said.

"Sorry," Abbey said before she turned back to Chloe. "I don't know how you managed to keep this to yourself for so long in the first place."

"We were careful," Chloe lied.

"I'll get to the bottom of it when I meet him," Jessica promised.

A hissed breath escaped her. "Dammit. I forgot to ask. Sorry, Jessie."

The succubus arched a brow. "Slipped your mind, did it? Wonder what you two did when you got home."

The other women laughed good-naturedly while Chloe's cheeks heated.

"Sunday," Jessica said, blowing on her coffee. "Tell your wolf he can either make a reservation or I'm showing up on his doorstep."

"Sunday should work," Chloe agreed. At least, for her. She'd have to talk Kieran into behaving civilly for an evening and not snapping at her like he'd done last night.

His dismissive expression rose in her mind's eye. He'd looked at her like she was nothing. No one. Minutes after he'd had his tongue in her mouth. Was she really so dismissible?

"Chloe?" Abbey said.

The concern in her friend's voice had her raising her head. All three of the women watched her with worried expressions.

"What?" she asked.

"It's just…" Tasha started.

"You look sad," Abbey put in.

"You never look sad," Jessica finished.

She forced a smile to her lips. "It's nothing," she assured them. "Just a tiring day."

None of them looked convinced.

"Do we have everything set for our mixer next week?" she asked instead, changing the topic with all the subtlety of a sledgehammer.

"Well, we did," Tasha said. "If the intake numbers keep skyrocketing like this we may need to move it to a larger venue."

"I'll mention it to Vivian," Chloe said as she made a mental note. "Abbey, I assume you've roped Lucian into coming?"

"You really think Vivian would let me leave this office without promising her favorite show pony would be in attendance?" Abbey rolled her eyes. "She made me clear his schedule months in advance. Melissa and Tarian will be there, too. Gotta keep our high profile matches in full view of our clients, after all."

"Which I suppose means you'll be bringing Kieran?" Tasha pointed out.

Chloe blinked. She'd been worried about Kieran meeting Jessica. The idea of him assisting her at a singles mixer was too ludicrous to imagine, but there was no denying his absence would raise eyebrows, especially with their other elite matches showing up. After all, he was supposed to love her. Lucian loathed prancing around Fated Match parties, but he did it with a smile because Abbey asked him to. If their relationship were real, Kieran would do the same.

"He's very busy these days," Chloe hedged.

Abbey snorted. "I see your busy and raise you an elder. Lucian controls all the vamps on the east coast. You know how hard it is to get him to take a night off?"

"And we appreciate his dedication," Vivian said, breezing

into the break room. "I'm sure Chloe will be able to convince Kieran. Now, ladies, there's a waiting room full of clients."

"Break over," Jessica muttered.

Chloe downed the last sip of her coffee and set the cup in the sink. She was about to follow the other three women out when Vivian caught her arm.

They waited until they were alone before the siren closed the door.

"I take it this charade is live now."

"Yes," Chloe replied. "We met a few of his pack last night."

"And in less than twenty-four hours we have this flood of clients. Excellent. This might not have been such a bad idea after all. Make sure Kieran is at the mixer. We need to milk his presence for all it's worth before he's gone."

Inwardly Chloe winced, but under Vivian's close stare she ensured her facial expression remained cool and calm.

"I'll do my best. He's not an easy man to control."

Vivian waved her hand airily. "Darling, that's why lingerie was invented. I have faith you can get him there. Now, let's get back to work and sign as many of these clients as we can before the clock strikes twelve."

Chloe followed Vivian out, not looking forward to the conversations she'd have to have with Kieran in the near future.

She'd worked late on purpose, but even with the rush of popularity, the doors of the Fated Match office were eventually closed. With no choice but to face the music, she returned to Kieran's penthouse. Her own personal key was nestled in her palm, to be returned upon completion of the contract, of course.

Outside the door, she paused. What could she expect when she walked inside? Her mind ran through the options. Stony silence was always a favorite. Or he could pretend like everything was normal. There was the possibility he was still angry at her prying. Or maybe he simply didn't care enough to act any differently, and she was over-thinking everything.

"Buck up," she told herself. "No one gets the better of a witch." Rolling her shoulders back, she unlocked the door and stepped into the beautiful home.

A mouth-watering aroma lingered in the air as she kicked off her heels by the door. Dropping her purse on the side vanity, she followed the delicious scent to the kitchen.

Once again, Kieran was cooking. Currently examining something in the oven, he gave her the perfect vantage point to drink in her fill of him.

Not good, she scolded herself. *Be professional, aloof. Show him he didn't hurt you.*

Crossing her arms, she leaned against the doorjamb and waited for him to notice her presence.

But she should have remembered a wolf wouldn't need sight to sense her.

"Have you eaten?" he asked as he straightened and shut the oven door.

"No."

Wiping his hands on a dishtowel, he turned to face her.

Here we go. She mentally braced herself.

"I got something for you," he said, gesturing to one of the cupboards above the counter.

Puzzled, she walked to the cupboard in question and pulled the doors open.

Tea.

The three shelves within were lined with tea. Everything from no-name brands one could find at any grocery store to expensive blends from high-end shops. Green teas, white teas, blacks, and oolongs were neatly arranged for her viewing pleasure. She could drink multiple cups a day for a year and still not go through the amount Kieran had packed into this one cupboard.

Warmth spiraled through her before she ruthlessly forced it back. On the surface this might look like a sweet gesture, but underneath it was little different from the expensive black dress. He was buying her. Throwing money at a problem he didn't know how to handle.

Then again, she was just his employee. What did he care if she was happy or not when they weren't in front of an audience?

Not sure how to take this gesture, she turned to him and crossed her arms. "Nice present. Everything's fixed now, right?"

He sighed, tossing the dishtowel into the sink. "No."

She didn't move as he came closer and leaned back against the island across from the counter where she stood.

The silence stretched until she couldn't take the intensity of his stare a second longer. "Look," she said. "It's not like you said anything untrue." Hurtful, maybe, but not technically false.

"I lashed out."

"We are strangers," she continued, trying to talk over him.

"We're not."

"And you did pay a substantial amount to get me here." A fact she kept conveniently ignoring.

"Not to you."

"So I should have done a better job following your lead." The words were bitter on her tongue. Did she really have to diminish herself to fit into his world?

"Which would have ended in our exposure."

"I'll keep things professional in the future."

He moved then, crossing the small distance between them to lean an arm against the counter on either side of her.

Trapped within his arms, she had no choice but to stare up at him.

"Last night I was an ass," he said. "And I hurt you in order to avoid your questions."

"We all have things we don't talk about," she replied. "I'm too nosy." She tried to focus on his words, really she did, but all her body cared about was how close he was to her. Heat pooled swiftly in her lower abdomen as her body urged her to reach out and pull him closer.

"Yes," he agreed. "But that's not a part of yourself you'll ever be able to change."

"Hey."

He leaned closer, running his lips over her cheek. "Not an insult, just a fact."

Her knees turned to jelly when he touched her with such care. Stiffening her spine, she refused to melt just because he looked a little contrite. She was made of stronger stuff.

"I learned my lesson last night, Kieran. We were blurring lines that can't be blurred for this deception to succeed. I'm not your lover and won't ever be."

"I'm sorry for last night."

She shook her head. "Some things you can't take back. Not with thoughtful gifts or gentle touches. You don't respect me. And beyond my body, you don't see me as something you need in any way."

"Wrong." The word was rough as he jerked back far enough to meet her gaze. "You are not an employee, you are a partner. One who hasn't had many qualms about reordering our story to fit your standards. If I didn't respect that, Chloe, I would have tried to stop you at the gallery." He reached out to tuck a strand of hair behind her ear. "As for needing you, it's true I want to get you in bed as soon as possible."

"Any woman would do—"

"No," he cut her off. "No other woman fills my thoughts

the way you do. No other woman would cause me to take the afternoon off to track down tea flavors I didn't even know existed." His hands clenched as if the words were paining him to say. "No other woman makes my wolf sigh in contentment every time our skin touches," he finished, his voice rough.

She blinked. Really? His wolf liked her? She'd heard weres' inner animals were incredibly picky about who they chose to relax around.

"And we're not strangers. I know you have a spot right behind your left ear that makes you shudder in pleasure."

"Doesn't count," she denied.

He smiled. "I know you are stubborn and moral. You believe in right and wrong and do your best to walk in the light. You love your job, and it's not because it's a paycheck. It's the helping you crave. The knowledge you've contributed to someone else's happiness."

She swallowed hard. "Paying attention, wolf?"

"You fascinate me," he replied, and she couldn't pick up any mockery in his words. "I've never met a woman like you, Chloe. In fact, I've actively avoided women of your ilk."

Bristling, she'd opened her mouth to cut him down when he laid a finger on her lips. "Women like you are far too complicated to be easily ignored. You pull at me until all I can think of is you."

The fight went out of her in a rush. "You can't say things like this, Kieran."

"Why?" he breathed.

"It makes it too hard to…" To remember he wasn't hers. To remember she was on very limited time and when the clock struck midnight, her fairytale would turn to ash.

"To treat this as a job?" he asked.

"Yes."

He nodded in understanding. "Then maybe stop."

Her eyes flicked back up to his. "I can't. Not ever. Because if I let myself lose track of what exactly it is you want from me, I'm going to get hurt."

His expression darkened. "I would never hurt you."

The words sounded like a vow he was making to himself more than to her.

She shook her head. "Not intentionally, maybe. But you're not the man I need and we have to remember that. Thank you for the apology. I appreciate the gesture. We can work together as a team for the rest of this contract."

Kieran looked like he wanted to argue but couldn't find the words. Patting his cheek, she forced herself to duck under his arm and escape.

"What's for dinner?" she asked, walking toward the stove.

A beat of silence rang behind her before he replied, "Roasted chicken and herb potatoes."

"Excellent. I'm starving." For more than food. Mentally, she shook her head at the thought.

Kieran watched her for a moment before sighing. When he moved toward her, his easy smile was back in place. "Grab the plates while I carve the bird."

Turning to follow his instructions, Chloe told herself she wasn't disappointed by his quick capitulation. Tonight had been the best possible outcome. They repaired their rift and were moving forward on more equal footing. Partners in crime, as it were.

There was no reason to feel upset that he hadn't pushed her toward more than a professional relationship. That he hadn't argued he could be the man she dreamed of.

Most of all, there was absolutely no reason to regret that she didn't have an excuse to crawl into his bed. Keeping her heart safe was the right choice. She wasn't missing out on anything.

Her inner voice snorted in derision.

Yeah, she didn't believe it either.

Chapter Nine

Chloe loved weekends. They were her break away from work, where she could focus on something besides helping others find the loves of their lives. Often she went out with friends, did her own recon for her elusive mate.

This Saturday, however, she sat in one of Kieran's deep, comfy recliners with a cup of tea in one hand and a book in the other. Her fake lover sat on the sofa staring intently at his computer screen. It was a scene so domestic she had to keep forcing herself to remember none of this was real. But the silent companionship wasn't awkward. Instead it was comfortable. Chloe couldn't remember the last time she'd simply *been* with someone. Not talking. Not engaging. Just a quiet part of someone else's world.

She turned the page with her pinky before taking the last sip of her tea. Closing her eyes, she savored the earthy taste of her oolong. Kieran really had outdone himself.

Not wanting to leave her comfortable position, she waved her hand and watched as the empty cup glided through the air to land gently on the coffee table in front of her. Task done, she turned her attention back to her book.

"I can feel when you do magic," Kieran said quietly.

Chloe glanced at her companion. "What?"

He tilted his head as if uncertain how to explain. "It's not an unpleasant sensation. More like something soft brushing along the very edge of my senses. It's you using your gift."

"I didn't know wolves could sense magic."

He shrugged. "I've never felt it this way before. Perhaps it's our close quarters."

Thinking back, Chloe tried to remember anything about species that could track a witch's power use. Usually it was only other magic users that could sense such changes. Not weres.

"Has anyone been able to do that to you before?" Kieran asked.

She shrugged. "No, but I live alone. You might be right about the cohabitation thing."

"Surely other witches would have mentioned it?"

Chloe looked back down at her book. "I don't speak to them often."

Other witches had covens, families. Even when they tried to include her, Chloe was always aware she was the outsider. Much like packs, it was rare for a witch to switch covens. Usually, the coven a witch was born into was the only option unless a witch married into another. Even then, there was a family connection to open a door.

She'd had no one.

While a baby might have been adopted into a coven, a grown woman wouldn't. After being rejected by a few groups in the sixties, she'd stopped hoping she'd find some magical family to fill the void inside her. Instead, she'd focused on creating her own bonds with other species more accepting of a lone witch. Jessica didn't care what sort of background she came from as long as Chloe could keep up with her at the bar.

But eschewing her people had some drawbacks. She'd had to learn about her magic on her own, with only books as a guide. Even after nearly a century of study, questions like Kieran's still stumped her from time to time.

"I'll research it," she said. "Let you know if I find an answer."

She glanced up at the wolf and found him watching her with sympathetic eyes.

Her fingers curled tightly on the spine of the book. She'd been doing her best to keep her distance from the tempting wolf but when he looked at her like that, her job just got harder.

"I'm fine as I am," she snapped, knowing he'd inferred more from her words than she wanted to reveal.

"Of course you are," he said evenly. "You don't need anyone else, right?"

"Right." She didn't long for the camaraderie he had with his pack. She didn't wish for a mate to wrap her in his arms. And if she did, the hero in her fantasies certainly didn't wear his face.

Kieran glanced at his watch and a smile tugged at his lips. "True as that might be, little witch, for the next few weeks you're not alone."

The air left her lungs. He couldn't have known how the words would affect her but they did. No one, in all her decades, had ever said them to her. But Kieran meant them in a very temporary sense and she had to be careful to remember that.

He looked up at her with a mischievous glint in his eyes. "How sporty are you?"

"What?"

"Saturday mornings a few of the younger wolves in my pack organize a soccer game in the park. Time with them will guarantee a smile on your face."

Warmth spread through her before she forced herself

to rein it in. Was he asking her to cheer her up or to set up another viewing op of their relationship?

His eyes displayed only eagerness.

"Do you usually join them?"

Kieran inclined his head. "When I can, since I'm so close to the park. I haven't been out in a few weeks due to work."

"I'm not the most coordinated sports player."

He nodded, looking back at his laptop. "Don't worry about it. I wasn't planning on being there today anyway. They won't be disappointed."

"No," she said. "I meant, you'll have to promise to overlook any instances of me running into trees and things as I attempt to play."

The smile he gave her was well worth any bruises she would acquire in this outing.

"I'll go change and be back down in a minute," she said.

"I'll let them know to expect us," Kieran replied as he reached for his phone.

As Chloe headed for her room, she wondered how exactly a werewolf match in the midst of mortals would turn out. Her nervousness was about the potential for supernatural exposure, she assured herself, and not because, once again, she was about to be judged by packmates that were important to the man living with her.

He'd planned to spend the day going over every minute detail of a new investment. Hours of work lay ahead of him—the reason he'd turned down the soccer game invitation in the first place. Though he loved to meet with members of his pack, business came before pleasure. Especially business that helped line the pack coffers as well as his own. He'd had a plan for his weekend the same way he had a plan for every other minute of his days.

But now he was walking through Central Park with a bouncing witch at his side.

Everyone needs a break now and then. He tried to rationalize the situation, ignoring the fact that he'd never been one to shirk a responsibility.

This is a chance to show off Chloe to more of the pack. It's a strategic outing. Good for our ruse.

Giving his younger packmates a chance to meet Chloe would help pave the way at the retreat and provide her with a few familiar faces to search out when they were in the woods. This work was more important than his investments if he wanted to protect his freedom.

That's all well and good, an inner voice whispered. *But that's not why you asked her out.*

No. He'd see the sadness in her eyes and wanted to do something, anything, to erase it.

Damned witch was wrapping him around her finger—a dangerous possibility he refused to dwell on too long.

"What are your packmates like?" Chloe asked.

"They're good kids," he replied. "Just relax. This is supposed to be fun."

"I am relaxed."

He arched a brow. The woman nearly vibrated with excitement and nervous energy.

"I just don't know what to expect," she defended. "I think we've covered that I don't regularly interact with werewolves."

"Be prepared for anything. Wolves are competitive and don't mind playing dirty in order to get what they want."

That brought a smile to her lips. "Good to know." She shot a pointed glance in his direction.

Unable to stop himself, he threaded an arm around her waist to pull her closer to his side. His sensitive hearing picked up her swift inhale, and the sound brought a smile to his lips.

"Just be yourself," he advised. "They'll love you."

She snorted at the words. "I think wolves are a little harder to win over."

He glanced down at her bouncing curls. She certainly wasn't having much trouble making him enjoy her company. Though cohabitation was necessary for his plan to look convincing, the past week with her had been far easier to adapt to than he'd anticipated. Too easy, in fact. He didn't want to get used to having her in his home when she was only a temporary addition to his life.

"Is that them?" Chloe pointed at a group up ahead of them.

"Yes. Are you ready?"

She took a breath and rolled her shoulders back. "Bring it on."

He leaned down, allowing his lips to brush against her cheek as he whispered in her ear. "Remember the point is to have fun."

She turned toward him, her mouth a breath away. "And to pretend to be madly into you," she whispered, low enough that no supernatural hearing would be able to pick up on their words.

"That too." His gaze dropped to her lips. So close. All he had to do was lean down a little and—

His arms were empty. Chloe grabbed his hand and pulled him off the path, into the bright, sun drenched field.

Though he had to smile at her eagerness, the lust riding his body wished she'd held still just a few moments longer.

The group ahead of them turned to watch their approach. Eight young adults gathered around, obviously enjoying being in each other's company. A soccer ball lay at their feet, waiting for a game to start up.

Glancing at the humans wandering by, he had to admit the group of weres didn't appear to be anything more than a pack of kids looking for a little exercise on a sunny day. But as soon as they spotted him, every one of them froze to attention. Eyes dropped to the ground and heads lowered in an automatic instinct as a more dominant wolf approached.

"Hello everyone," he greeted the group as they reached them. "Good to see you all."

Heads came back up and smiles lit the young faces.

"We're glad you could make time for us today," Kate replied.

"The pleasure is mine." And it was true. Looking at part of his pack, he couldn't regret taking a break from his computer today.

The group comprised some of the youngest of his family. Though they all looked like college kids, each had at least four or five decades under their belt. Still, they were young enough to depend on the pack for comfort and stability. He liked to make himself available to them whenever he got the chance.

"I brought an addition today," he said. "Gang, meet Chloe."

Eight pairs of eyes locked onto the woman at his side.

"Hi," she said. "Nice to meet you all. Thanks for including me in your game." Her smile was wide and friendly but he noted the hesitation in her tone as if she were unsure of her welcome.

"More the merrier," Kate said, glancing at her friends as if to see if the statement had their support.

"So how are we doing teams today?" he asked, pulling Chloe further into the group of wolves.

"Uh, well we had been planning on girls versus boys," Chad piped up, batting back the red hair falling into his eyes.

"But that might need to be adjusted," Sasha, the quietest of the group, said, staring directly at Chloe.

"Because I'm here?" Chloe asked. "Why does that make a difference?"

The younger wolves glanced at each other.

"The rules of the game prohibit fully turning," Kieran explained, "but anything the humans won't notice as unusual is allowed."

"It gets rough," Kate added.

"She's right. You need to be on my team."

Chloe looked up at him. "Why?"

"So I can protect you," he replied. His inner wolf growled in agreement. It liked the idea of keeping her close, keeping her safe.

He caught the female wolves rolling their eyes and the boys whispering to each other. No doubt about how they'd have to make allowances for a witch. It was to be expected, though. No one would expect Chloe to play as rough as they did. It wasn't in her nature.

He should have known from the way Chloe narrowed his eyes he'd made a mistake.

"How sweet," she said before snapping her fingers.

His legs shot out from under him, dumping him on his back on the ground. To a casual observer, it would have looked like he'd skidded on some dewy grass—well within the bounds of what a human wouldn't notice.

"But I think I have it covered." Stepping over him as if she didn't have a care in the world about dropping an alpha wolf, she walked over to the group of girls. "Play with me and there's no way we can lose."

"Done," Kate said, staring down at him with wide eyes.

He pushed to his feet with a barely contained growl. "No using magic on the ball," he ordered as the girls ushered her over to their side of the field.

"Wouldn't dream of it," she called back, a mischievous grin lighting her face. "Though that leaves all sorts of opportunities."

Pleasure rolled through him. All wolves liked to play, and

it appeared Chloe would make an excellent opponent.

As he joined his team to strategize, all thoughts of numbers and spreadsheets vanished from his mind.

"I can't believe you just did that."

"Why not?" Chloe replied to the girl who'd spoken.

"Sasha wouldn't say boo to a ghost," Kate said. "Still, it's not often anyone messes with the alpha."

Chloe snorted. "He might be strong, but he's still a man. Sometimes he needs a reminder he's not the boss of me."

Four girls stared at her with a look akin to awe.

"I can't imagine living with him," Sasha said. "Too scary."

"You do realize you turn into a creature with sharp claws and teeth," Chloe pointed out.

"Kieran's a different kind of scary," another girl said. "I'm Jenny, by the way. And if you can cause some of the boys to wipe out during this game, I don't care who you are, I'm in love."

Chloe grinned. "Well, I've got to bring something to the table. I'm not as fast or strong as you guys."

"The boys can be pretty rough," Jenny agreed. "But we give as good as we get."

"Kieran says you do this every week."

Kate nodded. "We're all young, according to the pack at least, and it takes more control for us to be able to handle our wolves. Events like this act as a stress release for us."

"Makes sense. You come and smash each other to bits then go home feeling refreshed."

"Something like that," Jenny said.

"It also gives us a chance to socialize," Sasha said. "Rachel and I are roommates." She waved to the fourth girl by her side. "But the others don't cross paths during their normal days."

"Well then, thanks for letting me drop in on your game. I appreciate it. Kieran has just started introducing me to his pack, and it's great to meet some people closer to my own age."

"My mom mentioned you were still in your first century," Kate said. "That's kinda amazing. I don't think I could handle being in a relationship with someone like Kieran. At least, not yet."

Chloe shrugged. "You never know what you're really capable of until you get dropped into a situation where you're forced to handle it."

Jenny sighed. "But falling for the alpha. How romantic."

"Like a Cinderella story," Chloe said. Or it would be, if any part of their ruse were true. "Still, we're not here to talk about boys. Let's play some ball."

The girls nodded, going over their strategy quickly as they moved to meet their opponents who waited in the center of the field.

"Ready?" Kieran asked when they were all in position.

"Ready," Kate replied.

Chloe blinked and the game was on.

They hadn't been exaggerating when they said they played rough. In the first few minutes, she caught quiet Sasha elbowing an attacker in the face when he'd tried to take the ball from her. The redheaded boy managed to swoop in when her guard was down and steal the ball. He then proceeded to race across the field at the speed that, while still within the bounds of human capabilities, was at least reminiscent of an Olympian.

Kate was hot on his heels and leaped through the air. Together they slammed into the ground as Rachel streaked by and took possession of the ball.

"I warned you," a voice whispered in her ear.

Turning, Chloe found Kieran behind her. "Sure you don't

want to switch teams?"

A flick of her fingers had him on the ground again. "Not on your life, wolf."

Leaving her fake lover behind, she dove into the game.

Though she couldn't run as fast as her teammates, sending a lick of magic to both feet made her kicks highly accurate. Not to mention she had the agility to dance around the boys as they tried to stop her from reaching her teammates. By the time her team had scored the first goal, the boys had developed a new strategy.

One that left Kieran in charge of blocking her.

Laughter escaped her as she tried to duck around Kieran only to have him wrap an arm around her waist and spin her back.

"No fair," she cried, feinting left in a move he easily countered.

"Says the woman using magic."

"Hey, you guys have all the super speed."

"Come on, Chloe!" Kate shouted as she raced past them headed for the boy's goal.

"Shoo," Chloe said, shaking her hands at Kieran. "Shouldn't you be chasing after the ball?"

"I think my team would vote you are the biggest threat."

"Little old me?" She dodged right and wiggled her fingers when he lunged for her. A root erupted from the ground to wrap around his ankle as she streaked away. His laughter followed her as she rejoined the game, stealing the ball away and aiming it for Sasha.

As the game wore on, Chloe realized this wasn't the average human match in more ways than one. The ticking clock had no effect on her teammates. Three hours after the start of the game they still played like they were fresh to the field, whereas her lungs were on fire. More and more she had to rely on magic to outwit her opponents, instead of her own natural abilities.

Kieran in particular showed no signs of tiring.

All that stamina. Think of all the ways one could put it to good use, her inner voice mused.

"Shut up, brain," she whispered.

"You're dragging, witch," one of the boys, Chad if she remembered correctly, yelled to her.

Calling on the depths of her energy, she raced forward.

"Last goal," Kieran shouted.

She refused to look at him, knowing the time limit had been set because of her.

The order merely amped up the energy of the others. Blood sprinkled the grass as the younger wolves fought each other for the ball. Determined to help her team, she chased after the others. One wolf lunged himself at her and she flicked her wrist, sending him flying past her as she pressed forward.

"Chloe!" Rachel called, kicking the ball to her.

Dancing around the others, she kept the ball out of the boy's reach until Kate was open. Aiming carefully, she let the ball fly.

The other woman charged toward the goal, ball firmly in control. Chad made a last ditch effort to stop her but it was too late. With a powerful kick from Kate, the ball soared into the net.

Shouts of triumph rose from the women as they gave each other high fives that would have broken a human wrist.

Chloe laughed at their success as she drew in some deep breaths.

"Looks like you won," Kieran said, jogging up to her side. "This time."

"Bring it on, wolf. We'll always take you down."

His expression was open and happy as he chuckled. "We'll see about that, witch."

She wiggled her fingers, but after three hours of being bested by her, he was ready. Wrapping his arms around her, he dragged her to the ground as he fell, rolling so he took the brunt of their impact.

"Cheat." She laughed as he rolled her back onto the grass, rising over her.

"I told you," he replied. "I can sense when you use magic. And this game has been a useful training session."

"Think you're unraveling all my secrets, hmmm?"

His eyes gentled as he looked down at her. "That would take lifetimes."

The smile slipped from her face as she stared up at him. A new awareness spiraled through her. One that whispered she was lying under him in a very compromising position.

"I'm not so complicated," she whispered.

"Oh sweetheart, I beg to differ." His lips came down on hers.

As always, she melted under his touch. Whereas before he'd kissed her with fiery passion, this time was different. The caress was light, tender. He kissed her as if she were special. Not just another nameless woman in the crowd.

Kieran's lips slanted over hers, deepening the kiss. Wrapping her arms around him, she was more than willing to give whatever he wanted.

Cheers split the air, and Chloe jerked back. The young wolves howled their approval. Heat flooded her cheeks as she looked back up at Kieran.

"Audience," she said.

"Lucky for you," he whispered into her ear. "Someday I'll get you alone when you have no excuses to make me stop."

A shiver ran through her. "Not on your life, Clearwater."

With a grin, he rolled off her and stood. Reaching out, he offered her a hand up.

"Thanks," she said, brushing off the leaves and grass

clinging to her shorts.

Their teammates descended on them with some good-natured teasing. Chloe grinned at the girls as she tried to remember the last time she'd enjoyed an afternoon as much as this one. She had her Fated Match friends, of course, but rarely did she ever let loose so completely. Maybe it was an age thing. Other than the very mortal Abbey, she had no friends under a century, and for the first time she wondered if she was missing out.

"You going to come out next Saturday?" Chad asked her.

"None of us will," Kate replied for her. "We'll all be at the retreat. You're coming, right Chloe?"

"Yeah, I'll be there."

"Awesome," one of the boys put in. "We can have a rematch and not have to worry about prying human eyes. We'll see who wins then."

"Any time," she shot back.

"Let me get your number," Sasha offered. "Then we can meet up during the retreat."

"Sounds great," Chloe said.

Phones appeared in hands as numbers were exchanged and saved. She'd even agreed to a coffee date with Sasha and Rachel after the retreat, before she remembered she wouldn't be around to keep it. As soon as the mating moon was over, she'd have to disappear from this life. Staying friends with Kieran's pack would pose too many complications.

Her eyes flicked to Kieran's and she saw the answering resignation in his gaze as he realized the same thing. They were from different worlds. When time was up, she'd have to go back to hers.

Waving good-bye, she headed off with Kieran back to the apartment. They walked in silence until they were far enough away from the other wolves.

"I enjoyed today," she said to break the silence. "Thank

you for suggesting it."

"You fit in perfectly," he replied. "They all took to you more quickly than I'd thought."

She chuckled. "That's only because they couldn't believe I had the audacity to stand up to you."

"Not many do."

"Your lovers must be able to."

He glanced down at her before looking away.

"Seriously? What, do you pick them for their ability to stay as far out of your way as possible?"

"Yes."

She blinked at the response. "Then what's the point?" As soon as the naive words were out, she wanted to take them back. "Right," she muttered. "Sex. Duh." She rolled her shoulders back and told herself to toughen up. "Well, don't worry. Another couple weeks and you'll be back to your carefree bachelor ways."

"And you'll go back to Fated Match."

"Yep. Exactly. Easy peasy." She'd forget about him and his built-in family. She'd stop dreaming about his kisses. Stop getting lost in a fantasy life she'd never have. Easy freaking peasy.

"As fun as today was, we should probably try to avoid mixing our worlds unnecessarily."

Pain stabbed through her. Keeping her expression serene, she forced herself to breathe past the hurt that again accompanied the reminder she wouldn't be welcome in his life after the full moon waned. "Right," she agreed. "We should have thought about that before coming out today." She didn't need yet another prompt that her only value was as a disposable commodity.

He ran a hand through his hair. "Yes. But I just wanted…"

When he trailed off she shot him a questioning look. "What?"

"You were sad," he said as if that were an explanation.

"So?"

He glanced her way. "So I wanted to see you smile."

Not mine, not mine, not mine, she forced her heart to remember. Because if he were hers, those words would have made her love him.

"Thanks for the thought," she said, her throat uncharacteristically tight. "I appreciate it. I had a blast today."

"And the news will travel to their parents and their friends. It won't be a complete waste."

She looked away, the barb finding a home. "I know you're a busy man. I'm sorry I took up your time. Not that it was my idea, I'd like it noted."

He stopped, catching her arm to slow her as well. "I misspoke."

"But you're not wrong." She caught his hand. "Really, thank you for today. And I know I won't be able to contact those kids again after we go our separate ways. It will be easier, I think, if we remember that going forward. I don't want to make relationships that will hurt to leave behind."

Like the one growing with you.

She would never say those words, but still, they hung in the air between them.

His gaze dropped to her lips as she tried to think of anything to say to break the intimacy she'd unintentionally created. One arm wrapped around her waist, pulling her up against his hard chest.

"This is what I'm talking about," she whispered, pressing her palms against his muscles despite herself.

"You want distance."

"Yes." *No.* Too bad she had no intention of letting her emotions rule her.

"Are you sure?" His head dropped until his mouth was a breath away from hers. It would be so easy to close that distance and lose herself in his arms. There were no witnesses this time. No one needed to know about her momentary weakness.

Her legs trembled before she locked her spine and stepped back, batting away his arms.

She ran a hand through her curls as she walked forward. *Focus,* she thought. *Think of Fated Match and not tangled sheets.*

"Since we were talking about exposure, there's one more hoop we have to jump through."

He fell into step beside her, slightly too close for comfort. "Which is?"

"My best friend wants to have dinner with us tomorrow, to vet you and make sure you're good enough for me."

He arched a brow.

"She's another woman who won't be impressed by the size of your bank account. You have been warned."

"All right. Let's go out to meet her. We can use it as more evidence of our public relationships. Two birds, one stone."

"I made reservations at Celeste's so there should be an audience. You'll have to make a good impression. Jessica is protective and if she gets a whiff that this is a fake relationship she will eat both of us alive."

"I can be charming when I want to be."

"Good," Chloe said. "Remember that tomorrow when you meet her."

When she introduced the man who melted her with his kisses to a gorgeous sex demon. Her step faltered, and for the first time, she wondered if more was at stake tomorrow evening than merely keeping their cover.

Chapter Ten

"Chloe, we need to leave."

"Be down in a minute," she called through the open door. Running back to the mirror, she twirled around to inspect the black slacks and red blouse she was currently wearing. It looked nice and professional.

And boring.

Swearing under her breath, she pulled the shirt over her head and tossed it into the closet. She never took so long to think about what to wear to meet Jessica. The succubus had been her best friend for years, knew all the secrets she shared with no one else. Had Kieran been her real boyfriend, she would have looked forward to introducing him to one of the most important people in her life.

Instead she was trying to find an outfit that could outdo a sex demon.

"This is useless," she grumbled as she pulled on a different blue shirt. This one was far more form fitting and boasted a deep V that accentuated her cleavage. Twisting before the mirror she nodded her approval. Better. Still, something was missing.

"Hair," she said, waving a hand before her face. Her clipped-up, sleek hairdo disappeared, replaced by bouncing curls that cascaded over her shoulders. Definitely sexier.

Deciding she was as ready as she'd ever be, Chloe grabbed her purse from the bed and rushed downstairs.

Kieran was pacing before the door, looking perfect as always, this time in a charcoal suit. He looked up as she reached the ground level, and the appreciation in his gaze chased away some of her nerves.

"Wow," he said.

Chloe tucked a curl behind her ear. "Jessica will expect me to make an effort," she said. "Since you are the first guy I've taken the time to introduce her to in ages."

It was as good an excuse as any for why she'd felt the uncharacteristic need to compete against a succubus. Kieran wouldn't let any attraction he had for her friend show, but she was still introducing him to the exact type of woman he preferred. Jessica was, of course, every man's fantasy.

"Well, you look amazing," he said, pulling her close and pressing a kiss to her temple. "We need to rush, though, if we're going to make our reservation."

Chloe let him usher her out of the apartment, trying not to think too deeply about the small touches and caresses he'd been showering on her since the soccer game. He'd said she needed to get used to him touching her more intimately before they showed up at the retreat on Friday. His people would expect them to be a lovey-dovey couple, and for that, she had to be comfortable being close to him.

But every time his lips brushed against her skin she had to stop herself from stepping closer, from pressing their bodies together and lifting her face for a kiss she knew he'd give her.

"Jon is waiting," Kieran told her as he guided her out of the building toward his town car. He kept a hand on the small of her back as they walked and the thin material of her shirt was no match for the heat radiating from his palm.

Ignore it, Chloe scolded herself. *Focus on surviving the night.*

"Hello, Jon," she said as she reached the waiting driver.

"Miss." He inclined his head as he held the door of the car open for her.

As gracefully as she could, she slid into the seat and shimmied over to make room for Kieran.

The spacious backseat didn't feel small until Kieran took his place. When Jon shut the door behind him, Chloe was acutely aware of the intimacy the dark space created, especially with the divider up.

"So tell me about your friend," Kieran said as the car pulled out into traffic. "What do I need to know?"

"I met Jessica soon after I started at Fated Match. We hired her to man the front desk."

"An old friend then."

"My oldest," she replied. Technically she'd known Vivian longer but she wasn't sure anyone called the siren a friend. "Jessica is older than me, of course. She's far better at using her gifts than I am."

"Which are?"

"Men," she answered drily. "She's an expert on reading men so whatever you do, don't give her any reason to be suspicious."

"I will act thoroughly in love with you," he replied, looking out the window.

Staring at his profile, Chloe wished she were with a man who didn't have to "act." She was barely a century old. Far too young to be thinking about forever. But this time with Kieran was making her realize she liked coming home to another person. She enjoyed hanging out with him in the kitchen while he cooked, or in the living room where they'd watch a movie in companionable silence. After decades of being alone, she liked having someone else she could depend on.

Maybe that was the problem. She might be young, but she'd never had the life others her age had. They'd been part of families, covens, or packs. They'd had people to turn to for support.

But she never had. Oh, she'd had friends and lovers she cared for. None of the men in her bed had ever made her feel like she wanted a life with them. They'd been a way to push back the loneliness, and she'd never heard any complaints, but now she wanted more. She wanted…a partner.

A mate.

"Damn," she breathed before she realized she'd said the word aloud.

Though the sound had been the slightest whisper, Kieran heard.

"What?" he asked, turning to her.

"Nothing," she said quickly. Too quickly. "Just thinking."

"About what?"

"Not your business." She turned to look out the window. "We should be there in a few minutes."

"Chloe—"

"Stop," she said in a low voice. "You have your secrets. Let me have mine."

She concentrated on the world outside her window and not the werewolf at her back. Talking wouldn't help. Not when her realization was still so raw. All she wanted was to leave Kieran behind and turn to her best friend to help unravel her thoughts. Jessica was twice her age and showed no signs of wanting to settle down. Surely she could help talk Chloe out of this.

But she couldn't ask for advice when she was supposed to appear to be exactly what she wanted to talk about—a woman seriously courting a mate.

Thankfully, the car slowed to a halt before Kieran could ask any more questions she didn't want to answer.

"We're here," she said, pushing from the car before Jon could come around to open her door.

What was that about? Kieran curled his fingers into a fist. When he'd turned to her for a split second he'd seen a look on her face that had been heartbreaking. Something about the way she stared at him had been so…lost. Sad. Chloe should never look that way. She should be smiling and happy, carefree in the way he'd always admired about her.

But her easy grins were growing less and less frequent around him. Was it something he was doing? Something that was taking the joy out of her eyes?

His wolf snarled at the thought. Once again his attention was wounding his companion. This was why simple relationships were better. Then there could be no chance of his cursed affection hurting anyone who mattered.

And for better or for worse, Chloe mattered.

There was no chance to ask her more questions, not that she looked in the mood to talk. Especially since she was already halfway up the restaurant's stairs and he hadn't even left the car.

"I'll call when we need a pick up," he said to Jon before leaping from the car.

It took him no time at all to catch up to her, though when he put his hand on the small of her back he felt her flinch.

What the hell had he done?

"Your table is this way," the maître d' said, leading them into the posh restaurant. Soft light lit the spacious room. Dark wood tables with creamy tablecloths filled the space. Wicker ornamental trees decorated the walls with white fairy lights woven through each. The effect created an ethereal forest without compromising on taste. He could see why she would like a place like this.

The maître d' stopped at a table set for three and held out a chair for Chloe.

"Thank you," she said as she slid into her seat.

Kieran took his place and waved the maître d' off. "We're waiting for one more," he said in explanation.

Alone, he watched her pick up the menu and start perusing her options, pointedly ignoring him.

"Is there anything I should avoid doing when your friend arrives?" he asked, hoping to prompt his date into conversation.

"Don't flirt with her and we'll be fine."

His brows rose at the snippy comment.

Chloe sighed and set down her menu. "I'm sorry," she said. "That was rude."

"Are you feeling all right?" he asked, watching her rub the top of her nose. "We can reschedule if you want to."

"No, better to get this over with. Jessica will wonder if I cancel at the last moment."

Right now, he didn't give a damn what the faceless Jessica thought. All he could focus on was the unhappiness of the woman before him.

Her predecessors had never made him care in such a way. If they'd been having a bad day, they hid it so he wouldn't be bothered. After all, their relationship hadn't been about feelings. He'd always appreciated the pretense, not wanting to be bothered with the daily goings on of their lives. It was just another way of keeping his distance, ensuring no one got close enough to make him care.

Ensuring he never made another mistake like he had with Lisette.

He'd been happy in his superficial world until his little

witch had come crashing into it, determined to tear down his walls regardless of whether she had the right.

And despite his best efforts, he cared. More than he should. Seeing her sad unsettled something within him that he hadn't felt since Lisette.

Apprehension snaked through him. He was on dangerous ground.

Chloe glanced up at him with her bright green gaze. "I'm sorry," she repeated, rolling her shoulders back as a smile slid onto her face. "I don't want to ruin the evening. Tonight will be fun."

With anyone else he would have accepted the obviously fake words. But with Chloe it worried him that her smile didn't reach her eyes.

"We can go," he repeated. "I care about you more than making an impression on your friend."

She blinked, the faux smile slipping. "This impression is important to our game."

Doesn't matter. The words were on the tip of his tongue before he called them back. What was he doing? She was right. Keeping up appearances was more important than either of their personal feelings.

Chloe looked over his shoulder and a resigned expression crossed her face. "Besides," she said, "Jessica's here."

Turning in his chair, Kieran glanced behind him…

And saw a cover model striding toward them.

The woman was tall, with wicked curves clothed in a skintight gold dress. Black tresses were pinned away from her flawless porcelain face, and stunning blue eyes locked with his.

Kieran didn't need to check to know every male in the restaurant watched Jessica's approach. She moved with confidence, despite the high stilettos on her feet. The woman managed to look dangerous and sexy all at once. As she grew closer he shook his head to clear it. Ogling over another woman in front of Chloe was not an option.

But when he looked back at his date, he realized she'd been very aware of his reaction.

"Jessie," she greeted, rising to hug the model. "Right on time."

"I couldn't wait to meet your man," Jessica replied, in a throaty voice made to whisper dirty words.

What is going on with me? Kieran frowned. He appreciated gorgeous women as much as the next man, but Jessica wasn't the one he wanted to go home with.

The two women took their seats, as he tried to figure out what was happening. Compared to Jessica, Chloe's brand of beauty couldn't compete, yet when he looked at the witch, warmth spiraled through him. She might not be as flashy, but she was beautiful in her own right. He loved the way her lips curled when she looked at him and thought he didn't notice. Or the tiny lines that furrowed her brow when she thought too hard. Or the way her fingers danced when she wasn't paying attention, as if they ached to do a little magic.

Glancing at Jessica, the warmth inside him disappeared. The woman might be breathtaking but she couldn't hold a candle to his witch. So why did she cause such a reaction in him?

Jessica held his gaze, her eyes filled with some knowledge he couldn't quite put his finger on.

"Kieran," she purred. "A pleasure to meet you." She leaned toward him, giving him a view of the swell of her breasts.

"Any friend of Chloe's is a friend of mine," he replied, concentrating on controlling the desire pulsing through him. He didn't want this woman. His wolf whined and paced within him. Neither of them understood what was happening.

Until everything clicked into place.

Chloe had said Jessica knew men. Jessica, a woman made so flawlessly perfect no man could resist her. One who inspired dark, sexy fantasies in every male she met.

"Succubus," he said.

Chloe blinked while Jessica leaned back, a satisfied smile on her lips.

"Guilty," she said.

"Turn off your charms, or it will be a lot less nice to meet you."

Her smile turned into a grin, and immediately the desire pulsing through him dissipated. She was still stunning, but he didn't feel any need to reach for her. Turning his gaze to Chloe brought the heat pounding back.

"Not many men can resist my lure," Jessica said, placing her napkin in her lap. "You must really love Chloe."

Chloe's gaze shifted to her empty plate.

"I know what I want," Kieran said, his eyes on his pretend mate. "And no offense, Jessica, but you're not it."

"Of that I'm very glad." She held out her hand to him. "It really is nice to meet you now that I know you care about Chloe."

"So I've passed the first test, hmm?" he said as he took her hand.

"Yes, but don't worry. I have many more."

He returned her smile, not minding that she was protective of Chloe.

"What are the specials tonight?" she asked as she reached for her menu.

With a grin, Kieran waved over their waiter. He might be in for a long night.

Chloe watched her dining companions with bemusement. When she'd first seen Jessica she'd wanted to sink into the floor. The succubus had pulled out all the stops tonight, making Chloe's efforts to clean up seem like a child trying to imitate her mother with smeared makeup and too-big high heels. Jessica could be drop dead gorgeous when she wanted to be — after all, it was a survival tactic — but in the work place she usually toned down her gifts. Dressing in purposefully baggy clothes with little makeup helped her do her job without every male she interviewed falling for her. In fact, it had been a while since she'd seen her friend in all her sex demon glory.

Every eye in the restaurant had been on her when she walked in. More than one man had been smacked by their date as they openly drooled after the succubus. Even Kieran had been unable to look away.

But unlike the other men, he'd fought the attraction long enough to correctly deduce Jessica's nature. Chloe had never seen that happen before. She hadn't lied when she'd said Jessica had mastered her gifts. Men simply did not get away from her.

Especially ones not really in love. How had Kieran done it?

Now the pair appeared relaxed, carrying on a conversation as if Jessica hadn't just tried to seduce Kieran and he hadn't managed to break her spell. Even for a magical being, this was a weird night, Chloe thought, as she rubbed the bridge of her nose.

When the waiter came to take their orders, she automatically picked the first dish off the pasta selection. Food didn't matter. Figuring out her date and her best friend did.

"You guys are leaving at the end of the week, right?" Jessica asked Kieran, reaching for her wineglass.

"Yes. On Friday, to beat the weekend traffic."

"Sounds like it will be a fun party." Jessica turned her way. "Tasha and I divided up your files. Everything is set for you to be spirited away into the forest."

"That sounds great," Chloe said.

Jessica whistled. "A couple's retreat in the woods is pretty intensive. You sure you guys are ready for that?"

Kieran reached across the table to catch her hand. "We're ready," he said, pressing his lips to her knuckles before releasing her.

"This is the moon mating thing Tasha is so excited about, right?"

"Mating moon," Kieran corrected. "I'm sure there will be a mass exodus of werewolves from the city this weekend. Those who can get away will try to, especially the larger packs with territory of their own to go to."

"Yes, we're planning for a lighter caseload in the next couple weeks," Jessica said. "It works well, as it gives us a chance to go through our annual audit. First time in years Chloe won't be there to supervise, though. She never dates werewolves."

"Is that so? Who does she usually date then?"

Jessica waved her hand. "A few witches, a few non-predatory weres. I think there was a griffin in there somewhere. And a couple humans."

"Really?" Kieran's eyes flicked to her.

"She's never really had a type. Well, not a species one anyway."

"Jessie," Chloe hissed.

Her friend just tossed a grin her way. "What Chloe goes for is on the inside."

"Ah," Kieran said. "So am I her type?"

Jessica snorted. "Hardly. Part of the reason I was so concerned."

"What do you think I'm missing?"

"Well," Jessica said, eying Chloe. "She likes smart men."

Kieran arched a brow.

"Yes, yes, on that front you qualify," Jessica said. "But she also likes honesty. Someone she can trust and laugh with. Someone kind." She thought for a minute before adding, "Fidelity. That has always ranked high on her list. And you, wolf-man, didn't seem to fit that bill."

"Not until I met Chloe," he said smoothly.

Chloe reached for her wine and drained the glass. "We need more alcohol," she declared. "Immediately."

Jessica laughed as Kieran signaled to the waiter. "Am I embarrassing you, darling? That's what best friends are for. Besides, after months together I'm sure Kieran knows you through and through." She turned to Kieran and said, "Chloe is terrible at keeping secrets."

She rolled her eyes behind her friend's back. If only she knew.

"Do you enjoy working at Fated Match?" Kieran asked, taking pity on her and steering the conversation in a new direction.

"It's a great gig," Jessica replied as the waiter refilled their wineglasses. "I love having a job that makes a difference. It's not like a human dating agency. When we make matches, they last centuries. That's a pretty awesome feeling."

"I can imagine."

"Chloe has a wall of matches in her office. Every couple she's helped bring together earns a place of honor on the wall. She and Vivian vie to see who can make more matches since they've been at this the longest. Though just between us, I think Chloe is the clear winner. Her matches adore her. You should see how many weddings she goes to in a year."

"A wall of matches, hmm?" Kieran asked her.

"I like to remember them," Chloe said defensively.

"Plus she's an utter romantic." Jessica took a sip of wine and murmured appreciatively at the flavor.

"Yes, that I picked up on my own."

Her gaze flicked to his. He had?

"You can see why we at the office are protective of her," Jessica said. "She's part of our family."

Chloe blinked. She'd worked at the office for several decades, but in that time, staff and clients had come and gone. She hadn't really thought of it as being part of anything other than a team.

Though Jessica was oblivious to the effect of her words, the intensity of Kieran's gaze proved that he wasn't. To cover her moment of shock, she reached again for her wineglass.

By the time the food arrived, Chloe was embracing her decision to use alcohol to cover her embarrassment. Jessica was regaling Kieran with yet another story that prominently featured Chloe. He was getting a crash course on her past, which wouldn't be a problem if they'd actually been going out for a year and he had some frame of reference for these stories. As it was, he was either getting the inside scoop on her most embarrassing moments or having to sidestep questions that had the potential to reveal how little he really knew about her.

"Jessie, you should tell him more about your succubus gifts. I'm sure that's a topic everyone is interested in."

Jessica sliced a bite of steak and popped it into her mouth. "Trust me, Kieran is far more interested in the stories I can tell him about you," she said when she finished chewing.

"Just you wait until I'm isolated in the woods with *your* family," Chloe hissed in warning to her date.

He tossed her an unrepentant grin. "Jessica, why don't you tell me what Chloe was like when you first met her."

Jessica took another bite as she thought about her answer.

Chloe sighed and spun some pasta onto her fork. Her

friend would no doubt launch into yet another tale about her chipper personality.

"Sad," Jessica said at last.

They both turned to stare at the succubus, who shrugged. "Fated Match didn't have many staff members that stuck around long in those days. All Chloe had was Vivian, and she's about as cuddly as a sea witch."

"I'm never sad," Chloe scoffed.

This time *she* was the recipient of two stares.

"But," Jessica said, ignoring Chloe's protest. "In the time since you've officially come into her life I've noticed her being far more content than she has been in years."

"That's ridiculous," Chloe said.

"Is it?" Jessica shrugged. "You always wanted stability. A real home. What else do you call finding your mate?"

She looked at her plate. Jessica wasn't saying anything wrong—not if her audience really were a couple in love, planning on forever. But Kieran wasn't that. Instead he was a man paying for her time, and humiliation scalded her. She knew good and well she wasn't the kind of girl he normally wanted, and Jessica's talk of her need for commitment was just underscoring that fact. As if she needed a reminder Kieran would never be hers.

"Excuse me," she said, pushing back her chair. "Too much wine. I'll be right back."

Not meeting either of their gazes, she pushed to her feet and quickly navigated the path to the ladies' room.

She breathed a sigh of relief when she stepped out of the main dining area and into the long washroom, with its dark wood doors on one side, and glass trough sink and massive mirror on the other.

Walking to the sink, she leaned on the glass and looked into the mirror. Pink colored her cheeks, thanks to the wine she'd consumed. But her eyes looked different. Less sparkle.

Less hope.

Jessica had said she was sad when they first met and maybe she was right. So much of the time she focused on being cheerful, being happy, and maybe the reason was that if she didn't look for the positives, the negatives would drown her.

"Chloe?"

Her breath caught when Jessica stepped into the bathroom with her.

"Hey," she greeted, straightening from the mirror.

"I'm sorry," her best friend said without any further urging.

"For what?" As far as she could tell, Jessica had been a delight tonight. She was the one dragging the mood down.

"You obviously don't want me sharing so much with him. I'm sorry. I just thought these were things a mate should know."

"You're right," Chloe agreed. "A mate should hear all these stories."

"Then what's the problem?" Jessica walked closer. "Are things not working out between you two?"

Chloe hesitated, wanting so much to confide in the one person who had never betrayed her. Never lied to her. Never treated her the way she was treating Jessica right now.

"It's just the mating moon," she said instead. "I'm nervous about meeting the family."

"Honey, you don't need to be. They'll love you. Just like he does. I know I wasn't the biggest fan of this match when I first heard it, but I think I was just upset you hadn't trusted me." The succubus frowned, looking down. "And truth be told, maybe a little jealous. I'm far older than you, and I've never gotten so close to finding my mate."

"But you don't want to be tied down," Chloe said, surprise coloring her words.

"I don't," Jessica agreed. "I love my life, my independence. But you've seen the same stats at work I have. Our kind usually either find mates early or late in life. I missed my chance at early, and lately I've been wondering if I'm one of the unlucky ones who has to wait centuries to find their matches."

"Of course you're not," Chloe said. "Matches just show up when you're ready. You know that."

Jessica sighed. "I do. But being wanted for just my body is starting to grate, for all that I need the energy to survive."

"If you want to seriously start looking for your mate I can help you," Chloe offered. "We'll revamp your account tomorrow if you want."

Jessica smiled. "I'll think about it. But for now we need to get through tonight. What can I do?"

"So you approve of him now?"

A small embarrassed smile curved her lips. "I changed a dozen times before meeting you tonight trying to decide if I wanted to come as the friend ready to support you no matter what you were walking into, or as—"

"A sex goddess ready to do battle on my behalf and reveal my date to be a player with no morals?"

"Yes. But he didn't want me, Chloe. Sex is my arena. I can sense lust a mile away, and what my magic inspired in him can't hold a candle to what he naturally feels for you."

Chloe drew a shaky breath. That was good for their cover, bad for her willpower.

"I like him. He's not who I would have picked for you, but maybe that's for the best. You need a little shaking up."

"He's definitely doing that," she murmured.

"Just tell me my boundaries, and let's go back to our meal."

"No more revealing stories," she said. "You can talk about work, what's in the news or yourself. No more spotlight on me."

"Scout's honor," she promised. "And if I say anything untoward just kick me under the table."

Jessica looked so serious Chloe had to smile. Reaching out she dragged her friend into a tight hug.

"Thank you for looking out for me," she said.

"Come on," Jessica said, stepping back. "We're not exactly being subtle. Let's go back to your man."

My man.

If only.

Chapter Eleven

"**D**o we count the evening as a success?" Kieran asked as they entered the penthouse.

"Jessica liked you," she replied, kicking off her heels next to the door. "She's no longer worried you're impressing me with your paycheck."

"Excellent." He watched as she drifted toward the living room instead of retreating to bed. For once, he wasn't annoyed a partner wanted to string out their evening. Extra moments with Chloe never seemed to grate.

She collapsed onto the beige sofa as she waved her hand in the air. A handful of the dimmer lamps flared to life, bathing the room in a cozy, soft glow.

"You had an eye-opening meal," she said.

"I did," he agreed, moving toward her with careful steps. "But you wish I hadn't."

Her eyes followed him as he grew closer. "I don't like you knowing intimate details about my life that you don't need to be privy to."

He nodded, remembering how he'd reacted the first time

she'd tried to pry into his past. "Except this meal made me realize the exact opposite," he mused. "There were points in the conversation where I should have known things about you, things a real lover would. We were saved due to the brevity of the interaction, and Jessica being worried about rocking the boat with you. Neither condition will occur at the retreat."

She shrugged. "What's your point?"

"My point is the same one you made the night we went to the gallery. You said we needed to know each other better. Know inner workings and secrets."

"Yes, I did. Then you shot me down."

"I was wrong." The words stuck in his throat. Had he ever uttered them before? If he had he couldn't remember. He was used to always being in the right. Even if others disagreed, few voiced their displeasure as Chloe had a penchant to do.

But in this case, he'd had everything backward. He'd thought this ruse could be accomplished while he and his partner remained strangers. Never had he thought this enterprise would require the true intimacy of a relationship rather than a facsimile of it.

"You were wrong?" she repeated. "Can I get that in writing?"

"Be kind."

The stare she leveled at him was not exactly friendly. "What happened? You heard a few Chloe stories and decided we needed to bond better?"

Exactly. What's more, he'd liked hearing the stories about her past and her work. He'd been privileged to see a side of her reserved for the friends she loved.

And dammit all, but he wanted more of it.

"Yes," he answered simply.

A beat of silence reigned before she shook her head. "We're supposed to be professional."

"Wolves don't do professional. Not within the pack." He stepped closer to her. "Bringing an outside lover to a wolf gathering is…intimate. I don't want to spill my secrets to you any more than you do to me. But meeting Jessica showed me that it's an eventuality we need to be prepared for."

Chloe hissed through her teeth. "You already know more about me than I know about you. This is a game I'm way too sober to play."

"Then let's fix that." This, at least, was a problem he could handle. Going to the sideboard, he grabbed two shot glasses and a decanter of whiskey from the cart.

"What are you, nineteen?" she demanded as he walked back to her.

"No," he replied. "I'm four hundred and twelve. And that was your first question, which means you have to take a drink." He dropped onto the couch by her side and poured out the first drink.

"Wait, what?"

"We need to know uncomfortable facts that we'd only share with long-term lovers. As we are not in that kind of relationship, we need a shortcut. Alcohol loosens tongues." Or at least he hoped to God it would. They needed to know each other's secrets. Logically, he understood that. But he'd rather walk on nails than speak of Lisette. If the whiskey couldn't help then they were both doomed.

"We can't drink wine like adults?"

"Takes too long," he replied. "Ask a question, get an answer, take a shot. Quick, painless, and we'll be unconscious before we can regret the mistakes we make."

"Where'd you get this idea?"

"Tonight, when I saw you loosen up as Jessica and I plied you with wine."

"Then you have an unfairly sober head start."

"Fine," he said and poured himself a shot and downed

it before she could protest. The whiskey was a familiar burn running down his throat. Some immortals had a high tolerance for alcohol, to the point where they could drink gallons without the slightest buzz. Kieran wondered at his partner's tolerance. Immortals with more human physiology tended to have similar weaknesses. If he were playing completely fair he'd admit it would probably take far more questions to get him drunk than her, but a smart hunter never gave away any advantage.

"Tell me about the last man you slept with."

She inhaled sharply. "Not exactly easing into this are you?"

If there was one thing he'd learned tonight, it was they didn't have time. In a week they'd be surrounded by his packmates, people eager to know every minute detail of their relationship. They weren't ready for that, and if they kept their secrets so closely guarded, they never would be.

"We need to know the details people might ask about. Exes are common fodder for interrogation," he explained.

"That means I'll be asking about yours."

Despair spiraled through him, though he kept his expression blank. "I know."

And he'd have to answer. He needed to be as open as he was asking her to be. He tossed back another shot at the thought.

"You'll really answer?" she breathed, obviously intrigued despite herself. "Anything I want to know?"

"Anything," he agreed before he could regret it.

"Might be worth a headache in the morning," she mused, eying her full shot glass. "Fine. My last ex was a griffin named Edward. It only lasted a few months."

"Why?"

She shrugged. "I lost interest. He was nice enough. Did all the right things. It was me who walked away." Pointing to the bottle she added, "I answered your question, drink up."

Inclining his head, he tossed back another shot.

"My turn," she said. "Tell me about your ex."

Ah, a brief reprieve. Chloe needed to learn when playing with wolves to have a care for her words. "She was a model named Candy," he said. "Seriously. It was on her birth certificate."

"That's not the ex I meant."

"Then you should have been more specific." He handed her a shot. "Bottom's up."

Sighing, she drank down the fiery alcohol.

He took a minute to think about his next question. What did he want to know about her? *Everything*. He pushed the thought away and tried to focus on the specific details that might come in handy. He could ask her more about her lost coven, perhaps details of her past relationships.

But the question that emerged from his lips was far from planned.

"In the car, why did you look so lost?"

The smile slipped from her lips. "That has nothing to do with our ruse."

"Doesn't matter. I asked you a question, you answer. That's how this works."

"And if I don't want to respond?"

"Three shot forfeit."

She gaped. "That will put me on the floor. Plus you can't change the rules once the game has started."

"Of course I can." His wolf paced inside him. Just like the man, it wanted answers. Wanted to figure out the inner workings of Chloe. If he were a gentleman he might retract his question, given her discomfort, but as soon as the thought crossed his mind he dismissed it. She was a puzzle he had to figure out. One way or another he'd hear her confessions, even if it meant giving a few of his own.

"Tell me the truth," he repeated. "What were you thinking about?"

She wanted to tell him to back off. Her realizations about her own desires had nothing to do with his plot. But she'd agreed to this game, and the alcohol was already flowing insidiously through her veins. Truths she'd regret tomorrow seemed a small price to pay for information she wanted today.

Take a page out of his book. Distance yourself from your emotions. Just lay out the facts.

"I realized I want to find my mate," she said, chin up. "When we are through with our ruse, I'm going to start actively searching for him."

The smile slipped off Kieran's face. "You want to settle down?"

She shrugged. "I didn't think so, but these few weeks made me think otherwise. I suppose I have you to thank for that. If I hadn't met you, I wouldn't have realized I was ready for something real."

"If not for me, huh?"

Reaching for the decanter, she poured him another drink. "Yeah. At least something positive is coming out of this." She held the glass out to him.

Saluting her, he tossed it back.

"Now, tell me about her. The woman you don't want to talk about."

He sighed, setting the shot glass back down on the coffee table. "Lisette," he said. "Her name was Lisette."

Chloe swallowed at the pain she heard in that simple sentence. Who had this woman been to him? Whatever had happened, it had obviously been brutal enough to leave scars. "What happened?"

"What always happens," he replied. "We loved too hard. The drama that fueled our passion grew too unstable. It overwhelmed our lives. Every little thing blew up into a fight until eventually, we forgot about the love and only focused on the anger."

She swallowed hard. "Did you leave her?"

He smiled, staring at his hands. "She left me. At least, I suppose that's what you can call screwing another man in our bed."

"What?" she breathed. "That's just…" Chloe shook her head. "Unconscionable."

"We'd been growing apart for a decade," he replied, his voice unnaturally even. "It was inevitable."

"Parting, maybe. But not so cruelly."

His gaze rose to hers. "I wasn't the alpha when we first got together. For years we were happy, until my father decided to step down. When you're immortal, there are only so many lifetimes you can do a job before you tire of it. He was at the end of his reign, and I was ready to take my place as head of the pack. But that time of transition put…"

"Pressure on your relationship," she filled in. "You had new responsibilities, and Lisette wasn't your only concern anymore."

"She wanted to lead, but she didn't want to be tied down to the needs of the pack." He shook his head. "There's a reason ruling alpha pairs are rare. Not everyone is cut out for such a relationship."

Chloe scoffed. "That's nonsense. If a curve ball gets thrown into your relationship, then you adapt. At least you do if it's worth fighting for."

Dark eyes caught hers. "We've already established, my lovely witch, that you think differently than other women."

"Not most other women," she said, sliding closer to him. "Maybe differently than 'Candy' but only because I care."

"Yes," he murmured, running a thumb along her jawline. "You do. About everyone. Strangers, friends. You care more than you should. Why?"

"Is that your question?" she whispered.

"Yes."

Chloe gazed up at him, knowing she was too close. "I don't know. Maybe it's because of the way I grew up. I had no one. I was nothing. I grew up during a war, watching people waste away in front of my eyes. Everyone matters, Kieran. No matter how insignificant they might seem."

"So you fight to bring people together," he mused. "And you keep a record of your successes. Because every match matters."

She nodded, unable to speak.

Both hands cupped her face. "How did you survive?" he whispered. "So naive, so hopeful. How did the world not crush you?"

"It tried." Again, and again.

"But you fought back. Just as a wolf would."

"I'm not a wolf."

"No," he agreed. "Just as strong as one."

The words brought a real smile to her face. "I think," she said, "that might be the nicest thing you've ever said to me."

"Really? Then I've been remiss."

Her breath caught as his gaze dropped to her lips. It'd be so easy to give in and close the space between them. Too easy.

"You need to take a shot," she whispered. "I answered your question."

He leaned back. "And I answered yours." Pouring two glasses, he passed one to her. "Cheers."

Their glasses clinked in the quiet room, then she choked down the alcohol. Already she feared she was in trouble. Never one to hold her liquor at the best of times, a couple drinks of hard liquor on top of wine would push her past her usual boundaries.

And nothing good would come of losing control around her tempting wolf.

"Why the models?" she asked as her next question. "Why pick the women who don't bother you?" It was an answer she thought she knew but wanted to hear from his lips.

"Because I don't care," he replied. "Actively. I do everything I can think of not to care about those around me. I would die for my pack, but when it comes to my personal life, I want to take the easiest way out I can find."

"Sex with no strings," she said. "Companionship without conflict."

"I've been alive far longer than you, sweetheart. I've seen centuries of indifference and brutality. I was born to be a warrior. Raised to do battle to protect my kin. After all the years I've lived, an easy out is...calming."

"I don't believe you," she whispered with a courage she wouldn't have had sober. "My friend is mated to a vampire twice your age, and the years never weighed on him until he lost someone he cared for. Just as you did. It's not your immortality that makes you shy away from relationships. It's Lisette."

He set a shot in front of her before saying, "You know this because of your expert insight? Tell me, Chloe, in all your decades have you ever been in love?"

Her gut response was to say no. The word even started to form on her lips before she silenced it. Had she ever been in love? Not with any of the men who had come before Kieran, certainly. They'd never managed to be exactly what she needed.

Yet in the past two weeks, this werewolf had. He'd seen when she was sad and done his best to correct it. He'd known when she needed something and went out of his way to provide it. They'd laughed as she'd never done with another.

Depended on each other in ways she'd never known, even if necessity dictated it. When something happened during her day, Kieran was the one she wanted to call. He was the man she thought of every night before she slept. The one who crossed her mind as soon as she woke.

Had she ever been in love?

"I don't know," she answered before tossing back her shot. "Probably not."

"Probably?"

She shrugged. "It seems coldhearted to look back over the men of my past and say I never loved any of them. I've lived more than a lifetime without forging such a deep connection. Surely there's something wrong with that picture."

"For humans, perhaps. For immortals that's very normal."

She shook her head. "I want to know what it means to think about one person. To want them, worry for them, trust them. I want to know what's it's like to be bound to another person."

"Because it's something you've never known," he finished for her.

She smiled, knowing it was probably not a happy expression. "It's a foundling's dream, I suppose."

"To have a family."

"To belong," she corrected. "Even if just to one person." Chloe reached forward to pour his drink. "It's not something you've ever had to deal with."

He'd been born into a ready-made support system. Even when his parents had been busy she doubted the darling heir to the pack had ever been alone. He'd have had playmates, companions, and friends.

"Wolves are never alone," she said. "Pack before all, right?"

"True, we're always with others." His gaze flicked to hers. "But that doesn't mean we don't understand loneliness."

Her breath froze in her lungs at the stark expression on his face. He might have had the family she'd always dreamed of, but Lisette had injected desolation into his idyllic life all the same. Maybe, even in a small way, he understood some of what she'd been through.

He tossed back his drink. "Your turn."

"Do you think you'll find someone?" she asked. "Eventually, I mean? Someone both you and your wolf approve of?"

Silence stretched as she waited for him to answer. Unnerved under his dark gaze, she said, "Three shot forfeit remember."

"I think my wolf is capable of trusting again," he replied.

She nodded, reaching for her drink.

"But it's the man I'm unsure of."

She paused, glancing back at him.

"That's a sad statement, Kieran."

"Lisette was a sad experience, Chloe."

"You've been apart for years, though, right?"

"Over a century."

"Then don't you think it's time to try again? To take a chance, but this time on someone worthwhile?"

"And how do I decide that?" he replied. "Consult an oracle I suppose."

"Or trust your instinct. Aren't you wolves supposed to be good at that?"

"In theory."

"Surely in all that time you've met someone that interests you. Beyond the bedroom, I mean."

"I know what you mean."

Chloe toyed with her glass before leaning forward. "You found me because your pack was asking you for something they needed. Something you didn't want to give. Maybe you picked the wrong path. If they needed a mated alpha so badly in order to stabilize the pack, maybe you need it, too. Ever think of that?"

"Every day," he replied, raising her hand with the glass toward her lips. Dutifully, she downed the drink.

"Which duty do I follow? The one to my pack that would see me mated to the next available female wolf, whether I loved her or not, or to my destined mate who may or may not show up for another couple hundred years."

"Or tomorrow," she said. "That's what we tell our members. Your mate may be centuries away or she may be right next to you. You never know until you try."

He slid closer to her along the couch. "Right next to me, hmm?"

Chloe swallowed and turned away. "You know what I meant."

"I do." His fingers threaded through her hair, caressing the curling tresses.

She glanced back at him. "I'm not interested in being the next Candy."

"I'm not looking for her replacement."

"Then what are you looking for?" The words were a whispered breath.

"I think," he murmured. "I'm looking for you."

"For how long?"

"I don't know," he said. "Does it matter right now?"

No, her body cried. She wanted to leap and see where the current took her. Kieran was being more honest with her than he had ever been before. Surely that counted for something.

So what if she regretted her decisions, when whiskey was the deciding factor?

"Now that you've found me," she said, shifting closer, "what do you want to do to me?"

A golden ring appeared around his irises. Awareness threaded through her. She was playing a dangerous game, one she would greatly regret in the morning. Whiskey courage or no, she wanted what she'd been fighting against since he first kissed her.

Chloe cast a leg across Kieran's lap, moving to sit facing him.

"Yes," he purred. "I want you like that."

"Just this?" She ran her hands slowly down his chest. "Liar."

The hard planes of his muscles tensed under her fingertips as his hands moved to cup her hips. Heat radiated from his skin, making her want to rip away the fabric and enjoy the body that lay beneath.

Sober, she might have resisted the desire, but right now she couldn't quite remember why she hadn't allowed herself to make the most of Kieran's presence in her life.

Her fingers flew to the buttons of his shirt. Within seconds they were free from their bindings, the material gaping around his golden chest.

"Better," she purred, pressing her palms to his skin.

He hissed a breath. Had he been waiting for this skin-to-skin contact as much as she had? If so, she could do better than her hands.

Bending, she pressed her lips to his chest. Her tongue lapped out to taste him.

"This is a bad idea," he said as his fingers delved into her hair.

"Terrible," she agreed, moving to flick her tongue over one nipple.

Power flooded her when his muscles contracted in pleasure. Usually she was uncertain with a new lover. She wanted to know what they preferred, needed to make sure she colored within the lines. But with Kieran, she did what she wanted. She touched where she craved, and he let her. This strong alpha, who was in charge every moment of his life, sat back and allowed her to play as she would.

Her fingers drifted along the waistband of his slacks. With a teasingly light touch she trailed along his abdominal muscles, her hands moving lower and lower. One hand dipped to cup the rock-hard erection pressing against his pants.

"Clothes are such a hassle," she whispered against his throat, licking over his thundering pulse.

"Agreed," he said, his voice hitching when she stroked him.

Chloe lifted her head to see his eyes. Gone was the thin ring around his irises. In its place was the pure, golden gaze of a wolf on the edge.

"Hello there," she said to the animal staring from Kieran's eyes.

"I told you both of us liked you," he said, leaning forward to capture her mouth.

She groaned as she parted her lips for him. He tasted of whiskey and sex as he took charge, plundering the depths of her mouth. She should have known an alpha of his power could only be so good for so long. It wasn't in his nature to relinquish control to another.

But as he rolled her to the floor, rising over her, she found she had very little problem with letting him dominate her. Not with his heady kisses clouding her mind with pleasure.

He pressed one leg between hers, fitting his body over hers. She clawed at the hanging shirt, pulling it from his body without breaking away from his mouth.

Her hands ran over the naked skin of his back. He was as perfect as she'd expected. Hot, hard, and hers, at least for now.

No wonder his past lovers had been willing to live off the scraps of affection he tossed their way. A woman would go to great lengths to keep a man like this in her bed.

Don't think about them, her inner voice whispered. *They aren't here right now.*

Not wanting to wait, her fingers rose to the buttons of her own shirt. Chloe was pretty sure she lost a few of them in her haste to strip, but didn't care.

Kieran helped her pull the blue material from her body before pushing her down with one hand. He rose over her, staring down with glowing eyes.

"Beautiful," he said, his voice gruff.

"I get better," she replied, pulling down the straps of her bra. She wasn't sure where her inner temptress had been hiding all these years, but she was glad the vixen had finally made an appearance. Keeping her gaze on him, she unhooked the bra and let it fall free. Twining her arms over her head she arched her back, her breasts on full display.

"Are you sure you don't have some siren blood in your background?"

She laughed, relaxing under him. "Who knows?"

Kieran cupped her breasts, running his thumbs over her sensitive nipples. Need spiraled through her. She'd known how good it would be in his arms and still fought against their attraction. Such a foolish decision.

When he replaced his hands with his mouth she threw back her head, enjoying the sensations of his tongue lapping over her hardened nipple. More, she wanted more. Her remaining clothes constricted her. She wanted them gone, wanted his naked body moving over her, in her. Her patience was coming to an end.

"Let's move this to the bedroom," she said.

Kieran stared down at her with glowing golden eyes. "Hell, yes."

She grinned, trying to roll up.

"Dammit," he muttered. "Wait, witchling. We can't."

She snorted, sure he was kidding. "Then we can stay right here." Her hands slid down his chest.

A happy fog filled her mind, getting rid of the nagging

voice whispering that this was a mistake. She didn't care. Right now pleasure pulsed through her body, and she wanted to return the favor.

Her hand moved lower to cup his cock once more.

"Christ," he swore.

"You've had centuries to perfect your seduction," she whispered in his ear. "But there's something to be said for raw enthusiasm."

"Don't I know it." A growl rumbled from his chest but she didn't mind in the least. Other women might find looking up into the eyes of a wolf unnerving, but she liked his inner animal just as much as she liked the man.

"I'm right here," she purred against his ear. "Asking you to take me." Her fingers stroked him as she spoke.

"You are making it damn hard to do the right thing."

"Our opinions of 'right' differ."

He grabbed her hands and pulled them up, trapping them against her chest so she couldn't touch him. "You're drunk."

"So are you."

A grin flashed across his face. "Maybe. However, I'm sober enough to know you'll hate me in the morning if this continues."

"I don't care about what happens in the morning."

"But I do, sweetheart." His forehead dropped against hers. "I'm not taking advantage of this situation."

She let out a growl of her own. Using a touch of magic, she reversed their position until he lay beneath her. Chloe pressed her hands against his chest as she sat astride him. "I'm not some innocent miss unsure of what she's getting herself into. I know exactly what I'm asking of you."

He gripped her upper arms and drew her down toward him. "Can you promise me you won't regret this tomorrow? Won't blame me for it?"

She frowned. No, she couldn't. But what was worse was

the knowledge she was half naked in front of him and he was still pushing her away.

Where had she gone wrong? He'd wanted her just a few minutes ago. His tongue on her body hadn't been an illusion.

Had he decided she didn't have enough experience for him? God knew he outnumbered her when it came to past lovers. Maybe there was something about her he found wanting.

"You don't have a noble bone in your body," she said, dropping her hands from his chest. "Why are you holding me off, when I'm offering exactly what you've wanted from me since we met?"

His breath hissed out between clenched teeth. "I want more from you than a drunken tumble."

"Who are you and what have you done with Kieran Clearwater?"

"I told you," he said, pulling her close. "I'm not looking for another Candy."

She looked down at him, seeing the gold bleed from his eyes. Here she was, all hot and bothered, and his lust was cooling.

Shame spiraled through her. She was begging a man who didn't want her.

Idiot, she berated herself. *Fool.* They'd shared some alcohol-fueled confessions and she'd made them into more than they were. He'd said himself he hadn't known what he wanted from her. Well, it seemed pretty clear that he'd figured it out.

Nothing.

Not even her body.

"Bastard," she hissed, pushing herself off of him.

"Because I'm saving you from a decision you'll make us both regret?"

She rounded on him. "Don't ever think you can make

decisions for me, wolf. I can take care of myself. Far better than you will ever believe."

"Chloe, I'm not rejecting you—"

A harsh chuckle escaped her. No, it wasn't rejection. He was doing this for her own good. Maybe he even believed it. But she knew he was doing it because his interest had cooled and he wanted an exit that wouldn't hurt their partnership. Couldn't have her storming out two weeks early, could he?

Holding out her arms, she twirled in a slow circle. "Hope you enjoyed the view," she said, snapping her fingers. Her shirt flew over her arms and buttoned itself up. "Because you will never see it again."

She scooped her bra off the floor and strode from the room.

"Chloe," he called after her.

She didn't pause as she raced up the stairs. Didn't hesitate when she threw herself into the shower to wash away every trace of his touch.

And she certainly didn't think twice about the tears trailing silently down her face.

Chapter Twelve

She was right. He was a damned idiot.

Kieran sat in his chair, staring at the files on his desk that required his attention, and couldn't summon the will to throw himself into work. Oh, he'd tried. But after catching the last of many calculation errors, he'd admitted defeat.

Work was not going to erase the memory that haunted him.

He pushed out of his chair, pacing the length of his office. Never before had he had a problem separating his personal and professional life. Whatever drama he got into stayed outside the office. This was his haven. A world he could command and order as he pleased.

But Chloe's face refused to leave him. The look of pain and disappointment in her eyes continued to slice through him half a day later.

"I did the right thing," he said to himself. The noble thing. She was right that it went against his hedonistic nature, but he hadn't wanted to break whatever it was growing between them.

Though trying to protect her may have done that anyway.

Claws ached to explode from his fingertips, a sure sign of his rising agitation.

His plan had been sound in theory. Alcohol had loosened both their tongues, allowing them to share revelations they never would have offered otherwise. If it had stopped there, they'd both be calling last night a win.

But when she'd climbed on top of him, all thoughts of talk had flown from his mind. What was it about the witch that made him crave her like a damned drug? It wasn't his way to get hung up on any woman. He'd lusted after potential lovers before, but he'd never pursued anyone the way he wanted to chase Chloe. Usually he took a what-will-be-will-be approach to his love life. Often the women he wanted had little problem with falling into his bed. The few who'd turned him down had then been dismissed from his mind with very little contemplation.

Maybe it was their prolonged proximity that was tying him in so many knots. Once Chloe was out of his life things would go back to normal.

Except he couldn't imagine weekends without her curled up on the armchair, tea in one hand and a book in the other. He'd have to go back to solitary meals and a life that revolved around the office—neither of which had ever bothered him before now.

"It's the mating moon," he said aloud. His instincts were all over the place.

His thought lacked the conviction it'd once had.

He ran a hand down his face. Chloe didn't want temporary. She'd told him so last night. He was to thank for her newfound desire to find her mate.

The universe had a twisted sense of humor.

Even if she hadn't discovered her wish for a permanent companion, he'd known right from the moment he'd met her that she wasn't the type of girl to settle for a relationship of convenience. No, anything with Chloe would be tangled and complicated.

And no doubt vastly rewarding.

Which left him with a decision. Did he want to repair what he'd broken last night? The hurt, angry Chloe he'd seen might not be a delight to spend time in a cabin with, but she'd also pose no threat to his solitary life. Right now the woman wouldn't touch him with a ten-foot pole.

It'd be the easy way out.

Except the pain in her eyes gnawed at him every time he closed his. She'd taken his concern as rejection, and after the lonely life she'd lived, he could just imagine what that was doing to her.

She's my employee, my pretend lover. I shouldn't care. Hell, Chloe was taking up far more of his time than his real girlfriends ever had.

That truth did nothing to quell his desire to make things right.

He glanced backward at his phone. She was a few button presses away.

"Dammit," he cursed, stalking to the cordless. Other men might be able to ignore their partner's pain but he didn't seem capable of it.

Here's hoping she didn't dismiss the call when she saw who was on the other end.

Some things magic couldn't fix. Chloe's pounding head was one of them. The embarrassment clinging to her like a second skin was another.

Leaning her forehead on the desk, she closed her eyes and wished she were anywhere but work. Drinking on a Sunday night. Recipe for disaster.

Not quite as bad as waking up with a clear memory of exactly what had happened the night before.

She groaned, not exactly sure what was worse—telling her flighty would-be lover she wanted a mate, or the fact that he'd turned her down when she'd offered herself up on a silver platter.

Oh, he might have said perfect words she was desperate to believe, but in the harsh light of day Chloe figured the alcohol was probably affecting him as much as it had her. Even intoxicated, Kieran had managed to stop and push her away. He might have said he needed her as something more than his next superficial girlfriend but when push came to shove, he hadn't wanted anything from her at all.

And that pain cut through the worst of her embarrassment like a knife.

It was a blessing he'd stopped when he had, she told herself. He'd kept them both from making a mistake. Better he realized she wasn't what he wanted before she'd ended up crossing a line she couldn't come back from.

It didn't matter that he didn't want her as much as she wanted him. She'd always known they wanted two different things out of this partnership. Better to get this job done and get away from him as fast as possible. Then she could focus on finding her mate, which obviously wasn't the delicious alpha. Her mate wouldn't push her away. Not ever.

Her mate wouldn't find her lacking.

The phone rang, cutting through her morose thoughts and making her wince at the shrill sound. Pushing herself up with a groan she grabbed the receiver.

"Fated Match, pairing mates together since 1704."

"Chloe."

Her body went from sluggish to alert with that one word, spoken in a voice she recognized all too well.

"Kieran," she said. Her instincts demanded she slam the receiver down, but logic stopped her. She could play this cool. Be an adult. So he'd turned her down. She could rise above and be mature. Couldn't she?

"You were gone when I woke today."

"Early shift," she replied, not wanting to admit she'd set her alarm so she could avoid bumping into him in the kitchen. Last week she'd enjoyed the domesticity of getting ready for work together, watching Kieran making them breakfast while she'd prepared the tea and coffee. Today, though, she'd wanted a chance to lick her wounds before she saw him.

"We need to talk."

That was the last thing she wanted to do. No doubt he'd be kind, explaining exactly why this was a bad idea for their charade. She'd nod along, all the while knowing if she'd been Candy or any one of his other nameless lovers he would have taken her every which way, until neither one of them had the strength to move.

"We can do that at home," she said. "I'll be back by seven or so."

"And leave you spinning worst-case scenarios in your head all day? I'm not a dumb man."

She sighed, leaning back in her chair. He wouldn't let this go. Fine. She could handle it. "What do you want to talk about? I'm busy."

The one lone file on her desk mocked her. Vivian had taken one look at her sorry, hungover self and banished her to her office with barely anything to work on.

"Last night…"

"I told you alcohol was a bad idea."

He snorted. "It was a brilliant idea. You never would have told me the things you did last night. Not without dating for far longer than we have been."

"And you wouldn't have mentioned Lisette," she snapped.

"It's not as if you're any more open about your thoughts than I am."

"I don't regret our confidences."

No, just stripping her body bare. "Then why are you calling?"

"I want to apologize for what came after."

She squeezed her eyes shut. Even though she'd seen it coming, it still hurt that he regretted the fiery embrace that was imprinted on her brain. He'd told her that he'd been looking for her and then pushed her away, all in the space of minutes.

"Apology accepted." Her tone was harsh even to her own ears. She wanted this conversation over.

"You're getting things twisted again, aren't you?" He sounded amused. The bastard. "Sweetheart, I'm only apologizing for pushing you away. I didn't want to take advantage of a situation you'd regret this morning."

"Convenient excuse," she said. "Just call things as they are. We were on track for what I thought would be some pretty epic sex and you lost interest."

His snort of derision mocked her. "Is that why I've been hard as iron all day?"

"Your own fault."

"Yes," he agreed. "I let things get out of hand. Whiskey or not, I should have stopped everything the moment you climbed on top of me."

Her cheeks heated at the reminder that it'd been her actions that started them on the path to the awkward conversation they were now engaged in.

"If we'd had sex last night, how would you have felt today?"

She wanted to say she'd have been perfectly fine, but the words died on her tongue. In truth, she would have berated herself for her poor decision. She would have cursed the alcohol she'd drunk, and probably cursed the wolf in her bed for taking advantage.

"You would have regretted it, Chloe. We both know that."

"And you cared about that so much you restrained yourself?" she asked, her words dry.

"Yes, that is exactly what happened."

She blinked. "You don't walk away from things you want, and you've been trying to get me into bed since I first moved in."

"I told you things were different with you. I meant it. When you finally yield to me, witchling, you're not going to have anything you can blame for your decision other than lust."

A flare of hope sparked to life within her. He sounded sincere. If he was telling the truth, then he cared about her. Far more than she'd suspected. Cared enough to protect her from herself, even when it went against his desires.

He'd put her needs first.

"Do you believe me?"

She chewed her lip. "I want to."

A chuckle sounded through the phone. "Chloe Donovan, I swear to you on my pack that I want you with a goddamn need I haven't felt in decades. If I had my way, we'd be having this conversation at home right now, and once you believed I only stopped because of the alcohol in your system, I'd carry you to bed. Hell, we probably wouldn't make it that far. Not that I'm opposed to bending you over the table and introducing you to such pleasure you wouldn't remember your own name, let alone your reservations."

Heat flooded her cheeks. "I believe you," she hissed. "Stop that."

"Good. Then believe this, I'm done trying to separate business and pleasure. You can try to resist, my witch, but I'm going to do my very best to seduce you."

Her mouth went dry. "I was clear about what I wanted, Kieran. That hasn't changed just because I'm in possession of all my faculties now. I don't do temporary."

"I know. Hurry home tonight, Chloe. I've been dreaming of kissing you again."

The line went dead.

She stared at the phone in her hand. What did he mean, he knew? Knew she wanted a mate and was happy to ignore that fact, or knew and still wanted to pursue her?

"Damn the man," she breathed, returning the phone to its cradle.

Kieran on his best behavior had been hard to resist. How was she supposed to survive the next two weeks with the wolf turning every ounce of charm and determination he had on her?

"I'm in trouble," she said, dropping her forehead back to her desk. Last night might have gotten her the secrets she wanted, but it also gave her a taste of what she was missing.

A taste that just made her crave more.

He heard the door close as he pulled the meatloaf from the oven. Chloe was right on time. As he portioned out dinner on to two plates he listened for her movements. Usually she kicked off her heels and made a beeline for food. Tonight, she lingered in the hallway.

A grin curved his lips as he walked the plates over to the island. Looks like she wasn't as sure of her self-control as she wanted him to believe.

Even after their phone call he'd been haunted with memories of her half naked and spread out beneath him. He deserved a bloody medal for having the self-control to turn her down. Not that she'd thanked him for it.

Just as she wouldn't thank him for seducing her if he didn't want to keep her.

He went to fish out some utensils from the drawer as he thought about that quandary. Chloe wanted something real, something long term if not forever. And he…

Lisette had broken something in him. He wasn't sure he could handle the kind of relationship Chloe would need to thrive. Wasn't sure he wanted to find out if the man he'd been with Lisette was still buried somewhere inside him.

But Chloe was worth the effort to find out, wasn't she?

His wolf let out a happy whine of approval within him.

"I know you like her," he whispered to himself. The damn beast had been overjoyed last night. Kieran couldn't remember a time when the two halves of him had been so in sync, so focused on the pleasure of one woman. His wolf wanted to keep her. It was the man holding them back.

"Smells great."

He turned to see Chloe slip into the room, her back pressed against the doorjamb.

As always, she looked good enough to eat. Her dark suit complemented her curves, even as it gave her an air of professionalism. How did her male clients manage to sign up for Fated Match without trying to catch her eye?

"Long day?" he asked, crossing his arms.

She shrugged. "Vivian had me on grunt work."

He eyed his partner, noting how she hugged the doorway. Did she think he'd pounce if she got too close? A wolfish smile tugged at his lips. Probably. He wasn't even sure she was wrong. Still, Chloe would bolt if he moved too fast, and though he'd always run from commitment, he didn't want to chase her away.

A mess of contradictions aren't you, Clearwater?

"Hope you like meatloaf."

"Yeah." She stepped forward, moving toward her usual chair.

As she did, Kieran grabbed the teapot off the counter and

headed toward the mug beside her.

"I figured you wouldn't want wine tonight," he explained as he poured her a cup.

"Smart man." Chloe wrapped both hands around the mug and inhaled the earthy aroma, closing her eyes in pleasure.

It was her favorite oolong. That he knew that fact had surprised him. Usually he never noticed such small, personal details. But with Chloe he knew which tea she preferred, what chair she liked to curl up in, what food made her sigh in delight. Necessity might account for learning more in their brief time together than he normally would have, but not for the desire within him to know her. Her likes and dislikes, her motives and fears. He wanted more than just a bedmate.

Which was a damn complication.

A couple more weeks. If they could just survive a little longer then…

Then what? He'd try to date her like a normal man?

The wolf inside him growled. It didn't want such a temporary arrangement.

Too bad. You are not in charge here.

Grabbing his own glass of water, he joined her at the island.

"So," she started, eying him carefully. "If you're in a good mood, I have a favor to ask."

Anything. "What do you need?"

"It's a work thing. We're having a mixer for our members and Vivian wants me to bring you."

He blinked. "Go to a work event?"

She nodded. "Two of our other high-profile couples are coming, and it would be a coup for the agency if you came, too. I know it's not really up your alley. But hey, a room full of sexy singles. You might find someone you want to pursue after the mating moon is over."

He growled, not liking those words at all. "Chloe," he

reproved.

Green eyes flicked up to his before she let out a long sigh. "Sorry," she said. "I'm on edge." Rubbing the bridge of her nose she tried again, "Will you come with me? Please? My friends expect me to bring my lover, and if you're not there it will raise questions I'd really rather avoid answering."

"This is important to you?"

She nodded. "I love my job and mixers are a great way of bringing people together."

Yes, thanks to the previous night he understood a little more why she did what she did. Chloe took pride in her work. It was part of who she was. If she was asking for this favor after the awkwardness of last night, then he was sure this was important to her. "I'll be there."

Surprise showed on her face when she looked back up at him—surprise that slowly melted into a true smile of pleasure. How could anyone deny her anything when she smiled like that?

Unable to help himself, he reached out to run a finger down her cheek. "There's much I'd do for you, Chloe, if you'd just ask."

Stay with me. The words were on the tip of her tongue. But of course, that was not the type of request he meant. No, Kieran would want her to ask for sexy times in the shower or bouts of sex in the bedroom.

She looked down at the delicious food she'd barely tasted. "Thanks," she said. "It will help to have you there."

Picking at her food, she searched for a way to get back to the easy camaraderie they'd enjoyed before yesterday. For all Kieran's teasing and taunting, she'd never been this nervous with him before. She wanted to ask what he'd meant about his vow of seduction. She needed to know—if she yielded, would she get more than a couple of nights.

But there was no easy way to frame such a question.

Deciding avoidance was the better part of valor she pushed her half-eaten plate away.

"I'm not very hungry tonight," she said by way of explanation. "I think I'll turn in early. I need to research harpy etiquette. I'm signing up a pair tomorrow, and they are not a species you want to annoy."

"I've met a few in my time. Let me know if you need any firsthand accounts."

"Thanks," she said, conscious of the fact she would have picked his brain had they had this conversation two days ago.

Hopping off her stool, she headed for the door.

"Oh, Chloe, just a moment."

She turned to see he'd followed her.

"Did I forget something?"

"Yes."

Wrapping his arm around her waist, he pulled her tight against his chest and claimed her mouth with his.

Chloe gasped, surprised by the sudden kiss, and he took full advantage of her dropped guard.

He kissed her with a passion that awakened an answering need within her. Even knowing it was a mistake, she twined her arms around his broad shoulders and tilted her head to give him better access.

Together they waltzed backward until she hit the wall. Kieran crowded into her space as his hands slid down her sides to rest on her waist. She wanted more, wanted his hands to run all over her body. His lips slanted across hers, sending all the sensitive nerve endings into overdrive. Rising to her tiptoes, she tried to get closer to him.

Then as suddenly as the kiss started, it was over.

Chloe blinked, her arms still wrapped around him.

"Much better," he purred.

Ripping herself from his arms, she spun on him. "What the hell was that?"

He leaned against the wall, arms crossed, and a lazy smile on his lips. "That," he said, "was on both of our minds."

"Is this how you seduce your lovers?" she taunted, drawing a hand through her hair as she tried to catch her breath.

"No," he said, his smile dropping from his face. "This is how I seduce *you.*"

She glanced up at him, hearing the sincerity in his words.

"I don't like when we're at odds," he continued.

"So the plan is to kiss me until I'm comfortable?"

The boyish grin was back. "Did it work?"

To her surprise it had. He'd done what she'd been thinking about all day, and it stabilized her equilibrium. It assured her last night had not destroyed the growing intimacy between them, hadn't irrevocably altered their relationship.

Her teasing, charming wolf was back.

Biting back her own smile, she closed the distance between them and balanced herself with a hand on his crossed arms. Rising on tiptoe, she stopped when her mouth was a breath away from him.

"Poor wolf," she whispered. "Wanting what you can't have."

She danced away when he tried to reach for her. "Be good," she chided. "I have work to do."

Kieran's warm chuckle followed her as she headed for the door.

"All work and no play makes Chloe a dull girl," he called.

Might be true, she thought, her lips curving. Even so, there was no hiding from the fact that in a few days they'd be away from the city and far from any thoughts of work.

Alone in the woods with a tempting werewolf. She wasn't sure if the thought worried or excited her.

Chapter Thirteen

"Where's your wolfish arm candy?" Jessica asked, her arms full of a Fated Match banner.

"He's meeting me here later," Chloe said. "He's been working late these past few days to offset what he'll miss when we're away."

"A retreat to the woods," the succubus sighed. "Romantic."

"Need a hand with the banner?"

"Please."

Holding out her hands, Chloe let her magic flow around the pink and white paper. The banner floated into place over the bar, it's ties knotting automatically to the ceiling hooks.

"All right?" she asked.

"Looks good."

Chloe dropped her hands as the banner unfurled to read, *Singles Mixer by Fated Match.*

"We're fully booked. It should be a good night," Jessica said, glancing at their sign-up sheet. "Kieran's appearance will help with word of mouth, too. Thanks for roping him into this."

"Didn't take much convincing at all." Indeed, Kieran had tried to be as helpful as possible, even when she made him practice all her friend's names on endless repeat. He had, for all intents and purposes, been a model boyfriend this week. Though he did make use of any opportunity to pull her close for a kiss or a caress. If she wasn't careful she'd get used to the happy smiles that greeted her arrival in a room, or the light pecks that accompanied her departure in the mornings.

"Problem," Tasha said as she walked into the room. "The bartender is out of O neg."

"Drat," Jessica murmured. "We'll have to have someone do a blood run. We've got at least ten vamps on the guest list, and that's the most popular blood type."

"No worries. I'm calling Melissa right now," Abbey said, trailing Tasha. "She can grab some on her way over with Tarian."

"A vamp and a necromancer. I still can't believe they're mates," Tasha said.

"Stranger than a human and a vampire elder?" Abbey teased.

"Or a witch and an alpha wolf?" Jessica put in.

Tasha sighed. "Well, when you put it that way."

Jessica slung her arm over Chloe's shoulder. "See? You and your weird relationship are in excellent keeping. Fated Match seems to breed them."

"If everything is in place I'm going to open the doors. Members will be descending on us any minute," Abbey said.

True to her prediction, at exactly eight o'clock the first guests arrived. Chloe moved into place by the door, greeting the members as they came in. Usually Vivian handled this particular job but she was running late. Besides, with any luck, Chloe would be in charge of the agency in a few months. She'd be doing this all the time.

The thought brought a real smile to her face. The drama

with Kieran sometimes made her lose sight of the bigger picture. She wanted this agency that brought people from all walks of life together. Making families answered a calling within her she couldn't describe.

Behind her, she could hear her teammates mingling with the singles, easing their way and making appropriate introductions. Supernaturals rarely had evenings like this, where they could be exactly who they were without fear of prying human eyes.

"Chloe, nice to see you again."

She glanced up at the tall man before her. He stood ramrod straight, his dark hair impeccably styled and his clothes fit to perfection. When he turned his blue gaze to her she shivered, despite the fact she'd met him many times before.

"Lucian," she said in greeting. "Good of you to come."

"My mate made it clear if I didn't, I would be sleeping on the couch for a week," he said, his lips twisting in amusement. "A wise man does not cross Abbey when she's focused on a cause."

"I just saw her over in the corner. I'm sure she'll be happy to see you."

The ancient vampire's gaze was already locked on his errant lover. "Thank you," he said to her without glancing in her direction.

Chloe watched him move toward his mate as if he couldn't stand to be away from her for another second. What would it feel like, she wondered, to be that drawn to another? She spent her days waxing poetic about the mating process, but she had no firsthand experience. Abbey looked at Lucian as if there were no one else in the room. When the two of them touched, she could almost feel the love vibrating between them. She wanted that for herself.

Though when she pictured her future mate, he only wore one face.

"Deep thoughts?"

Two words, and her body leaped to life. Turning, she found her own date standing by her side. His eyes were focused on her, humor in their amber depths.

"Just thinking," she said to Kieran.

"About mates."

He said the words easily, in no way looking like a man about to bolt for the hills. What a difference a few weeks made.

"Yes."

He nodded, moving closer to her. "Well, since this evening is about romance, we should make a good show of it. Kiss me, witchling."

People were moving past them, guests she should be greeting, but she couldn't muster the will to care.

Grabbing his lapels, she pulled him down. Her lips pressed against his in a kiss that was far more decent than she wanted it to be. But they were in public and eyes were on them.

He wrapped one hand around her waist, the other cupping her cheek as he returned the caress. His lips were soft against hers, the touch gentle. It was a kiss that had less to do with passion than it did with companionship. A hello between lovers.

When he drew back, his gaze was locked on hers.

Drawing in a shaky breath, she told herself the kiss hadn't affected her. It didn't matter at all that he'd kissed her as if she were important to him.

As if she was special.

"What do you want me to do?" he asked her, his voice soft.

Take me to bed. "Ah." She swallowed. "Stand here with me while I welcome people. Our were clients will be thrilled to see you."

"As you wish." His expression clearly said he'd heard the

words she hadn't voiced. Still, he moved into position by her side, smiling at the people who came through the doors.

Just as anticipated, the gossip about both Lucian and Kieran being present spread throughout the bar. Glancing over her shoulder, she saw Abbey and her mate holding court in the corner while most of the single werewolves were eying Kieran.

"You have fans," she whispered to her partner.

"I didn't notice," he replied, equally soft. "I have eyes only for you."

She snorted at the old line, but even so, warmth spread through her chest. No doubt a month ago he'd be prowling through the bar looking for his next conquest.

White-blonde hair flashed across her vision, heralding Vivian's arrival.

"Kieran," she said, shaking his hand. "Good of you to come."

"Always happy to help, Vivian," he replied.

Vivian's cool stare flicked to her. "Look who I found outside." She gestured to the couple by her side. "I heard there was a blood shortage."

"I brought all I could," said her friend as she entered. "I hope it's enough."

Chloe accepted the bag from her and glanced inside to see a number of containers of blood. "It's perfect. Thank you, Melissa." She passed the package to Vivian who strode toward the fridge behind the bar.

The red-haired vampire grinned. "Looks like a good turnout."

"Your presence helps with that," said Chloe.

Melissa's amusement didn't fade. "They just want to see how a necromancer and vampire survive without killing each other."

"Very happily," her companion said, wrapping his arms

around his mate's waist.

"Tarian." Chloe greeted him with a smile. "Fair warning, Lucian is in the corner."

The necromancer frowned. "So much for a relaxing evening."

Melissa elbowed him in the stomach. "Be polite to my father."

Tarian rolled his eyes before holding his hand out to Kieran. "I hear you're the Clearwater alpha. Welcome to the club."

"Club?" Kieran said, returning the handshake.

"Men who love Fated Match girls," he clarified. "I met my mate the first time I stepped foot in that agency."

It's true. Chloe had been there when Melissa and Tarian had first met. For a brief moment she'd considered vying for the necromancer's attention, but it had been clear from the very first that he had eyes only for Melissa.

She glanced at the man by her side, wishing their story had been similar.

"I hear Jessica got to meet your boyfriend properly," Melissa whispered to her, moving closer to her side. "Unfair friend favoritism."

"I'm sure Abbey filled you in," she whispered back. "We're very new to the public scene."

Melissa nodded. "I also heard he's whisking you away to a pack retreat. When you're back I insist on a dinner. I'm sure Abbey is just waiting to hear all the details, too."

Chloe smiled at her friend. "Absolutely," she said, wondering if it was a promise she'd be able to keep. If Kieran ever wanted a serious relationship, she'd be proud to introduce him to her friends.

"I'm going to go say hello to my father," Melissa said. Glancing at the man behind her, she asked, "Coming? Or are you going to hide at the bar and pretend you haven't noticed him?"

"Where you go, I go," he replied, bending down to press a kiss to her cheek.

"So we're invited to a dinner?" Kieran asked as the other couple walked off.

Chloe glanced up at him. "After the moon. Don't worry about it."

"They seemed like a nice pair. I'll look forward to it." He turned to smile at an incoming wolf, who stared at him like she'd just seen a movie star.

Chloe stared at her date, her jaw nearly dropping. Had he casually referred to the possibility of them staying together beyond their deal?

Could he want her for longer than the charade?

Hope fanned brighter within her. The moon was fast approaching. Maybe she didn't need to dread its arrival as much as she had been.

It turned out Kieran was a natural at the matchmaking game. Vivian had relieved them of doorman duty, wanting the latest feather in her cap to mingle with the crowd and talk up the services. Chloe had thought that a tall order, considering Kieran hadn't officially used any program at Fated Match, but the wolf had been a good sport. He was charming as he conversed with the singles in the bar, encouraging them to extend their contracts and suggesting introductions to other supernaturals milling about.

Chloe sat on a barstool watching him work his magic. He might be an investment guru, but she'd bet the beer in her hand at least one of the pairs he'd introduced would be calling her up tomorrow to schedule official dates.

"He's doing well," Vivian said, appearing by her side.

"Who would have thought."

The siren plucked the beer from her hand and took a sip before passing it back. "Tomorrow you leave for the woods."

"Yep. We're almost there."

"Still planning a big break up after the moon has waned?"

She hesitated, not knowing how to reply.

Vivian sighed. "That's what I thought. Didn't heed my advice, did you?"

"Abbey and Melissa beat the odds," she replied. "Maybe I am one in a million, too."

The look the siren leveled at her was equal parts pity and disbelief.

"Shut up," she said, taking another sip. "I can hope if I want to."

"Yes, you can," Vivian replied. "I've got you on the schedule the Monday after the moon. Let me know if you need more time."

To cry my heart out? she wondered, looking at her flawless boss. The other woman obviously thought she was headed for disappointment.

"Thank you," she forced herself to say.

Kieran caught her eye as he threaded his way toward them. "Your mixer appears to be a success, Vivian," he said when he reached them.

"Yes," she replied. "Thank you for your appearance. You've helped us enroll quite the numbers this week."

"I'm glad this worked out for all of us."

Vivian's eyes flicked to her before she smiled once more. "As am I." Inclining her head, the siren drifted off into the crowd.

Kieran leaned against the bar next to her. "I can see why you like this job," he said. "Spotting the similarities between people and setting them on paths to each other is oddly satisfying."

She clasped his arm. "We do these mixers a few times a year, and it always results in some great matches. Supernaturals simply don't have many chances to mingle with their own kind. Two mates can be living in the same city, sometimes on the same block, and never meet one another."

"You're doing good work," he said, patting her hand.

She nodded, watching the crowd. "Kieran?"

"Hmm?" He looked down at her.

"The dinner with Melissa. Did you mean it?"

Understanding lit in his gaze. A soft smile curved his lips as he reached out to tuck a piece of hair behind her ear.

"I like your world," he said. "Seeing what you do, how you bring these people together. You give them a chance at happiness. Maybe I want the same opportunity."

The din around them ensured semi-privacy, even from those with acute hearing, so she didn't have to censor her words. "You want me beyond the mating moon?"

"My wolf does."

It was a non-answer, and they both knew it.

"What about the man?" she said.

He blew out a long breath. "He does, too."

A smile started to tug at her lips, but he caught her hand, shaking his head. "I still don't know what I can offer you, Chloe. I'm not sure I can ever be what you want."

The words had an ominous ring she wanted to ignore. "Time," she replied. "All I want right now is time."

His eyes gentled as he raised her hand to his lips and pressed a kiss into her palm. "Being with you isn't like being with anyone else."

Even Lisette? The words hung on the tip of her tongue. But Kieran's expression was open and happy. She didn't want to dredge up painful memories.

"Me too," she replied instead. "You're unlike anyone I've ever known."

He leaned close until his lips brushed her ear. "Just think of how good the sex will be."

With faux outrage she pushed him back, only to realize he was laughing. Though she'd heard the sound before, it still brought an answering smile to her lips.

"One track mind," she said. "This is what happens when you're without a lover for too long."

He shook his head. "No, my witch. You're just special."

Her heart twisted at the simple phrase. How many times had she wanted to hear those words since they'd met? Even though she'd heard it straight from his mouth, it still seemed unbelievable. The powerful alpha and the orphan witch? It sounded like a fairytale, a perfect fantasy.

One that would hurt when it shattered.

"What?" he asked, his smile sliding from his face.

She shook her head, not willing to offer up that particular confession. "Time. Promise we'll have more than just the retreat."

He pulled her into his arms, resting his chin on the top of her head. "We'll have more than the retreat, witchling. I might not know much, but I know that."

It wasn't the promise she'd hoped for, but for now, it was enough.

Chloe closed her eyes, breathing in his earthy scent as she tried to forget the fact that the days that separated them from their future would be the hardest of their whole charade.

Chapter Fourteen

Leaving the confines of the city never failed to excite his wolf. This time, though, his inner animal was practically doing back flips the closer they got to pack territory. Even his human half had to admit he was excited. The retreat was something they all looked forward to, and this year was no different.

What's more, he was eager to see Chloe's reaction to his people. No doubt a tough road lay ahead of her, but she had the mettle to face it.

"Wow, you guys have a lot of space," she said, pressing her nose to the window as they drove across the Clearwater land.

Pride swelled within him. The pack property had been in the family for as long as he could remember. Though acres of forest stretched out all around them, it was the heart of the property they were driving through.

Cabins appeared along the main road, signaling their journey was almost over.

"If you look to the left you'll see the dining hall," he told her as they drove through the center of the retreat. "It doubles as a meeting lodge, and as a day care for younger cubs."

Continuing the drive, they passed a lake equipped with canoes and kayaks on the shores, a fire pit with bleachers for dozens of people, and paths leading into the dense forest ringing the retreat.

"We're getting farther and farther away from everything," she commented.

"The alpha's lodge," he replied. "It's the farthest from the others."

"Why?" she asked, looking back at him.

He bit back a grin. "Privacy, sweetheart. Everyone around us has supernatural hearing, remember?"

Her cheeks glowed red as they pulled to a stop before the last cabin on the road. He couldn't help chuckling as Chloe practically threw herself from the car.

Following suit, he stepped out on to pack land and drew in a deep breath. Part of him loved the city and the elegance and vibrancy it offered, but another side craved open spaces just like this. He couldn't wait to let his wolf run free without having to worry about observers.

"It's beautiful here," she commented as she pulled her duffle from the trunk.

"Just wait till you see more of the land." He grabbed his own bags and followed her up the cabin steps.

"Is there anything else I need to be on guard for?" she asked as he fished for his keys. "What if I forget something?"

He smiled at her nerves. She'd demanded a list of all the major players in his pack and spent hours each day memorizing each and every one. If Chloe was one thing, it was thorough when she set her mind to a task.

"You'll be fine," he assured her. Though she might be a jumble of nerves, he was remarkably calm. Logically, he should be worried about any slips, but he couldn't help think his pack would love this witch once they came to know her.

Unlocking the door, he pushed it open. "Welcome to Camp Clearwater."

Inside the cabin was a charming, if rustic, living space. Looking around the familiar room he knew the fey Chloe had tried to set him up with would have had kittens if forced to stay here. The woman at his side merely examined the place with a smile.

There was a small sitting area to the side of the door. It boasted a wood-burning fireplace able to make the cabin warm and cozy on even the coldest days. Though there were no electronics such as computers or TVs in the building, there was a kitchenette in the corner, with a stove and fridge. Chloe walked across the colorful throw rug to reach one of two doors in the far wall, one opening to the washroom and the other to the only bedroom.

She turned back to him and crossed her arms. "So I take it you're sleeping on that tiny chaise in the sitting room?"

"No, sweetheart," he said, crossing the room to her. "I'm sleeping next to you." He entered the bedroom and tossed his bag on the far side of the bed. "Unless, of course, *you* want to sleep on the chaise."

He sat on the bed as he watched her glance around for an alternative sleeping option. As he'd planned, she found none.

"I could have brought a sleeping bag had you warned me," she said at last.

His grin was unrepentant. "Exactly."

Rolling her eyes, she dragged her duffle to her side of the bed. "You better not be a cover hog."

"You can always kick me if I steal them. Or better yet, cuddle up closer."

"Shameless," she murmured, perching next to him on the bed.

There wasn't much space in the room beyond the mattress and two chests of drawers. A wide window was cut into the far wall, with light curtains hanging on either side.

"This is rather cozy," she said.

"Very." Unable to keep from touching her, he let his hand drift to her nape, toying with the lose tendrils of hair falling free of her bun.

A soft smile curved her lips as she allowed the caress, but it was quickly chased away by her worries. "What if I screw up?" she whispered to him.

A curious tenderness gripped him. "Has it not occurred to you, Chloe, that the lie we are telling gets smaller with each passing day?"

She shook her head. "You don't love me," she denied. "And we haven't been dating as long as we've claimed."

He shrugged. "I agree it would be far better they never discover the truth, but wolves don't place the same emphasis on time as you do. I've seen couples declare themselves under a mating moon having known each other for far fewer days than we have. When our wolves know, they know. We're trained from childhood to listen to their voices."

"What's it like?" she asked. "Is it a voice in your head?"

He'd never tried to describe the animal that was his constant companion in life. How did one explain a presence that was as natural to him as breathing was to her? "More like…feelings, sounds," he tried. "My wolf doesn't speak as you or I would, but I understand him all the same."

"Another way in which you're never alone."

He fell back on the bed, his arms cast out on either side of him. "Trust me, after a few days with my pack you'll be wishing for solitude."

"Spoken like someone who has never been abandoned," she quipped.

Though the words were teasing, the sentiment underlying them was real and painful. Grabbing her arm, he dragged her down onto the bed with him.

For a moment she lay stiffly by his side, then her body started to relax into his. Wrapping an arm around her seemed to be the most natural thing in the world.

"While you're here, you'll never be alone," he said.

"I'll have to enjoy it while I can." He frowned at the words, but she'd already moved on to another thought. "Your whole clan is here for the retreat?"

Allowing her to change the subject, he nodded. "Most of them. Some members are abroad or too far away to make it, but the majority try to come when they can. It's the only time in the year we're all together, after all."

"Are you really okay with this?" she said, tilting her head up to see him. "Lying to your friends, your advisors?"

He was silent for a long moment. "They didn't give me much choice," he said at last. "The last three women they pushed me toward were unacceptable."

"Why?"

He exhaled. "Their candidates housed very submissive wolves, which in theory makes sense. It's widely believed a larger gap between dominance levels in wolves leads to a happier mating. Two alphas or two submissive wolves don't balance each other out. They are constantly hampered by the similarity of their inner animals. It's what tore me and Lisette apart."

Her small hand pressed against his chest, over his heart, and he reached up to tangle his fingers with hers.

"Having watched that train wreck," he went on, "my advisors decided I needed a docile mate. They keep sending women after me who have far less dominant wolves."

She snorted. "That would bore you silly in a month. You need someone who can go toe-to-toe with you."

His arm tightened on her. "Exactly. But I also need someone who doesn't raise the hackles on my wolf."

"You should have looked to the rest of the supernatural world earlier if that was your criteria. You need someone strong without an inner animal chained to the dominance hierarchy of a pack."

"Perhaps," he agreed, his fingers stroking up her arm. "Outsiders are rarely welcomed into a pack. And almost never into a ruling pair."

"So you're telling me I'm in for a hell of a ride while I'm here."

"Yes." He turned to look at her. "When we made this bargain I didn't really care about how hard this time would be on my fake mate."

"I'm tough," she replied. "That's why you picked me, isn't it? I can hold my own."

With her so close, smiling so widely, he had no choice but to lean over and kiss her. Need pulled at him, but he did his best to keep himself in check. This was neither the time nor the place to give in to his baser instincts. Not with his pack waiting for them. Even so, he allowed his lips to trail over hers, enjoying a brief taste before he had to pull back.

"I'm glad you're here," he told her, meaning the words more than he should.

Her cheeks were a rosy pink as she smiled at him. "Because I'll be able to play this part convincingly?"

"No," he replied. "Not just because of that."

Her lips parted silently as she stared up at him. He drew his thumb over the smooth skin of her cheek, marveling at how perfect she looked lying next to him here. No other woman would have fit so easily.

"We should go," she whispered. "Let the others know we're here. Right?"

The question sounded as if she were hoping he'd disagree with her. If only he could.

With a sigh he pulled them both up. "Yes. They will have seen the car. No use hiding."

She nodded, drawing in a deep breath. "Then let's go get

started."

Time to put their ruse to the test and see if his pack really would believe he'd fallen head over heels for a witch.

In her teenage years, Chloe used to have nightmares that she'd walk into a room of her peers and silence would fall, all eyes on her, as if they knew the secret she was trying to hide.

Today she lived that fear.

When she entered the main hall, her hand clasped in Kieran's, a room full of werewolves eating dinner were stunned to silence. Chloe stared at the rows of tables, packed full of people who had been laughing and talking when they'd walked in. Now she could have heard a pin drop.

Undaunted, Kieran pulled her forward to the head of the hall. As she followed him, the weight of dozens of eyes landed on her.

Show them your mettle, she instructed herself. He'd had picked her because he needed a woman who could stand up for herself, even against a room full of disapproving wolves.

Lengthening her stride, she caught up to Kieran so that he was no longer pulling her along but instead walking shoulder to shoulder. Lifting her chin, she tightened her grip on his hand and strode with purpose. She'd spent years living from meal to meal, sleeping in doorsteps and clawing for any scrap of safety. Werewolves were nothing compared to that fear.

Together they halted before the assembly.

"Thank you all for coming," Kieran said, raising his voice so that it carried to every corner of the hall without needing a microphone. "The Clearwater pack has had another successful year with pack revenues rising nine percent. We've also welcomed fourteen of our young into adulthood this year. I'm also happy to report, all twelve couples who declared themselves at the last mating moon are doing very well. I hear there is even a babe on the way for the Larsens."

A tentative round of applause followed what Chloe assumed to be the annual recap.

"I am pleased to see so many of us have managed to make it this year," he continued when the applause died down. "This is a sacred time when we can come together as a pack. Relationships can be reforged, new love cemented by ties of mating, and our community strengthened by our time together." He glanced her way before continuing. "You all know I am not one to share private details of my life, but I am going to make an exception tonight. You have a right to know why a non-wolf is present at our gathering. Chloe Donovan is a witch, it's true, but she'd also the love of my life."

She fought to keep her face impassive and not flinch at the false declaration. If he'd meant the words, she would have been beaming with pride.

"Though we will not be participating in this year's mating moon due to our cultural differences and beliefs, I am hoping to woo her into staying by my side. I trust each of you will help me in my quest and welcome her. I know if you do, you will come to love her as I do."

Chloe was so focused on the crowd that she didn't notice Kieran reaching for her until he bent her backward, his mouth on hers. Feeling herself falling, she automatically wrapped her arms around him, responding instinctively to the hunger in his kiss.

Thunder pounded in her ears as his mouth slanted over hers. It took several seconds to realize it wasn't in her head, but the roar of the pack pounding on the tables.

Pulling her back to her feet, he called out, "Let the retreat begin!"

More cheers. She pasted a smile on her face even as she

made careful note who was applauding and who was stonily silent. Most of the howls came from what she assumed to be younger wolves. One table in the corner was silent, their disapproving eyes on her. There she noticed Julie and Darrel from the art gallery.

The senior wolves. Obviously they did not approve of a witch trying to win their alpha. She'd known going in not everyone would want her here. At least now she saw where her opposition lay.

By the direction of Kieran's gaze, the wolf was picking up on the same thing she was.

"Ready?" he said to her.

"Always," she replied.

Tossing her a grin, he led her toward the senior table while the noise levels in the cabin returned to where they'd been before her surprise appearance.

"Alpha," the wolves murmured when they approached.

"It's good to see you all," he said. "Chloe, allow me to introduce you to my advisors. They help keep the pack stable."

"It's a pleasure to meet you all."

One chair had been set at the end of the table, obviously for Kieran. She glanced around to see where she could sit but the benches were completely full. Before she could wonder where she'd be eating dinner, Kieran gestured to one of the wolves who seemed to be on serving duty.

"Another chair," he said.

The man bowed and hurried away to carry out the order.

"Chloe can sit beside me," Julie said with a smile. "I'm sure we can make room."

"Thank you," he replied. "But I rather she stay beside me."

Even she could see those words were like gas on a fire. As a chair was set beside Kieran's at the head of the table, she could see this move was winning her no friends. After all, in the eyes of the pack she wasn't his mate, just his girlfriend. She had no claim to the respect an alpha's partner could demand.

Still, she took her seat, not wanting to cause more conflict. Plates of food appeared before them like magic and, despite her nerves, her mouth watered in anticipation.

"Has everyone arrived?" Kieran asked one of the men at his side. "Traffic delayed us."

"A few families are due this evening. We'll leave the guide fires lit until midnight."

"Chloe."

She turned to her left and saw a familiar face at her side.

"Niall," she said with an honest smile. "It's good to see you again."

"I wasn't sure you'd really come."

She smiled, falling into her role. "Kieran took some convincing but I held my ground. I'm done hiding in the shadows while he decides whether we're serious or not."

"Good for you," he said, pointing a fork at her. "So what do you think of this gathering so far?"

"That was quite the welcome. Do all Kieran's guests stun the entire room to silence?"

Niall chewed a mouthful of potatoes as he watched her. "He hasn't brought anyone to the retreat. Not since…"

"Lisette," she said, thanking her stars she'd been filled in.

Niall's expression lightened. "Yes, since Lisette. She broke him pretty badly."

Chloe dropped her gaze to her dinner. "I'm putting him back together."

"Then this might be an eye-opening week for you, witch."

She swallowed a piece of chicken before replying, "He's worth it."

As she ate she found her words were no lie. The line between her role and her desires was growing more and more blurred. One thing both sides of her agreed on was that Kieran was a man worth fighting for.

Chapter Fifteen

Though she'd retreated to the cabin after dinner to give Kieran a chance to catch up with his people, there was only so much one could do alone in the woods.

Chloe lay on the bed, staring up at the wooden ceiling. Beyond a pack of cards and a few worn books, there wasn't any sort of entertainment up here. Wanting to really immerse herself in this experience, she'd left most of her technology at home, figuring the lack of wifi would make it largely obsolete anyway.

Now she wished she'd loaded her cell with games.

Sighing, she pushed herself off the bed and did yet another circle around the cabin's interior. It had been hours since dinner. Surely Kieran was done with his meetings for the night.

"They can't expect me to stay cooped up in here," she reasoned, grabbing her hoodie. A walk around the camp would do her good, as long as she stuck to the main paths.

Mind set, she shrugged into the sweater and stepped out of the cabin.

Cool night air hit her as she jogged down the steps. All the paths around the camping zone were lit with small garden lamps so at least she didn't need to worry about falling down a hill.

The stars twinkled overhead as she walked along the dark path. Though not yet full, the moon's light helped illuminate the woods. It was beautiful here. It'd been years since she'd ventured far from the city, and she was beginning to understand the desire to travel, to see new and changing sights. Maybe she'd been caught in a rut. One Kieran was succeeding in shaking her out of.

Rounding the bend, she saw a group of dark shapes milling before the main hall. Chloe paused, not wanting to intrude. She was about to turn away when a hand shot up into the air, waving at her.

Adjusting her course, she closed the distance between her and the group. Excitement practically vibrated in the air. Whatever they were doing, the wolves were in high spirits.

"Hey," the waver called, pushing her way to the edge of the group.

"Kate," she said, recognizing the young woman from Kieran's soccer group.

"You made it."

Chloe stopped beside her. "To what?"

"It's the opening of the mating moon season," one of the nearby wolves told her. "We always play a game."

"Cool," she said. "I love games."

That earned her a few more smiles, though she could have sworn from the knowing looks in the women's eyes she was missing something.

"Yes, you do," a deep voice rumbled in her ear as hands descended on her shoulders. "But I'm not sure you want to play this one, my Chloe."

She leaned back into Kieran's touch, not surprised to find

him in the crowd. "Why not?"

"Gather around everyone," Darrel called out. "We're about to start."

Chloe moved with the crowd, rising to her tiptoes to see the older man.

"The rules are simple. Our lead runners will get a five-minute head start before their partners give chase. Should you need help, simply howl; someone will be along to assist you."

That instruction brought a round of chuckles from the crowd.

"We run?" she asked, frowning.

"And we chase," Kieran said into her ear. "Still want to play?"

"But that's the objective? How do we win?"

Snickers were quickly covered all around her.

"That's two different questions, dear," the woman by her side said.

"There's a natural spring in the middle of the woods," Kate explained. "Beside the pool is a white flag. If you reach it, you win the game."

"Got it," Chloe said.

"But no one ever reaches the flag," one of the nearby men said.

"Why?"

All around her couples exchanged lust-filled glances.

"Oh," she whispered, understanding dawning. This wasn't capture the flag, this was the werewolf version of foreplay. No one ever reached the flag because that wasn't the objective of the game. Glancing around she realized there were no children present. This was definitely an adult pastime filled with only happy couples.

"Told you this wasn't your kind of game," Kieran whispered to her.

No, it wasn't but how did she extricate herself without sending the message loud and clear that she didn't want to have sex with their alpha in the woods?

"Witches are too weak for such activities," Darrel said as she tried to puzzle out a solution. "You can wait with the younger wolves inside the main hall."

She stiffened. "I beg your pardon?"

"I'm merely stating fact," he replied. "In a few minutes these woods will be filled with wolves. Do you really want to sprint through them?"

No, but there was no way she'd admit that to her biggest fan.

"No one here would hurt me. Kieran would eat them if they tried. Plus once I got my hands on them I'd turn them into something far less pleasant than a wolf."

Good-natured laughter answered her words as Darrel's frown deepened.

She spun to face Kieran, giving her back to the upset wolf. "Bet you I can reach the flag before you reach me. If I win, you escort me back to the main hall like a gentleman."

It was a good plan. If she won the flag, the game was over, for her at least. No one would question why she'd then march out of the woods alone.

But the look in Kieran's eyes was far from understanding. Heat snapped in his dark gaze as a slow smile curved his lips. "And if I win?"

She swallowed.

Reaching out, he caught her hips and pulled her close. "I'm sure I'll think of something."

Staring up into his hungry face, she realized she'd made a tactical error. Challenging him may have gotten Darrel off her back, but her taunt had been very public. His people would be expecting him to win.

And Kieran was not one to lose on purpose.

"Kieran," she whispered in warning, for his ears only.

"Hush," he said with a grin. "You should know better than to dare a wolf. We love to play with our mates."

The words arced through her like lightning. Judging by his stunned expression, it'd caught him by surprise, too. Chloe didn't need to turn her head to hear the whispers rippling through the crowd. No doubt Darrel would be glaring daggers at her.

Trying to cover his slip, she said, "I don't know where the pool is and everyone else does. Aren't I at a disadvantage? You could run straight there and lie in wait."

"The pleasure comes from the chase," one woman said to her. "He's not going to cheat himself out of the best part, never fear."

"All runners to the starting line," Darrel called.

The crowd started to split up as she glanced at her partner.

"Go," Kieran said, looking more like his old self. "I'm counting on you giving me a good chase."

She tossed a few curls over her shoulder with a mock scoff. "The day a wolf can catch a witch is the day the sun rises in the west."

Kate grinned at her as she tugged Chloe to the starting line. "Run to the left," the girl whispered. "The pool is about a mile in, but trust me, it'll be a long mile with a wolf like Kieran on your tail."

Chloe nodded her thanks as she glanced around at her fellow runners. Though she'd expected the crowd to be all women, it appeared to be a mix of both sexes.

Dominance, she realized. Whoever had the more submissive wolf in the relationship ran first, giving the stronger predators the chase their wolves craved.

"Who's your partner?" Chloe whispered to Kate.

"Trevor asked me if I wanted to play tonight," she replied with a shrug.

"Are you dating?"

Kate cast her a questioning look. "No."

Chloe blinked, once again reminded of the difference between their races. Weres were so tactile that sex was more sport than love.

"On your mark," Darrel called.

The frenzied energy picked up as the runners took their positions.

"Get set."

She glanced back at Kieran to see his heated eyes on her.

"Go!"

She took off for the tree line, zipping around the people in her path. The dozen of those running had barely gone the length of the cabin when clothing started flying. Chloe jumped over a discarded blouse as the woman who had tossed it transformed into a wolf right before her. The sight nearly sent her tumbling to the ground. In a shimmer of light, the woman was replaced by a charcoal gray wolf that streaked past her at double the speed.

All around her the runners were transforming, jetting off into the woods. Kate cast her a happy wave before morphing to a small brown wolf.

Alone, Chloe crashed into the trees and realized that while the rest of the inhabitants of these woods could see in the dark, she was outmatched.

"Think, think, think," she said. The clock was ticking down. Kieran would be after her soon.

"Light." Snapping her fingers a small blob of light appeared. It bounced several feet in front of her, chasing back the gloom. Unfortunately for her, it would also be visible from a distance.

"Take me to water," she whispered to the ball, adding a touch more magic.

The light hesitated for a moment before zipping off to the

left. Not wasting any time, Chloe raced after her guide.

Luckily, the forest was clear enough that she didn't have to battle through thick brush, but still, even pushing herself as fast as she could go, she'd never beat a determined werewolf.

Veering away from the light ball, she shrugged out of her hoodie and hid it under a pile of leaves. Hopefully the scent of it would draw her tracker away from her main path for a few precious minutes.

What she needed was a way of masking her scent, she thought as she ran back on track. Darrel was right about one thing. Her near human body had her at a disadvantage in chase games.

Movement raced by her right side, though a flash of white fur assured her it wasn't Kieran. That glimpse of another wolf reminded her she was not alone out here—as did the happy yips and growls rising on the air, hinting that several of the couples had already given up the hunt for the white flag.

Not alone out here. A smile curved her lips. Perfect.

Pausing long enough to concentrate, Chloe pressed her palms together as whispered words dripped from her lips. Magic surrounded her, coating her skin in a comforting mist as it twisted under her command. Slowly she drew her hands apart as the shimmering power took solid form.

Opening her eyes she grinned at the two identical versions of herself staring back at her. Though made of magic and not flesh, they would pass as her twins right down to her scent.

"Run," she commanded them. "Don't let Kieran catch you."

Mute, her doubles nodded before dashing off in opposite directions, each with their own blob of light leading her. Let Kieran try to figure out how her scent trail had managed to break into three separate paths.

Triumph surged through her as she pressed onward. She might not be as fast as a wolf, but she was just as canny.

In wolf form, his other half was far stronger than normal. All it wanted to do was run straight after Chloe, to hell with giving her a fair head start.

She's not like us, Kieran tried to convince his wolf. *Give her a chance at least.*

He padded through the forest moving with near silence. Large black paws instinctively avoided the twigs that would snap and the leaves that would rustle. After centuries of practice, he could be a deadly hunter when he wanted to be.

Lifting his nose, he inhaled the myriad of scents filling the air. There were those from the woods, those from the pack, and somewhere, one from a witch. As he walked he tried to unravel Chloe's path. In his wolf form, every sense was heightened. He heard the scratching of a field mouse running for its hole. To him, the woods were not dark but lit with the type of light humans would see at twilight. It allowed him to see the cracked branches caused by someone fleeing. The breaks were too high to be caused by a wolf, which meant they had to have been hit by someone of mortal height.

Padding over to the tree, he inhaled deeply. Lavender and magic. Chloe.

He would have grinned if he could. Every good intention to give her a chance by chasing slowly dissolved. She'd wanted to play a hunting game. Time to learn what it meant to be prey.

His claws dug into the soft earth as he shot forward. Though he was fast in human form, it was no match for his wolf's strength. Trees flew by as he raced through the underbrush, following Chloe's unique scent.

The trail led him to a discarded hoodie.

Clever girl. Pride swelled within him. She wouldn't make it too easy on him. Just like an alpha female—when she was challenged, she played to win.

Too bad I have the advantage. Leaving the hoodie behind, he backtracked until he caught her scent once more. Again he took off, racing after his witch. This time it wasn't long at all until his keen eyes picked up the soft glow of a light source.

Got you. Slowing his speed, he prowled through the brush. Sure enough, the tiny glowing blob of light bounced over a curly blonde head. Chloe glanced behind her, as if sensing her danger, before sprinting forward.

Giving into his wolf's desire, Kieran raced after her at full speed. He jumped onto the path, seeing Chloe whirl to face him.

Her jaw dropped in shock as he launched himself at her, transforming in mid air so that human hands hit her shoulders.

Or would have if she'd been corporeal.

He fell through Chloe to hit the ground hard. Turning, Kieran caught a hint of a smile before the apparition vanished.

"Magic," he breathed, laughter bubbling up within him. And he'd thought Chloe would be easy prey? More the fool him.

Transforming into his wolf self, he raced backward, trying to find the spot where Chloe's scent had split into magical bodies. He was wasting time trying to decipher this riddle, just as she must have intended. One way or another, though, the witch was not going to best him.

The lavender left from her shampoo intensified, and he came to a halt. Sniffing the ground, he discovered three trails all leading in three different directions.

Clever, clever, clever. If he chose the wrong path he wouldn't have time to double back again before she reached the pool.

Two choices. Both seemingly identical.

Except one path made the hair on his body stand just a touch on end. The change was so slight he never would have noticed had he not been concentrating. Chloe's magic.

Anticipation surged through him. He had her. This time, she wasn't going to escape.

T he soft bubble of a brook drifted to her ears.

Almost there. Chloe pushed her tired body faster. If she was going to continue hanging out with wolves she was going to have to start some sort of exercise regimen. Her human body put her at too much of a disadvantage.

Her breath rasped from her in pants as she jogged around a fallen log and burst into a small clearing.

There, by the end of the pond, a white flag waited.

"Success," she whispered, starting across the clearing. Looks like she'd shown her wolf a thing or two.

At least, she thought she had, before a large, black body exploded from the trees.

Chloe jerked to a halt, eyes on the massive wolf before her. He dropped to his haunches, sitting between her and the flag. By the amusement in his dark eyes, it could only be Kieran blocking her path.

Though she wanted to win, she couldn't help taking a minute to admire the sheer beauty of him. Never before had she seen his wolf form, and it was impressive enough to rob her of breath. Yes, he possessed the claws and teeth to do serious damage, but she didn't feel in danger. Instead she wanted to run her fingers through the glossy black fur and see if it felt as soft as it looked. He was as majestic in this form as he was captivating as a human. It didn't seem quite fair that something so beautiful could exist.

Though he might take her breath away, she still had no intention of losing to him.

"Don't suppose you'd consider letting me win?" she called to the wolf.

He gave a sharp yip in response.

"That's what I figured. Okay then, you've been warned." She laced her fingers in front of her, stretching out her hands in a warm up.

She couldn't go through a werewolf, but that didn't mean she couldn't go *over* him.

Chloe launched herself forward. She raced at the surprised wolf, who did nothing but wait for her to come to him. At the last moment she cast out her hands, releasing her magic.

Her feet left the ground as she jumped, flying over the stunned wolf below. Propelling herself through mid air, however, was not the easiest thing to control. Her landing was going to be rough but it'd be worth it if she managed to get her hands on the flag.

A body collided with her as she dropped down to earth.

"No," she cried as she was rolled away from her goal. "Tricky wolf."

"Devious witch," he replied, trying to pin her to the ground.

Chloe twisted beneath him, seeing the flag an arm's reach away. Writhing and kicking, she pushed herself free long enough to grasp madly at the flag.

Her fingers touched the smooth flagpole before Kieran grabbed her hips and yanked her back.

"Too slow, wolf!" She laughed, waving the flag in her grip. "I win!"

"I caught you before you grabbed the flag. I win," he replied, rolling her onto her back while he rose over her.

"Nuh-uh. That's not how the rules work."

"How would you know? You've never played before."

"I say I take this flag back to the main camp and get the wolves to vote on who triumphed here."

"They're my people. I'll win for sure that way."

"I'll take my chances."

Chloe looked up at the man blocking out the moon's light. There was no annoyance on his face, just good-natured humor and something darker. Something hungrier.

"I want it noted I had the hardest quarry this year," he said.

"You're the alpha. Isn't that how it's supposed to work?"

"When it's right," he replied.

Chloe ran her hands up his arms, realizing she was touching naked skin.

"I think you lost something along the way," she breathed.

"One downside of the transformation. Can't take clothes with us." He shifted, pressing himself more intimately against her. "Are you complaining?"

She should be. Instead she shook her head.

"You knew what you were getting into when you participated tonight." His head lowered, his mouth a breath away from hers.

"This is a bad idea," she whispered.

"Then push me away."

She closed her eyes as his hands slid over her hips. His hard erection pressed against her, leaving little doubt about how he wanted this encounter to end.

Kieran ran his lips over her throat, sending pleasure shooting through her body.

The wolves did get one thing right, she mused. Streaking through the woods had gotten her adrenaline pumping and the idea of giving in to her desires was far too tempting to ignore.

Besides, why was she still resisting? He had promised her the end of the deal wouldn't be the end of their affair. So what if she gave in now instead of once the moon was over? The end result would be the same either way.

"Tell me again," she whispered to him.

Kieran drew back, staring down at her in the moonlight.

"This is more than a single night," he said, needing no prompting to know what she needed to hear. "Trust me, witchling."

"I do. More than I should."

His mouth came down on hers.

Chloe bit back a moan, giving herself up to his expert touch. His tongue traced the seam of her lips, demanding entry. She didn't have the will to deny him.

His tongue invaded her mouth even as he rocked against her. Dimly Chloe wondered whether they should be concerned about their location. She'd never been into voyeurism and a whole host of wolves were trying to capture the flag beside them. At least, on paper they were.

Kieran broke away from her mouth to press his lips to her throat, tickling the sensitive skin.

Turning her head to give him better access, she looked out at the dark wood.

White flashed through the brushes.

That same wolf. Looked like they had an audience after all.

"Stop," she whispered.

"Why?" he replied, grinding his body against hers.

She bit her lip as her hips automatically moved with him. "Someone is here."

"Want to go back to the cabin?"

Trek a mile through dark woods while wanting to jump the naked man at her side every second? Didn't that sound like fun?

"Let me get a hand free," she said, wiggling out from under him. Raising a hand to the sky, she whispered a simple spell.

Blue magic shimmered over them in a dome before fading from view.

"Privacy spell," she said. "Now you're all mine."

Mine. That was his line.

Kieran stared down at the woman under him and tried to rein in the lust pounding through his body. All he wanted to do was strip her bare and run his lips over every inch of her creamy skin.

Gripping her T-shirt, he tugged it over her head in one smooth movement.

"Too many clothes," he said.

In response, she snapped her fingers. The clasp on her bra popped open and she wiggled beneath him until the material fell from her.

"Magic makes everything better," she said, grinning up at him.

"Perfection." He drew his fingers down her body, tracing invisible designs over her skin. "I could stare at you forever."

"I'm hoping for something a little more physical than a stare."

"And I never leave a woman wanting." He dipped his head to capture one of her taut nipples in his mouth.

A moan escaped her as he lapped his tongue over the sensitive flesh. She writhed beneath him, and it was all he could do to focus on the task at hand and not sink into her as he longed to do.

"More," she whispered as he transferred his attention to her other breast.

Her fingers delved into his hair, holding him close to her. A quick glance at her face showed her head thrown back in pleasure, her eyes closed. Had he ever seen such a beautiful sight?

Whatever was happening between them, this was about more than sex. Never before had he experienced the raw, primal need to claim a woman as his own. Both his human side and his wolf agreed.

Chloe was theirs.

Shifting down her body, he ran his lips down her torso, reveling in the smooth skin beneath his fingertips. When he reached the top of her jeans he sat back to pull them from her body. She was more than happy to help, wiggling and kicking her legs free.

Task accomplished, she lay before him with only a scrap of black lace covering her from his view.

"Off," he ordered.

Reaching down, she shimmied out of her panties without the slightest hesitation.

Kieran sat back, just looking at her in silence. It had never made sense before, that some people could be happy looking at one body for the rest of eternity. But now he understood. He doubted there would ever come a time when looking at Chloe would leave him anything other than desperate.

Propped up on her elbows, she stared back at him, arching a brow as if daring him to find fault with her. Such a ridiculous notion.

"I've said it before," he murmured.

She arched a brow. "Said what?"

"Where have you been all my life?"

The grin that curved her lips seemed to light up the dark glen. "Silly wolf. I told you the right woman was out there."

"And you're always right," he teased, prowling back over her body. "I can almost hear that becoming my mantra in future years."

Years. Had the word really come out of his mouth? He saw her blink in surprise but didn't want to give either of them the chance to think too much. Right now was a time for action, not words.

He ran his lips over her navel as he pressed her thighs apart.

"Kieran," she breathed.

He cast her a grin before moving between her legs. The first touch of his tongue had her arching off the ground.

"More," she begged.

He traced along her slit, flicking over her wet folds. Her hand reached down to tangle in his hair, a wordless encouragement he had no intention of ignoring. Each stroke of his tongue had her breathing hard, squirming against his mouth as her pleasure built within. When his teeth grazed her clit he heard her muffled cry of pleasure.

"Again, again," she chanted.

He continued his sensual torment, every instinct attuned to her pleasure. He wanted to bring her to the brink, have her desperate for one more touch, but not let her crash over that edge.

"Please," she cried, rocking against his mouth.

With a last lick, he pulled away.

"No," she protested when he climbed back up her body.

"Don't worry, sweetheart. We're nowhere near done."

He maneuvered himself between her legs, which she eagerly opened to accommodate him. His cock pressed against her, ready to drive into her heat.

"Damn," he whispered, pausing at a thought that should have occurred to him before any of this started. "Birth control?"

She snorted. "I'm a witch. I drink a potion every month. We're good."

"Magic," he murmured, leaning up to kiss her. "Such a blessing."

"Please," she repeated, undulating against him. "Now."

Reaching down, he guided himself against her. "Ready?" he whispered into her ear, nibbling on her ear lobe.

"Since the day you walked into my office," she confessed, staring up at the man who, in just a few more moments, would no longer be a pretend lover.

He thrust forward, forcing a cry from her lips. Chloe arched her back. Nothing was small about her were, and it took her a moment to adjust to the feeling of him so deeply seated within her.

"All right?" he asked, trailing his lips over hers.

"Yes." She tilted her pelvis up toward his. Hearing his swift intake of breath brought a smile to her face. Bending her knees, she drew him in deeper even as he shifted to withdraw.

Chloe tossed her head back when he drove back into her. Each stroke was sure and strong, timed to her responses. She'd had some lovers who treated sex as a race, uncaring of whether or not she crossed the finish line with them. Not Kieran. His intense gaze watched for every movement, heard every moan. He matched his motions to her rising pleasure, ensuring a wave of need within her.

Chloe did her best to meet his thrusts, rising to meet each one. Her arms wrapped around his shoulders to hold him to her as she writhed underneath him.

"Almost," she panted into his ear. His strokes increased in speed, matching the rising desire in them both. She rocked beneath him as she strove to wring that last missing drop of pleasure.

He drove deep within her and she shattered. Her cry reverberated in the dark woods around them as her orgasm crashed over her. Wave after wave of indescribable sensation battered her body even as she heard Kieran roar his own fulfillment. Every inch of her skin tingled with pleasure.

As she lay beneath her lover, reveling in the aftermath, she couldn't stop the smile clinging to her lips. Kieran's hot breath panted against the skin of her throat as he sought to catch his breath.

"Worth it," she breathed, staring up at the stars above them.

No matter what happened next, she would never forget her werewolf lover. Not even if she lived hundreds of years.

"Told you," he said, pulling her close. "I totally won."

Her laugher echoed in the clearing around them. "Says you. I'm hanging that flag in the main hall before we go back to our cabin."

"Mm." He nuzzled against her throat. "Let's do that immediately. The sooner we get back to the cabin, my witch, the sooner I can have you naked beneath me again."

Though she'd just survived the most intensive orgasm of her life, her body clenched at his words.

"Yes," she agreed. "That's a plan I can get behind."

As she gathered her clothes, Chloe knew she was in for a long night.

And looked forward to every second of it.

Chapter Sixteen

The sound of birds singing woke her.

Chloe opened her eyes, disorientation momentarily overtaking her. It took a minute to remember why sunlight was streaming into a cabin and not a penthouse. And a second more to realize the arm wrapped around her waist wasn't a figment of her imagination.

A smile tugged at her lips. For the first time in ages, she was waking up next to someone. The experience wasn't one she often repeated. Usually either she or her lovers would leave before sleeping arrangements came up. It wasn't that she disliked the intimacy, but she'd always slept better in her own bed.

Not so last night. Curled in Kieran's arms, she'd slept like the dead. There was something to be said for feeling all warm, safe and…cared for.

Trying to move as little as possible, she turned her head to glimpse the man behind her, only to find his brown eyes on her.

"You're awake?" she whispered, spinning the rest of the

way so that she faced him.

"Not long," he replied. His arm tightened around her waist to pull her closer.

Chloe pillowed her hands under her head as she watched him. "Are you trying to think of a polite way to hustle me out of bed?" she teased.

He shook his head. "You're exactly where you belong."

Yes, her inner voice agreed. For the first time in a century she was perfectly happy. Something deep inside her had clicked into place, banishing the worries that had followed her since the day she was born. Gone was the fear she'd make the wrong decision and lose the life she'd built, that she'd end up alone and scared once more. No matter how successful Fated Match grew or how secure her life became, those doubts had been impossible to scrub from her mind.

But right now they were silent.

Because I'm not alone anymore. The M-word would send Kieran running for the hills, but she didn't know any other way to explain what was happening to her. This wasn't about sex. She wasn't a stranger to taking lovers. Kieran was simply different. He was changing her, changing the direction she'd thought her life was taking.

She just prayed she was having the same effect on him.

"Deep thoughts," he said, brushing a thumb over her cheek.

"Yeah."

"Regrets?"

She shook her head. "Never. No matter how this plays out."

A grin split his face. "I'll tell you how this plays out. We get through a day full of my advisors snipping at our relationship then we fall back into bed tonight. Rinse and repeat until this retreat is over."

"And then?"

"Then we go home," he replied.

Home. A pang of longing squeezed her heart. "Yours or mine?" she asked.

An infinitely gentle expression slid over his face. "I have a feeling they are the same thing."

She nodded, her throat tight.

"We go home," he continued. "And turn this charade into a reality."

"A real relationship. I thought you were allergic to those."

"Me, too. Then I wound up in your office, and you took a wrecking ball to my life."

She propped herself up on his chest, staring down at him. "You say the sweetest things."

Her wolf smiled, curling her hair around his fingers. "I never thought I'd be saying these things to another woman ever again."

"Lisette did a real number on you."

"An experience like that…"

"Can break you to pieces," she said. Leaning down she pressed a light kiss over his heart. "Luckily, I love a challenge."

"I'll try," he promised. "To be whole for you."

She watched him silently. A tiny nugget of worry reformed. The truth of the matter was, her lover's heart had been destroyed before they met. As much as she wanted to believe she was enough to reform it, there was always the chance that some wounds were just too deep. What if he could never love her the way she needed?

"We have time," she said. Time to help him move beyond Lisette and look to the future.

"Time," he agreed. "Though not at the moment. We'll miss breakfast if we're not careful."

She groaned, dropping her forehead to his chest. "I don't want to move."

"Looks like I did something right last night."

Chloe pushed away from him with a roll of her eyes. "Laugh it up, wolf. I'll thank you to remember the white flag is hanging in the main hall. Everyone will know I won."

"I still contest that point," he said with a chuckle.

Yeah, she decided as she reached for her clothes. They'd both gotten exactly what they needed last night.

Her good mood lasted exactly until she sat down for breakfast with the older wolves. Niall smiled at her presence but the others treated her to stonily silent stares.

Round two, she thought with a sigh, cutting into the pancakes before her.

"The last of the stragglers arrived last night," Niall said. "Everyone's accounted for. At least those of the pack who planned on coming. There are still a dozen or so out of state."

"Good turn out this year," Kieran replied.

"We have your girl to thank for that. Everyone wanted a look at the witch that finally got you to commit."

Chloe glanced up from her food. "Please tell me you're kidding."

"Nope," Niall replied. "Highest numbers in five years." He leaned closer to her and added, "You'll be happy to know your popularity rose significantly when the others saw that white flag hanging over the stairs this morning."

"You all wanted to see your alpha lose?"

Niall shook his head. "I think they wanted to see someone unafraid to beat him."

"We're still deciding exactly who beat whom," Kieran put in. "I, for one, am looking forward to a rematch tonight."

Heat bloomed on her cheeks as she dug her elbow into her lover's side but that only earned her the chuckles of both men sitting beside her.

"The hunt is scheduled for tonight," Darrel's steely voice cut in. "You will be otherwise engaged, Kieran."

That cut the laughter short.

"Hunt?" Chloe asked quickly, hoping to diffuse the tension. "Sounds like fun."

Darrel's eyes flicked to her. "This is one event you will not be participating in, magic or no."

"Why do you assume—"

Kieran squeezed her hand under the table. "Think, Chloe," he whispered. "We're a group of wolves and these woods are full of life. Do you really want to run by my side as I take down a deer?"

"Ah, ick," she said. "Count me out."

The look on Darrel's face made her wish she was far more bloodthirsty than she was.

"What other events do you have planned for the retreat?" she asked. "I'm looking forward to meeting all of the pack."

Her dining mates exchanged glances at her announcement.

"Why not use this time to relax?" Darrel offered instead. "I'm sure your city life is hectic. Setting up all those dates and what not."

She narrowed her eyes. "It is," she agreed. "However, I came to support Kieran and meet those important to him. I'm not going to sit in my cabin and read the days away."

The man sitting next to Darrel cleared his throat. "I'm sure Darrel meant nothing of the sort," he said diplomatically. "We're just trying to think long term. There is no need for you to…tax yourself."

"Vance," Kieran growled in warning.

"Why?" Chloe asked. "Because I won't be around next year so you don't want to raise your pack's hopes?"

Vance met her gaze head on, not looking away. "Exactly."

By her side Kieran tensed. He'd leap to her defense if she let him, but he'd wanted to find a strong fake lover for a reason. Laying a hand on his arm, she turned to face the table. "Let me make something clear," she said, addressing all the advisors. "I know you don't like me and I don't particularly care. Yours is not the opinion that matters. Theirs is." She gestured to the rest of the room, the wolves happily eating their breakfast and chatting among themselves. "This pack is more than a disapproving group of ten. If Clearwater, as a united front, took issue with a witch being with your alpha, I might give the concerns some credence. All I am hearing right now is a bigoted group of old wolves refusing to step into the twenty-first century. I'm a witch. Big deal. My genes don't change the way I feel about Kieran, or the fact that I want to be a part of this pack."

Kieran squeezed her hand in encouragement when she paused. Smiling at him she said, "I have no intention of going anywhere, so I will spend this time getting to know the people who matter to my lover. And as far as I've seen, they are more interested in their alpha being happy than the magic in my blood. Perhaps you should take your cues from your people rather than your prejudice."

Silence greeted her words, but she wasn't blind to the anger in several pairs of eyes. It would take more than a handful of days to win these people over, but if she and Kieran had the time she hoped they would, then she'd crack them eventually. Right now, though, she had no intention of suffering through more thinly veiled insults.

"In fact, I think I'll start getting to know your pack this morning," she said to Kieran, leaning over to press a kiss to his lips. "Enjoy you're breakfast, darling."

He caught her when she would have drawn back, and deepened the kiss. Chloe smiled against his lips, feeling his approval. Warmth bloomed inside her to know she had a partner who liked when she stood up for herself, even though his wolf must have been chomping at the bit to do it himself.

"Try not to eat anyone alive," he whispered against her lips.

"I'll be good. Don't make your advisors suffer too much for this."

"Just a little," he agreed.

Grinning, she grabbed her plate and stood then scanned the other tables for a familiar face. Spotting Kate, she made a beeline for the woman. She meant what she said to Darrel. She wanted to get to know Kieran's people, and she couldn't do that with her lover attached to her side.

"Looking for a table?" Kate asked when she grew close.

"A little friendly conversation wouldn't go amiss," she said.

The group of women exchanged glances before they scooted down on the benches to make room.

"If you want to eat with us," one said, "then the price is the story of how you bested the alpha last night."

Chloe grinned as she took her seat. "That's a tale I'll happily tell a dozen times."

As she launched into the explanation of how she'd used her magic, she glanced over at Kieran. The approval in his eyes was impossible to miss.

Maybe this can work. Maybe I really can have a place here. Not just a lover, but a pack.

A family.

Chapter Seventeen

Chloe dragged herself back toward the main hall. Her day had been filled with more physical activity than she usually got in a month. After breakfast she'd volunteered to help watch the cubs. Little did she know just how much of a disaster-waiting-to-happen a group of weres under the age of ten could be. Though she'd spent exhausting hours running after toddlers trying to chew everything they could find, or to climb the tallest trees with their baby claws, at least the experience had allowed her to meet a number of the cub's parents. Some were reserved in their judgment as to whether a witch could integrate with their group, but none seemed morally opposed to her presence. She counted that as progress.

Once free of the children, she'd found herself in a kayak on the lake. The invitation had sounded fun in theory, except she'd forgotten to account for weres' endless energy. The group of kayakers circled the lake three times at top speed before they'd burned off enough steam. Chloe wanted nothing more than a nap by the time she returned to dry land. She'd never tell, but by the third lap, her magic had been doing more of the work than her muscles.

"Need to sign up for the gym," she muttered to herself as she went in search of a snack in the main hall. "ASAP."

"Chloe, over here."

Looking up, she saw the soccer group from the city perched on the benches outside the main hall.

"Hey guys," she said, adjusting her course to bring her to them. "Nice to see you all again."

"We're glad you made it," Sasha said. "The boys want a rematch."

Please let them say tomorrow. If she had to play soccer right now she'd probably face plant on the field before the first goal was scored.

"Out here I'm sure we'll be more than a match for your mojo," Trevor put in. "No prying eyes to limit us."

"I'll beat you any time," she replied, joining them on the benches. "As long as it's not in the next ten hours."

Eight sympathetic sets of eyes focused on her. "Wolf life a little tougher than you're used to?" Rachel asked.

"Let's just say if you guys could bottle your energy you'd all make millions."

Chad laughed, slinging his arm around Sasha. "It's just because everyone is in such good spirits. We haven't felt this fantastic in ages."

"Tell me about it," Trevor agreed. "I heard my parents wondering if you were good for the alpha but from what I can see, you're brilliant. This past month it's been like a knot in my shoulders has just vanished."

The other wolves nodded in agreement.

"What?" Chloe asked, blinking in surprise.

"It's a pack thing," Kate said, looking to the others as if to seek help explaining. "Weres are pretty connected to each other."

"And the alpha is at the head of everything," Sasha put in.

"When he is anxious, we all feel it. When he's happy, we feel that, too."

"You mentioned a month," she said to Trevor.

"Yeah. I know you guys have been dating for longer but it was a few weeks ago when it really clicked for all of us. Like a weight was just…gone."

Shock spiraled through her. Their relationship was having a direct effect on Kieran's people? That sounded…

Like something that happened between mates.

"I've slept better this past month than I have in years," Kate said, carrying on the conversation.

"That's why most of the pack is on board with the two of you," Chad said. "We haven't seen the alpha so happy in"—he looked at the group—"ever? Definitely not in our lifetimes."

"What about Lisette?" Chloe asked.

The group shrugged. "The way I hear it, she helped a bit but she didn't provide the same support to the pack that you have. You guys are made for each other," Trevor said.

"Are you going to declare your relationship at the moon?" Kate asked. "I know Kieran said you wouldn't, but why not? Surely you know by now whether you're meant to be."

"I…" Chloe didn't know what to say. Part of her wanted to argue it was too early. No one could know in a month if they were mated. But another part of her argued that mates always knew. It was instinctive, uncontrollable. If she and Kieran really were meant to stay together, they would know by now. Wouldn't they?

"Leave her alone, Kate," Rachel cut in. "You're so pushy."

"Like you weren't wondering the same thing," the other wolf replied. "It's the question on everyone's mind."

It was? Had anyone mentioned it to Kieran? The thought made her a little queasy. He was just getting used to the idea of a real relationship again. If someone mentioned eternity, who knew how he'd react.

"We haven't discussed it," Chloe said.

"Well, you've got time," Chad said. "That's the nice thing about immortality. Tons of chances to get things right."

He had a point.

So why did she feel like her time was quickly running out?

Kieran stood at the window of the main cabin, looking down at his lover chatting with the younger wolves. As usual, she was a mix of contradictions. One minute she'd stare down pack members hundreds of years older than her, and the next she seemed young and innocent enough to fit in with his weakest packmates.

Crossing his arms, he leaned against the sill, unwilling to take his eyes off her.

The padding of footsteps alerted him to Niall's presence before his friend appeared at his side. Together they looked down at the small group.

"You've got no intention to take a mate this week, hmm?" Niall said, breaking the silence.

"Witches and wolves. You know the complications."

The man he'd known since he was a cub let out a soft laugh. "I also know they don't matter if you love her."

"Of course I do," he said, the words coming automatically.

"Do you?" Niall asked. "That's rather fast."

Tearing his gaze away from Chloe, he examined his friend. "We've been together for months."

"Have you." It wasn't a question.

"What are you implying, Niall?"

"After the gallery, I did some digging," the other man said. "Six months ago you were lip-locked with a woman named Candy, and Chloe was seen dating a griffin."

A growl built in his chest he had to force back. "We were

taking a break. Couples fight. It wasn't serious."

"Do you remember what it was like to be a member of the pack instead of the alpha?" Niall asked, shifting gears. "How in touch you used to be with our leader?"

"Of course."

"I don't think you do." Niall ran a hand down his face. "Your parents were happily mated when you were a packmate. Their stability was the bedrock of the group. You've never known what it feels like to follow an alpha you can feel slipping away."

"I'm right here."

Niall looked back out the window. "Since Lisette you've been a wild card. We've all inherited your tension. Then suddenly, a month ago, something changed." Blue eyes flickered back to him. "I think that's when you met Chloe."

Claws pressed against his fingertips as his body wavered between preparing for a fight and the love he had for a man who had always been a brother.

"What will you do with your suspicions?"

Niall snorted. "Not a damn thing. I had your back when we were foolish cubs. Nothing has changed."

"Then what is the point of this conversation?"

"If I noticed, do you really think no one else has?"

He exhaled. "It doesn't matter. Once this retreat is over things will go back to normal."

"Will you let her go?"

He didn't answer. Didn't have one to give. Let Chloe go? It was an inconceivable thought. He couldn't imagine going home to an empty apartment or making it through the days without a guarantee that he'd get to see her, touch her.

They might have set out a month ago to fool the world into thinking they were meant to be, but now he rather thought the joke was on him. For better or worse, Chloe had wormed her way into a heart he hadn't thought he still possessed. He'd survived a catastrophic loss once. He wasn't sure he could do it again. He'd learned the hard way that love only brought pain. It was to be avoided at all costs. But Chloe didn't see the world that way. She didn't understand his damaged heart was the last thing she should ever want.

"The pack benefited from your relationship with Lisette," Niall said. "But I haven't felt this level of peace and solidity since your parents ruled."

"She's not my mate," he said, trying to ignore the fact that an outsider had brought the very harmony his pack had been missing.

"Why?"

"I can't be paired with a witch."

Niall shrugged. "You've proven pretty conclusively over the years that a wolf wouldn't work for you. You need a woman able to go toe-to-toe with you without challenging your inner animal. No were would be able to meet that need."

"I barely know her."

That earned him a chuckle. "You never looked at Lisette the way you've looked at Chloe these past days."

The words brought him up short. Was it true? He tried to picture what he and Lisette had had. It had been consuming, passionate to the point that nothing else had mattered. His world had narrowed to focus only on her. She'd been his darkest obsession. But had she been the love of his life?

"Time doesn't matter to your wolf," Niall continued. "Does it want to claim Chloe on the full moon?"

Yes. It wanted her more than it had ever wanted another. His wolf clawed at the edges of his consciousness communicating one single thought.

Mine.

"Maybe next year," he temporized, hardly able to believe the words had left his lips. After centuries of avoiding taking a mate, was he truly considering accepting that level of commitment?

Niall clasped a hand on his shoulder. "If I ever found a woman who could calm my wolf the way I suspect she calms yours, I'd claim her the first chance I got. Don't wait too long, brother, or you might miss your happy ending."

The hand left his shoulder as the other man turned to leave.

"Keep these thoughts to yourself, Niall," he cautioned.

"Always."

The footsteps faded as Kieran focused on Chloe once more.

She tossed her blonde curls over her shoulder, shading her eyes as she looked up at his window.

He raised a hand to wave to her. Her smile faltered for a moment before she waved back.

Mine, he mused again as she returned her attention to her friends. After centuries without a mate, the thought of taking one now was daunting.

But the thought of losing her was worse.

Do I love her? He needed her, lusted for her, liked her. But was it love? Could he even feel that emotion again?

But he knew enough of Chloe to know there was only one way she'd accept him as her mate. If he wasn't head over heels for her, she'd walk away without a backward glance.

Which meant he had to be very, very sure before he made a move that could destroy everything.

Chloe had meant to stay awake until Kieran finished his hunt. Truly she had. But despite her best intentions, she was asleep by the time her head hit the pillow. She'd pay for her exertions the next day when her tired muscles were forced back to life.

That time came far sooner than she expected, when lips running down her throat roused her to consciousness.

A body pressed down on hers as those clever lips trailed over her skin.

"Kieran," she breathed.

"You looked so tempting," he whispered in her ear. "I couldn't resist."

"Mmm," she said, raising her hands to frame his face. "Good."

His hair was wet against her fingers, signaling a recent shower.

"How was your event?"

"I wanted it over with," he replied. "My quarry wasn't in the woods."

"No, it was trying to recover from a day keeping up with werewolves."

"You weren't complaining about my stamina last night."

She grinned, wrapping her arms around his shoulders. "True. Going to try to prove your mettle again?"

"Wolves love a challenge." He kissed her before she could think of anything else to say.

Closing her eyes, Chloe relaxed into his embrace. Her tongue flicked out to tangle with his as he deepened the kiss. Desire woke within her, obviously not caring that she should be tired. All Kieran had to do was run his lips over hers and she was ready and willing to play any game he devised.

Her hand slipped between their bodies to find he'd come to bed naked.

"Thinking ahead?" she murmured as her hand closed around his already erect cock.

"A wise man is always prepared."

"Precisely why I'm wearing an easily removable nightie," she replied before doing exactly that. Tugging the cotton over her head, she dropped the dress to the floor and returned her attention to her lover.

"What do you like?" she asked as she stroked him.

"Everything you do," he replied.

Chloe pressed her lips to his jaw as she rubbed her thumb over the crown of his cock. The way his body stiffened in pleasure was gratifying to say the least.

"I take it that worked," she whispered.

"Again."

Grinning, she complied.

Her focus was broken when his fingers stroked along her slit. Tilting her head back, she tried to concentrate on bringing him pleasure while he did his best to distract her.

His thumb brushed over her clit before one finger delved into her. There was nothing she could do to stop the cry that erupted from her mouth at the sensation. When his free hand moved to play with her breasts, the rhythm of her hand faltered.

"Getting hard to remember what I was doing," she warned, rocking against his fingers as he pressed into her.

"Good," he said, running his lips up her throat. "Means I'm doing something right."

"Mm." A second finger joined the first to send spikes of pleasure through her.

"More," she told him. "Please."

He shifted his position, catching one of her legs and hooking it over his hip. Kieran slid into her without any more urging. Chloe bit her lip at the slow, steady rhythm he took. He rocked into her not with the frenzied passion of the night before, but with a tenderness that flamed her desire higher.

She moved beneath him to lock her legs around his waist. His guttural groan filled her ears as she pressed her heels into his back, driving him deeper into her.

"Just like that," she breathed, undulating under him.

He bent down to catch her lips as he rocked within

her. Framing his face with her hands, she returned the kiss with enthusiasm. Maybe it was their surroundings, but this embrace was far different from their first time under the stars. That had been a desperate, consuming need followed by a night of exploring every inch of each other's bodies.

This was different. Intimate. Kieran touched her as if she were precious.

Loved.

"Yes," she whispered as he increased his speed. "A little more."

They rocked together, striving toward their mutual release.

"Come with me, witchling," he whispered to her.

Chloe arched her head back, her fingers digging into his shoulders. So close.

A few more strokes were all it took. She flew apart in his arms as her climax over came her. Holding on to her partner, she tried to ride out the sensations flooding her body. Kieran's harsh groans filled her ears as he found the same release she had.

He collapsed by her side, pulling her close even as he stayed pressed inside her.

"Good way to wake up," she said.

Kieran rested his forehead against hers. "Agreed."

"Kieran, I—" She stopped, biting back the words the endorphins flooding her body pushed her to say.

"What?"

"Nothing," she murmured. Wrapping her arms around him, she nestled against his chest. "Nothing at all."

No need to borrow trouble. Not when lying in his arms was as close to perfection as she'd ever found.

Chapter Eighteen

The smile wouldn't leave her face. Chloe pulled her coat closer around her as she sat on a picnic table. The lake lay before her, sparkling in the sunshine. Kieran was meeting with a few of his advisors, and she hadn't wanted to be in the way. Besides, after the athletics of last night she needed a few hours to recharge before she'd be ready for soccer games and pack bonding.

A scratching noise reached her ears. Turning, she saw a white wolf trotting out of the woods.

"Hello," she called as the beautiful creature moved closer.

She'd seen most of the pack in their wolf forms, and while there were some with white patches, none were the pure snow white of this wolf.

"Who would you be?" she asked as it stopped before her. "I don't think we've met yet."

Even as she said the words, she remembered seeing a flash of white the night Kieran had chased her through the woods. Had this wolf been there?

"You're welcome to my coat if you'd like to change," she

offered. Not that weres had much of an issue with nudity. Still, she shrugged out of the coat and held it out.

The wolf tilted its head before it began to transform.

She could see the process a thousand times and still never get bored with it. Seeing a wolf change into a human was like watching an optical illusion you couldn't quite explain. Her eyes tried to reconcile two forms overlapping each other, but her brain didn't have the capacity to explain the phenomena. Instead she just watched in appreciation as the white wolf faded away, leaving a naked woman in its place.

"Thank you," the woman said, rising to her feet.

As she held out her coat, Chloe had to admit the woman was just as stunning as her wolf form had been. Long black hair hung to her trim waist. Every inch of her body was lithe and honed, with legs that seemed impossibly long. The woman took the coat and tossed it around her perfect body. It fell to mid-thigh and Chloe couldn't help but think it added another layer of sex appeal to a woman who looked like she'd stepped out of some lucky man's fantasy.

"I haven't seen you around," she said.

Clear blue eyes flicked to her. "I've kept to myself. It's been a while since I attended a gathering such as this."

"Well, you're welcome to join me," she said, shifting to the side.

Inclining her head, the woman climbed onto the tabletop with her.

"I've missed this place," she said. "I stayed away too long."

"It's beautiful," Chloe agreed. "I wasn't sure about coming here, but I'm glad I was able to see the Clearwater land."

"The alpha brought you."

She nodded. "We thought it was time his people met me."

"Because he's serious about you."

A soft smile curved her lips. "I hope so."

The nameless woman studied her for a long moment

before sighing. "It's been a long time since he was happy."

"Yes."

"So he told you his tale, has he?"

"Enough of it," she replied. "It's taken him a long time to get to the point where he can let someone else in."

"It was her fault," the woman said. "She was too young to be what Kieran needed. Selfish and undisciplined, she didn't understand what it meant for an alpha to rule."

"Did you know her?" Chloe asked. "Lisette, that is?"

"Oh yes. I knew her." She tilted her face up to the sun. "She's been traveling the world, you know. Trying to figure out what went wrong. She thought if she could fix herself, maybe she could fix their relationship."

A shiver ran down her spine. Lisette always seemed like a phantom presence. One she'd never come across in real life. She was a ghost from the past that Chloe had never expected to reemerge. If Lisette had spent decades trying to become what Kieran and the pack needed, she'd be a formidable opponent indeed.

One you couldn't best, her inner voice whispered. Kieran had loved the wolf to distraction for over forty years. A fake girlfriend couldn't compare to that kind of devotion in any way.

Not fake. Not anymore. He cares about me.

But he didn't love her.

"I hope she's had luck with her self-discovery," Chloe said, choking out the words. "Everyone deserves to find their happiness."

Blue eyes met hers. "Aren't you sweet?"

"Not sweet. Hopeful."

A smile touched the woman's rosy lips. "I can see why he is drawn to you. Your youth, your naïveté… It's like he found the anti-Lisette."

Her eyes narrowed. "Don't mistake kindness for

weakness," she said. "Just because I choose to see the good in people doesn't mean I won't fight for those I care about."

"And what would you do if someone tried to take Kieran from you?"

Magic coiled through her. While this wolf didn't appear to be a threat, she certainly wasn't a friend.

"I'd make them regret it," she replied.

Cool eyes studied her, as if taking her measure. "Yes," she said. "I think you'd try." The woman slipped off the table. "I should be on my way. Mind if I borrow your coat? I'll return it next time we cross paths."

"Take it," she replied. The coat was a small price to pay to send the woman on her way.

"I'll see you soon, Chloe."

As the white wolf walked away, Chloe realized she'd never asked the woman her name.

Nor given hers.

"There you are."

Chloe glanced up from her spot curled up on one of the cabin's armchairs to see Kieran entering the room.

"Sorry," she said. "I needed a little break." To think. To wonder if Lisette was a threat she needed to be on guard against.

To puzzle whether Kieran was the man she'd been waiting a lifetime for, or whether her desire to belong was clouding her judgment.

With a grin, Kieran collapsed onto the chaise. "You're only two days in. Just wait until we get closer to the mating ceremony."

Pushing from her chair, she crossed to the chaise and shimmied into place next to him. He automatically adjusted to give her room, wrapping an arm around her as she rested her head against his shoulder.

"You're doing well," he said, running his fingers along her arm.

"Thanks," she murmured.

"The older wolves are still standoffish, as you predicted."

"Doesn't matter," she said. "If you're happy, the pack is happy."

"And I am," he said, tipping her face up to his. "Very happy. Though I'd be happier if you lost a few of these clothes."

She huffed out a laugh. "You'll be missed."

"No one will begrudge me a little break."

Chloe rolled her eyes. "One thing I've discovered in the past few days is that you're always needed. Everyone wants a word with you."

"It's the one time of year we're all together," he said with a sigh. "For those who don't live in the city, this is their chance to touch base with me. Make sure any concerns are heard."

"You're good at your job."

"What I do in the city is my job. This is…"

"What you were born to do," she supplied. "And you take that responsibility seriously."

"There was a time when I didn't."

"Why?"

His fingers stroked her hair, and she closed her eyes, perfectly content.

"My father stepped down partly because he was ready but also, I think, because he wanted me to gain a purpose, a direction. Lisette wasn't pleased."

"I thought she'd like the power dating the alpha would give her."

He snorted. "Oh, she did. She just didn't like the responsibility that came with it. And I only saw her. She was my priority."

"It's okay to love a partner and care for your pack."

Silence stretched. "I'm not sure I can do both," he told her, his voice soft. "I can't lose myself the way I did with her."

Her breath hitched. Was this Kieran's way of telling her they could be together but love wasn't something that would ever enter the equation?

"Good relationships find balance," she whispered. "Yes, you're beholden to another person, but so are they to you."

"Would you leave me, Chloe, if I couldn't be that for you?"

Pain flared through her chest. "I don't know," she said to avoid the answer she deeply feared was yes.

He wasn't ready to talk about love. It wasn't a surprise. Really, it was too soon for both of them. But what hurt was the knowledge that he'd once loved someone so completely that it had consumed him. He was capable of the darkest kind of passion, but with her he still held himself apart, despite their physical intimacy. She didn't want their relationship to follow the pattern he'd set with Lisette, but she wanted to know that…

That someday she would be as important. More so even. She wanted a guarantee that there would come a day when someone asked Kieran about the great love of his life and her face flashed to his mind.

She wanted to be better than Lisette.

An impossible dream for wholesome, plain Jane Chloe Donovan.

The stranger's words at the lake crept into her mind. If Lisette were here now, would Kieran still hold Chloe with such tenderness? Or would she find herself once again passed over in favor of something, someone, better than her?

"We're borrowing trouble," she said, pushing out of his arms.

He caught her before she could leave. "I know I can't tell

you what you want to hear," he said.

"That's fine. It's still new."

"I do care about you Chloe. I like everything about you."

Like. Not love. It was too soon for that lack to hurt so much. What was wrong with her? Maybe the pressure of their ruse was finally getting to her. They just needed to get back to the city, back to normalcy.

But a part of her whispered, that wasn't the answer. That no matter how much time passed, she'd always be waiting for three little words her wolf might never say.

"Come on," she whispered. "We should be getting back to the group. I think I heard there were field games or something up next on the schedule. Everyone will be waiting."

She walked toward the door, only to be pulled back when he hauled her into his arms and kissed her.

Closing her eyes, she gave herself up to his touch. When his hands were on her body she could almost believe they'd be okay.

That it wouldn't matter if he never learned to love her.

H er kiss tasted of disappointment.

Kieran shook his head, trying to focus on the games being carried out on the field before him. No matter what he did, he couldn't shake the unsettling thought.

Inside his mind, the wolf whined. The woman it wanted was unhappy and there was nothing it could do about it.

I'll fix this. Once they were alone again he could—

What? Drive her into oblivion with pleasure and hope she forgot that this retreat that was all about love and commitment was happening to everyone but her?

You need to take a chance, Clearwater. Four hundred years and he'd never met anyone like Chloe. It couldn't be a coincidence she'd walked into his life right when he was facing the truth that he needed to find a mate.

"You are ridiculously easy to beat this year," Niall said, slapping a hand on his back. "Get your mind off your witch and focus on the game."

"One's more fun to think about than the other."

Niall laughed. "Women often are."

Shaking his head, he followed Niall back toward his team. A handful of "stations" were flung around the field, each with a task or challenge that the teams were racing to fulfill. The one before them boasted a tug-o-war rope.

"Come on," Niall said to his half of the team as they moved to pick up the rope. "Who wants to best the alpha?"

Kieran gestured to the four wolves by his side to take their places. He grabbed the rope with them and waited for the station monitor to blow her whistle.

With ten werewolves pulling on the poor rope from either side he was surprised the damn thing didn't snap in two. Still, he pulled with all his strength, grinning to see the strain on Niall's face. There was a reason he was the leader.

Inch by inch they gained ground, pulling Niall and his wolves ever closer to the middle line on the grass.

"A little more," he called to his team.

He should have been focused on Niall, would have been under any other circumstance, but an awareness brushed against his senses. His eyes shifted from Niall to the woods just as a figure came into view.

The rope dropped from stunned fingers, causing the other nine wolves to stumble off balance to the ground.

"What the hell?" Niall grumbled.

Kieran barely heard him. He only had eyes for the woman walking toward him.

"Christ," Niall whispered, moving to his side. "Is that who I think it is?"

She looked different and yet achingly the same. Long black hair hung free and unadorned down her back, swinging with each step. Her body was clothed in a simple white dress that brushed her ankles when she moved. It left little to the imagination, clinging to every killer curve he'd once spent a lifetime worshiping.

Leaving Niall behind he moved forward like a possessed man. Nothing mattered beyond getting closer to her.

Silence had fallen in the field. Every eye was on them. He didn't care.

Her lips curved in a smile that used to light up his world. The crystal clear of her blue eyes met his as she refused to let the dominance of his wolf cow her into submission. She'd always been like that. Beautiful, stubborn, strong.

"Lisette." The word left him like both a prayer and a curse. How could she be here now? He hadn't seen her since the day he'd walked out of their home. The memory of her clutching the sweat soaked sheets to her naked body still haunted his dreams.

"Hello, Kieran," she said, her voice soft and lyrical. "I've missed you."

"Her name," Chloe said to the wolf next to her. "What is her name?"

Pitying eyes turned her way. "Lisette," the man replied.

No.

The woman from the lake stood in the center of the field, staring at Kieran as is transfixed. Neither member of the pair touched but even so, Chloe could physically feel the longing between them. The anger and confusion.

Lisette had told her she'd wanted to get Kieran back. Apparently she was true to her word.

He's with me now. He doesn't want her. Disaster followed that relationship.

And love. A love powerful enough to make Kieran think it couldn't be replaced.

"What are you doing here?" Kieran asked, the words floating back to where she stood.

"I should think that was obvious." Her gaze shifted over his shoulder to lock on Chloe's. "Sorry, dear. I forgot your coat."

Accusing eyes turned toward her, including Kieran's.

"I didn't know it was her," Chloe tried, stepping back with raised hands. Because she hadn't asked. She'd just assumed no one in the pack would purposefully manipulate her, but Lisette was doing just that—making it look like she'd had forewarning and not bothered to share it with the pack. Or worse, with her lover.

"You are not welcome here," Kieran said, shifting so he was between Lisette and her.

"It's my pack, too." She stepped forward, moving within touching distance. "I missed you, Kieran. Did you miss me?"

"This isn't fair, Lisette."

"No," she agreed. "But it isn't just you I need to apologize to. I hurt the whole pack with my behavior. They deserve to hear my regret."

"We've been fine," he said. "Go back to whatever corner of the world you ran to."

"That's the point, my darling. I ran as far and as fast as I could and still I couldn't erase you from my mind. From what I hear of your exploits, I know it was the same for you."

"Those days are over."

"Do you know what I've spent decades doing, Kieran?" she asked, taking another step closer. "I've meditated in monasteries. Gone on vision quests and participated in every journey toward self-discovery I could find. I know I wasn't what you needed all those years ago, but things are different now. I'm different. I found a way to be both true to my wolf and strong for you."

She raised a hand to his face. "I lived in exile for lifetimes to prove I can be what you need. I can put the pack first. Are you really telling me I'm too late?"

Yes, Chloe fists clenched. *Tell her she'd far too late. Tell her you've found someone better. Tell her you love me.*

Kieran didn't move. Not when Lisette's triumphant gaze flicked to her. Not when the woman closed the distance to her former lover, and certainly not when she rose on tiptoe and pressed her mouth to Kieran's.

No. Pain tore through her. All around wolves alternated between watching the couple on the field and looking at her—the outsider witch whose position had just become superfluous.

Humiliation raged through her. She'd signed up to be a fake lover. It was Kieran who had pushed her to cross boundaries that should never have been crossed. He'd promised her she was more than a body, more than a replacement, and obviously hadn't meant a word of it. She'd wondered who Kieran would pick if he had the chance. Looks like she'd found out.

If hearts really could break, she was sure hers was in pieces.

Chloe took a step back, then another. Turning, she ran from the field as fast as she could. She didn't want to be there when Kieran wrapped his arms around another woman, didn't want to see him kiss her back. And she sure as hell didn't want to be there when he looked around to tell her they were over. The last thing she needed was to see the gloating in his advisors eyes as she was faced with incontrovertible proof that there was no place for her in this pack. She should have learned her lesson. Lifetimes of disappointment made it very clear she would never find a family of her own.

A mate of her own.

The camp was empty as she raced toward her cabin. Slamming through the door, she grabbed every piece of clothing she'd come with and threw it into her duffle. She needed to be anywhere but here.

Bag packed, she ran outside and stopped. They'd taken Kieran's car here. She had no way of getting back to New York. At least, not until the pack showed up with car keys, ready to take her to the nearest bus stop.

Collapsing on the steps she tunneled her fingers through her hair. There were no choices to be made. She couldn't strike out over miles of Clearwater territory. She'd have to wait. Which meant she'd have to face Kieran and listen while he described all the reasons why he was going back to Lisette. After all, the gorgeous wolf was all the things Chloe would never be. She fit into this pack, knew the people and the customs. And worse, she was the damned embodiment of any man's fantasy. Whereas Chloe was always the girl who was just a bit too short, a touch too plump. She couldn't compete with this woman from Kieran's past. Lisette was dazzling while she was…average. Boring. The perpetual Plan B.

But the fact she didn't measure up didn't mean she had no pride. She wouldn't absolve Kieran and wish him well as he went back to his former flame. He'd made her a promise that apparently only held out as long as she was the only show in town.

That's not true. He didn't look at anyone else while you were together.

So maybe she had been special. Just not special enough.

The sound of a car flittered past her morose thoughts, and she raised her head to see a gray sedan park in front of her. The door opened, and the last person she expected stepped out.

Darrel stared up at her, arms crossed.

"Come to gloat?" Chloe demanded, raising her chin.

"No," he replied and held out his hand. Car keys rested in his palm. "I thought you might like an escape."

She dragged a hand over her eyes before pushing to her feet. "Why would you help me?"

"I'm not. I'm helping the pack. This situation will be hard enough to navigate without having the witch our alpha wronged floating around camp like a heartbroken ghost." He looked away. "For what it's worth, you have my sympathy. I may not have wanted you for Kieran, but I don't approve of the way Lisette is handling things."

"You mean lip-locking another girl's man in front of the entire pack?"

"It was not well done." He pressed the keys forward. "Take them and find your way home. You can leave the car parked at Kieran's building, and I'll fetch it when I'm back in town."

Gingerly she accepted the offering.

"Thank you," she said.

"I'm sure at some point you will hear them in person, but on behalf of the Clearwater pack you have my apologies."

She didn't want them. Didn't want anything from this pack.

Moving around Darrel, she tossed her duffle into the car and climbed in. She didn't glance in the rearview as she drove away. There was no use in looking back. Not when the cabin she left behind represented a future she'd so desperately wanted.

L ips pressed against his. Lips that weren't Chloe's. There was no scent of lavender and magic, no contented sighs from his inner wolf. If anything, the damn creature was throwing fits that Lisette was daring to touch him.

His initial shock receded long enough for his hands to wrap about Lisette's arms and push her off.

"What are you doing?" he demanded, holding her back when she moved to press against him once more.

"Isn't it obvious?" she murmured. "I'm proving to you we can be what we once were. I swear to you, Kieran, I will never again make the mistakes I once did. The pack comes first."

"Does it?" he demanded. "You came here to ignite a brand new drama."

"No. I came for you."

He shook his head. In all the years that had passed, her antics remained the same. "You could have spoken to me privately. We could have discussed this like civilized people. Instead you ambush me in front of a field of our people."

Sorrow filled her eyes. "Maybe my actions were wrong," she said. "But my motives weren't. Think of it. We could be a true ruling pair. Alpha mates." She shook her head, reaching for him. "Why do you think I picked now of all times to come home? I'm ready, Kieran. I can be what you need."

Years ago he'd have given anything to have Lisette standing before him, saying these words. He'd mourned the loss of her like a death of a loved one. She'd turned him into a ghost of the man he'd wanted to be.

And she hadn't been the one to put him back together.

"Chloe," he breathed. How could he have forgotten his pack had not been the only ones watching Lisette's display?

Spinning around he scanned the section of the field she'd been standing in.

The space was empty.

He'd taken a single step when Lisette's hands were on him once more. "Let the witch go," she urged. "She's not one of us."

He looked back at his former lover and whatever she saw on his face had her taking a step back.

"Chloe is more of a leader than you will ever be, Lisette." He realized the truth of his words the moment he said them. "You aren't what this pack needs, but she damn well might be."

Glancing around at the frozen faces watching him he shook his head. "You're a member of the Clearwater pack and it's your right to be here. But I don't have to stay and listen to you wax poetic about a life we will never live."

Leaving her behind, he stalked toward Chloe's last location.

"Where is she?" he demanded.

The wolves before him cast out their arms, signaling their lack of an answer. Pushing past them, he strode toward the cabin. If Chloe was going to run, she'd pick a place she felt safe. He'd bet every cent he had that was were she'd be.

But when he got there all he saw was Darrel.

"She's gone," the other man said. "Back to the city."

"How?"

"I lent her my car."

His hand was around Darrel's throat before he could think twice. "Damn you," he growled.

The older wolf gripped his hand but didn't struggle, as he stood pinned to the side of the cabin.

"She wanted to leave," he wheezed. "Why would she stay?"

Kieran dropped his hand, his teeth grinding together. "All I needed to do was talk to her. Explain."

"That you wanted another?" Darrel scoffed. "You obviously don't know much about women."

"No," he growled. "I needed to explain I only want her."

Darrel blinked. "She's a witch."

"Like I give a damn. I'm going after her, Darrel, and if you are wise, you will ensure that, should I be lucky enough to bring her back with me, her return will be celebrated. Lisette is not, and will never be, my future."

But his maddening witch just might be.

That is, if he could repair what a ghost from his past had just shattered.

Chapter Nineteen

"Come in."

Chloe pushed into the Fated Match office, shutting the door behind her. This was one meeting she was dreading, but it was like ripping off a Band-Aid. Better to get it over with quickly.

Vivian sat at her desk, surprise on her face as Chloe dropped into the armchair across from her.

"Hello, Viv."

The siren dropped her pen and leaned back in her chair. "How bad?"

"Bad."

"Lose the check, bad?"

"Possibly." She'd run away, after all. Kieran might call that a breach of contract. On the other hand, her presence had become redundant. She'd held up her end of the bargain as long as she was needed. Surely he couldn't blame her for wanting to avoid more humiliation by being publicly cast aside.

"Hell."

Chloe braced herself, ready for whatever her boss tossed at her. At the end of the day it was her fault, her decision to leave. If they lost the money they needed to expand Fated Match it was because Chloe had dropped the ball.

But instead of yelling, Vivian pushed to her feet and walked to the silver cabinet in the corner. Opening the paneling, she reached for a decanter of dark liquid and poured a finger full into two glass tumblers. Returning to the desk, she held one out to Chloe.

Still expecting the axe to drop, Chloe accepted the drink and stared into the amber depths.

"Are you going to poison me?"

Vivian snorted, taking her seat. "We just lost thousands of dollars. We deserve a drink."

"I expected you to fire me."

White lashes shaded the siren's eyes for a moment before she turned her attention back to Chloe.

"You had your reservations going into this and I talked you out of them by offering what you most wanted. That doesn't mean I was one hundred percent sure we were doing the right thing."

"Did you come to any conclusions?"

"I'd say your presence here now is a pretty good indication that we bet on the wrong horse."

She swallowed hard, trying to keep herself together. No matter what she did, she was letting people down—left, right, and center. "You mean I shouldn't have let my emotions cloud my judgment."

"No," Vivian replied. "You should never have been in the situation in the first place."

Chloe blinked. "What have you done with my boss?"

Vivian lifted the drink to her lips. "Contrary to popular belief, I do have a heart."

She'd always just assumed there was a cash register in

the siren's chest, but sure, if Vivian was feeling forgiving she wasn't going to rock the boat.

"Tell me what happened," Vivian said.

A huff of self-derision escaped her. "Exactly what you warned me about. Turns out I'm not one in a million."

Her boss held out her drink for a toast. "Me neither."

Touching the glasses for an obligatory clink, she tried to process the startling confession. "You're dating someone?"

"Almost always," Vivian replied. "But that's not what I meant. I had my heart broken once when I was young. You have a choice ahead of you, Chloe."

"Which is?"

"One, you could let this crush you and become the sad lady with a dozen immortal cats in her house."

"Not an attractive option. What's door number two?"

"Let the heartache make you stronger. Grieve, and then come back wiser with the knowledge that you will never make the same mistake twice."

Like Vivian had, Chloe realized. Her icy boss hadn't been born without a heart. It had merely been shattered.

Just like hers.

"Did you love him?" Vivian asked.

Chloe tossed back the remainder of her drink, enjoying the fiery burn as it slid down her throat. "Yes."

"Damn."

"Yep."

"Well, take some time off. Do whatever you need to put yourself back together."

Somehow she didn't think a week of vacation time would cut it.

"When Abbey got dumped by Lucian you weren't nearly this nice."

Vivian shrugged. "Her romance endangered the survival of this agency. Besides, I hadn't known Abbey for fifty years. I hadn't built this business from the ground up with her."

"My, my, Vivian. Does this mean I'm your friend?"

"Probably my one and only," she agreed, lifting her drink in a salute. "I mean it, though. Take the time you need."

"I'm not sure how to put the pieces back together," she said, staring down into her empty tumbler.

Vivian was quiet for a long moment. "It happens gradually," she said at last. "One day you decide to get up, to go back to your life, and a little piece comes back. After a little more time passes, you smile and another shard returns. There is no magic recipe, Chloe. You can't cast a spell to numb the pain. Not even a witch as powerful as you."

"Do you think…" Her voice trailed off.

Vivian waited with uncharacteristic patience.

"Is it possible to have a mate who belongs to someone else?" It was the only explanation that made sense. How else could she explain Kieran meeting her every need without the reverse holding true for him?

The siren sighed. "We tell our members there is one perfect match out there, but in truth, you know as well as I that connections can be missed. Relationships broken. Promises betrayed. I want to believe mates always find a way back to each other."

"But you don't really."

"No," she said, her face expressionless. "I don't believe it."

Chloe set her tumbler onto the desk. "Thanks for the drink. I'll think about taking time off, but right now I need to be busy. I need…"

"To think about anything else," Vivian said with a nod. "I'll send you some easy cases to work on. If Kieran contacts the office, I'll handle it."

She inclined her head in thanks, knowing that seeing her wolf would snap the last thread of her dignity.

"I'll get to work then." Pushing from her chair, she

navigated to the door on autopilot. All she wanted to do was go home to the privacy of her apartment but if she did, she'd fall apart. She needed to keep moving forward. One foot in front of the other. That was the extent of her capability at the moment.

Anything else, and she'd break into a thousand pieces.

She spent the day staring at a single file. Though she'd told Vivian the truth when she'd said she didn't want to be alone with her thoughts, it seemed that thinking was all she was able to do.

As if on repeat, her brain kept playing the scene of Lisette and Kieran meeting once more.

On the one hand, logically, it was hard to blame him. He'd been very upfront about his intentions when she'd signed their agreement. Hell, he'd even been open about Lisette, eventually. Just because her heart had become involved was no guarantee his would have. He had the right to love whomever he wanted.

But on a far less rational side, she wanted to scream—to break things and make him hurt the way she did. She had thought...

She had thought he was her mate. As illogical and silly as it sounded, she'd thought they were the fairytale. The couple destined to be together. And he had thrown that all away for a woman who had already betrayed him once.

"His loss," she whispered, trying to focus again on the document before her. It was of a single witch looking for love in the big city. Shouldn't be too hard to match up.

The idea of finding love for someone else cut like a knife. Kieran hadn't just broken her heart. He'd ruined a job she had loved.

Tossing the file back onto her desk, she leaned back in her chair and stared at the ceiling. Maybe she really did need that vacation Vivian had offered. She had some money saved up. She could travel. A fling in Rome might push Kieran from her mind.

Except while he apparently had no problem replacing her, she couldn't imagine letting another man touch her.

The ring of her telephone forced her back to the present. Reaching for it, she tried her best to channel her former sunny self. "Fated Match," she greeted. "Chloe speaking."

"Hello, Chloe," said a female voice—one she'd only heard twice, yet would never forget.

"Lisette."

"You returned to the city."

Her instincts demanded she slam the phone into the cradle. Her curiosity, though, insisted she see why her rival was calling.

"It seemed best for everyone," she said.

"In theory, perhaps. In reality, it's caused a few problems."

"Oh?"

"Kieran is on his way to see you."

Chloe sat up straight. Her heart kicked into overdrive as the spark of hope she'd thought was dead flared back to life.

"He is?"

A soft sigh sounded through the phone. "You know how Kieran is. He might take a few wrong turns, but at his core he's an honorable man. He could never be with me until he'd broken things off with you. Officially."

He was coming to dump her. The battered flicker of hope was snuffed out once more.

"I don't want to see him," she said. "Tell him to turn around."

"Won't do any good. He's already on the road. I just thought a heads up was the least I could do, considering."

"Considering you came back into his life at the very worst time?"

There was a beat of silence. "Worst for you," she said, her voice not unkind. "Best for us. We're meant to be together. Surely you can see that. I'm sorry you were caught up in this, Chloe, truly I am. That's why I wanted to meet you by the lake. I needed to see what sort of woman you were. See if you were better for him than I was."

"As if you would have walked away."

Chloe could envision the other woman shrugging. "I don't know," she answered. "I was serious when I said I will put the pack first."

"It doesn't matter," Chloe said. "He picked you, right? Case closed."

She was silent for a heartbeat. "I realize I have no right to ask anything of you, but I'd like you to remember that when you see him. He might waver, knowing how he's wronged you. He might claim we're not going to try again. Please remember that he belongs here with us. Send him back."

"You are asking me to give my lover my blessings to be with another woman?" Surely her disbelief sounded in her voice.

"You called yourself kind. I'm asking you to be that for him, one last time. Do the right thing and let us all get on with our lives."

"Good-bye, Lisette."

The satisfaction she got hanging up on the perfect wolf was short lived. Seeing Kieran again was a bad idea. Who knew if she'd be strong enough to send him on his way as Lisette wanted, or whether she'd give in to the urge to turn him into a frog.

"I've got to get out of here," she said aloud. The confrontation coming her way was not one she wanted to have in an office with thin walls.

Nor was it particularly one she wanted to have in her apartment where she'd forever remember what would surely be an ugly scene.

So where? She couldn't stop Kieran's arrival but she could take charge of how the meeting went down.

Opening her purse, she stared down at the penthouse keys she'd yet to return. As good a place as any to stomp on a little more on her heart. It seemed fitting somehow that their relationship would end in the place where it had first begun.

He'd driven like a madman. Speed limits had been meaningless in his quest to get back to the city. Still, he hadn't managed to beat the night, which meant he'd have to wait before he could go after Chloe. No good would come from showing up on her doorstep at midnight.

Stepping into the elevator of his building he punched the button for the top floor. The time would be useful in other ways as well. For one thing, he could figure out what the hell to say to her.

Hours on the road and he still didn't know.

Seeing Lisette again had been a blow he hadn't been prepared for. Turning around and finding out Chloe had disappeared, though, was even worse. He didn't know what he could say. What excuse he could offer. All he knew was it couldn't end like this.

He stepped into the hall, rubbing the back of his neck. A week that had started so promisingly had crashed and burned, and it was all his fault.

Turning the key in the lock, he pushed into his apartment. The hall light was on. Odd. Had he forgotten it when they'd left days ago?

His keen hearing picked up the sound of someone

shifting. He wasn't alone.

Moving on silent feet, he slid around the doorway to the living room and looked out over the dark space.

A figure stood by the full-length windows, staring out at the glittering city.

The scent of lavender and magic hit him. Chloe.

"Lisette called," she said, not turning around. "She made it clear you wouldn't leave without talking to me, and I didn't think this particular meeting deserved an audience."

Kieran stepped farther into the room, conscious that he was in a very precarious position. His wolf leaped with excitement to see his lover again. The man, however, knew the dangers of a woman scorned.

"She shouldn't have contacted you."

Chloe shrugged, still not turning. "I might loathe her, but at least she had the decency to give me a heads up."

He rounded the sofa, prowling closer. "You left."

"I did. Breach of contract, right? Want your money back?"

"I don't give a damn about that." And he didn't. He'd double the agency's fee if she asked him to.

"Vivian will be relieved."

"Chloe, we need to talk."

She turned then to face him. Even with only the glow from the cityscape behind her he could see the steely look in her eyes. Gone was his fun-loving witch who saw the good in everyone. He'd done that. His need for her had erased the joy in her eyes. Regret stabbed him like a knife. Did he even have the right to fight for her if all he brought her was hurt?

"Leaving without a word? That was me not wanting to talk. You seemed to have missed that memo."

"I wanted to explain."

"Explain that you used me until a better offer came along? Got it. Thanks. Have a safe drive back to the camp."

"It wasn't like that at all."

She arched an aristocratic brow. "Seemed pretty clear when you kissed her."

"I didn't kiss her." He denied the accusation. "She kissed me."

Chloe rolled her eyes. "Really? That's the best excuse you can come up with. The two of you just sort of tripped and accidentally fell into a make-out session."

He ran a hand down his face, wishing he'd had time to rehearsal this bloody train wreck. "I pushed her away, Chloe. She wasn't the woman I wanted."

For a brief moment she paused, as if caught off guard by his words before shaking her head once more. "Not the woman you wanted? We both know that's not true. She's the love of your life. A wolf that can put you back together and you'll ride off into the sunset together. I know how this story goes."

"Lisette doesn't know how to heal," he said, taking a cautious step forward. "Though she's excellent at destruction, case in point this lovely conversation we're having."

"Don't blame this on her," Chloe snapped. "You're the one who made promises you didn't keep." She turned away from him, tunneling a hand through her curls. "I can't give you absolution," she said. "If you've come for forgiveness you're out of luck."

"I do want forgiveness," he replied, "but not for Lisette. I didn't touch her other than to push her away. What I want you to forgive me for is driving you back here. Letting you think for hours that you were second best."

A cold laugh escaped her mouth, one he'd never heard coming from her before. "Second best is getting to be a really familiar feeling."

"That's not what you are to me."

There was no hiding from the mockery in her eyes. "I'm the beard you bought for a month. Maybe at one time I deluded myself into thinking it was more but we both know the truth."

"The truth that you smashed through all my carefully crafted barriers? That you pulled me out of my monotonous, isolated world and brought me back to life?" He reached for her and she spun out of his grasp.

"Do not touch me," she said, her voice flat. "You do not have the right."

"Then tell me. What do I have to do to earn the right? Name it and it's yours."

She shook her head, backing away from him. "I won't let you do this to me again. You're not drawing me into another fairytale that will smash at my feet. Go away, Kieran. Go back to your pack and make your peace with Lisette. I'm done being everyone's consolation prize."

"I didn't choose her," he argued. "I didn't want her."

"For the love of God, man. You got the love of your life back. Go figure out how to make it work and leave me alone."

He growled aloud at the thought. "Lisette and I had a tempestuous relationship, it's true. But she's not the love of my life."

"Then who is?"

And then he knew. He knew exactly what he needed to say to win her back. Three little words, and his generous witch would forgive his transgressions. All he needed to do was be what she needed.

Except the words stuck in his throat.

His wolf whined, knowing they were headed for a cliff.

"Who, Kieran?"

His mouth opened but all he could think of were the times he'd heard his pledge of love tossed back in his face. Those little words had turned into daggers that had ripped into him again and again. They brought nothing but destruction and ruin to all they touched.

Speak up. Be what she needs.

Silence stretched.

Chloe looked away. "I'm done, wolf. Be with Lisette or don't. It no longer has anything to do with me."

"Anything else," he said, lunging forward. "Ask me for anything else. I care for you, Chloe. I want you by my side. You make me think of spending a future with you when I've never entertained such thoughts before. You're the one I want." He took a deep breath. "Be with me. Please. If you want me to beg, I'll beg. Just be with me."

For a long moment silence reigned. His heartbeat filled his ears as he waited for her response. He'd never thought he could ever want a true companion again, but that's what Chloe was. She was the one for him. He couldn't lose her now. His pride was a small price to pay for her forgiveness.

"You can say that," she said, her voice softer, "but you can't love me?"

"You don't want me to love you," he said, desperation tingeing his words. "Look at what happened when I loved before. It ruined an entire pack and sent my lover fleeing across the globe. I destroy the things I love."

The softness vanished as rage lit her eyes. "Bullshit. We are not your sordid past and I am not Lisette. You are more than one bad experience, Kieran, and if you felt for me the way I feel for you then three little words wouldn't be your Everest." She backed away from him. "I'm not going to keep fighting you. I can't. Let me go heal so that when my mate finally comes along, I do not push him away because of the scars you left."

The pain in her eyes froze the protest on his tongue. Again he was hurting someone he cared about. Being with him had turned his vibrant, happy witch into the desolate woman before him. His love was more curse than blessing, just as he'd always known it was.

"Good-bye," she said, with a finality that ripped into him like claws.

Spinning on her heel, she headed for the door.

He watched her go, unable to voice the words that would bring her back.

When my mate finally comes along, she'd said. Which meant she didn't view him as a possibility. Even though their relationship had started to heal the pack. Even though their touch calmed his wolf in a way he'd never experienced.

Even though he wanted her more than he wanted his next breath.

He ran a hand down his face. Chloe wouldn't waver. He'd seen her stubbornness firsthand. And being unable to give her the words she needed, he had no right to fight for her.

Hell, she'd be better off with a mate who was whole. One that didn't carry damage from the past.

And him? Maybe Lisette was right. They kept circling back to each other. Maybe that was the best he could ever hope for. Not a real mate but at least a partner to help protect the pack.

The idea of doing his duty left a bad taste on his tongue. Not even for his people would he participate in a mating ceremony.

Not if the woman at his side wasn't Chloe.

Chapter Twenty

Pounding filled her head.

Chloe groaned, pulling the covers up to cocoon herself. The sound dulled under the blankets.

Which meant it must be from the front door and not her brain.

"What?" she called, kicking her legs out of her cozy bed.

"Open this damn door."

Jessica. She sighed, shrugging on a housecoat. "Coming."

Padding to the door, she flipped the latch and let her friend in.

"Two days of silence," Jessica said, pushing in with a pair of coffee cups in her hands. "No texts. No calls. Nothing."

"Sorry." She grabbed one of the cups and led the way into her small kitchen. "I told Vivian I was taking her up on her offer of time off. Didn't think more needed to be said."

"The bastard broke your heart," Jessica replied. "Good girlfriends show up with chocolate and offer a sympathetic ear while you bad mouth the ex."

"Where's the chocolate?"

The succubus pulled a bag out of her purse and handed it over.

Selecting a Mars bar from the stash, Chloe gestured to the table. "You can stay."

"So who do I need to kill?" Jessica said, dropping into one of the empty chairs.

"No one. I'm fine."

"Yes, you look it. Three-day-old eyeliner is all the rage."

She stuck out her tongue before taking a sip of the decadently sweet coffee.

"What happened?"

Chloe opened her mouth to lie then caught herself. She'd been doing that too much since Kieran came into her life. The deal was over, the check cashed, according to Vivian. There was no need to continue the charade in her personal life.

"It's a long story," she said.

Jessica shrugged out of her coat and tossed her purse on a chair. "I'm all ears."

With a sigh, Chloe launched into her escapades with the world's sexiest wolf. She left nothing out. Not the relationship lies. Not the fact that she'd fallen hard, and definitely not the reality of Lisette's return.

When she finished, both their coffees were cold, and Jessica was silent.

"Say something," Chloe tried.

"Processing," Jessica replied. "On the one hand, I want to chew you out for lying to me for weeks."

She winced at the accusation.

"On the other hand, I want to hug you and tell you things will get better."

"Can we say the two cancel out?"

"I can't believe Vivian allowed this to happen."

"Kieran can be persuasive when he wants to be."

Jessica rolled her eyes. "His bank account can be." She

leaned forward on the table. "One thing I don't understand."

"Shoot."

"You said you loved him."

Chloe looked down at her drink. "I do."

"Not much."

Her head snapped up. "How dare you?"

Jessica shrugged. "The Chloe I know is a force of nature. She never gives up on those she cares about. Do you remember when we first met, and I found you annoying? You freaking wore me down until I admitted defeat and liked you."

She smiled at the memory. No way she was going to let her new co-worker keep her at arm's length.

"You fight, Chloe. That's one of the reasons your wolf picked you, is it not? So why aren't you fighting for him?"

"I don't fight battles I can't win. Lisette spent forty years with him."

"And that went down in flames. Did he say he was going back to her?"

"Of course he is."

Jessica just leveled a stare at her.

"He might not have stated it explicitly."

"What did he say when you told him you love him?"

She squirmed in her seat.

"Good God," Jessica muttered, rubbing the bridge of her nose. "You're a moron."

"Hey!"

"A loveable one. Listen up, witch. You are dealing with a man who was burned badly by love. Not only that, he's an alpha. A be-in-control-at-all-times wolf. If he did fall a second time you can bet he wouldn't go easily. Might not even be aware it was happening. He's certainly not going to say the words first."

"So what do you want me to do? Crash the retreat and declare my undying devotion to him?"

Jessica said nothing.

"He's not going to say it back."

"If that's true, then at least you know you tried every option. When you get back, I'll come over and bring you all the chocolate ice cream you can handle. But you're not allowed to fall apart until you try everything."

Chloe ran a hand through her hair. "When did you get so pushy?"

"I'm trying to channel what you would say to me if the positions were reversed. You always see the best in people, Chloe. It's your gift. Give him a chance to meet you halfway before you toss in the towel."

"The mating moon is tonight," she said. "For all I know he and Lisette will be officially declaring their relationship."

"Then I suggest you drive fast." Jessica's gaze flicked over her, and she added, "Maybe take five minutes and wash your face first."

She rolled her eyes even as she headed for the washroom. Was she really going to do this? The odds were sky high that she'd make a fool of herself.

Her reflection stared back at her from the bathroom mirror. Raccoon eyes aside, the witch looking back at her appeared as uncertain as she'd ever been.

Because nothing had ever mattered as much as this decision. If it worked the way she wished, she could end up with a mate. If it didn't…

"Chocolate ice cream is always there," she whispered to her reflection. "Men like Kieran don't come around very often."

One in a lifetime in fact.

She needed to make it count.

It had been easy to surf Jessica's enthusiasm until she was in the car. The drive to Clearwater lands had even been smoother than she'd anticipated, the hours filled with her talking to herself as she practiced how to make a last ditched effort to get him to love her.

But when she parked at the edge of the campsite, her courage deserted her.

The whole pack would be there tonight. Everyone would see if Kieran turned away from her and picked Lisette. Her heart would break all over again.

Already the full moon was rising overhead. If she was going to crash this party, it needed to be now before Kieran promised himself to another woman.

"You can do this," she whispered to the rearview mirror. "You are a strong, sexy witch who fights for those she loves."

Even if she did feel like an ant about to get squished.

Drawing in a breath for courage, Chloe pushed from the car.

The cabins were deserted as she walked down the dark paths. Though the lights were on in the main hall, no one was around.

The field. It was the only place close enough that could handle the whole pack all at once.

Her heart thundered in her ears as she changed course. Butterflies erupted in her stomach, fluttering so hard she felt queasy.

As she drew closer, she heard the chatter of a large group of people. Firelight flickered through the trees, guiding her path.

When she caught her first glimpse of the field she drew to a stop under a tree.

The pack formed a ring around the clearing with Kieran standing in the middle. A woman stood by his side that Chloe assumed was the pack priestess able to perform the mating ceremonies.

A couple stood in the center of the circle, holding hands as they grinned like loons at each other. Chloe couldn't hear what was being said but she saw the priestess's lips move. The smell of burning sage filled the air as the priestess bowed and stepped back.

The couple threw their arms around each other in a kiss that was so earnest it made Chloe smile, despite her worries.

The pack cheered the newly mated couple. Clapping and howls alike rose into the night air, the excitement palpable.

Moving closer, Chloe scanned the circle until she spotted Lisette. She wore all white again, standing out against the dark background. Her eyes were on Kieran but Chloe assumed if they'd been mated she would be by his side blessing the couples instead of relegated to the sidelines. She was in time.

If only she could figure out how to interrupt the wolves' most sacred ritual in order to steal their alpha away and declare her undying love.

This was a stupid idea. Just wait until the ceremony is over and speak to him after. As long as Lisette doesn't walk into the circle you're fine.

Not a bad plan, actually. She walked toward a tree where she'd be obscured but able to see the proceedings.

And stepped on the loudest cracking branch in the whole damn forest.

The wolves closest turned to investigate the sound. Everyone's jaw dropped when they saw her.

So much for subtle, she thought as they started to whisper amongst themselves, drawing more attention to her.

"I'm just going to watch," she said in a loud whisper. "Don't mind me."

But it was too late. The damage was done. The rumor of the alpha's returned ex spread like ripples in a pond.

Chloe cringed when Niall crossed into the middle of the

circle and said something to Kieran.

The brown eyes she'd grown to love swung in her direction, finding her even in the darkness.

Couldn't let me catch a break, could you, Fate?

An entire field of people turned to look at her. There was no escape.

Well, if I'm going to do this, might as well get this show on the road. Squaring her shoulders, she stepped forward.

The ring of people parted around her, in utter silence letting her pass. She glanced at Lisette to see the other woman watching her with what looked like resignation in her eyes. Not the expression she'd expected to see from her gorgeous rival.

The distance to the middle of the field seemed a thousand miles, yet all too soon she was closing in on her lover. His gaze had never left hers, but his expression gave no hint as to whether he was pleased or annoyed to see her.

The priestess gave her a gentle smile before retreating a few steps to give them the illusion of privacy, as if Chloe didn't know full well every wolf present would be able to hear them.

With no room left to walk, she stopped before Kieran. Though she'd practiced what she'd say hundreds of times, looking up at him wiped all the words from her mind.

"I forgot something," she said.

Kieran blinked. "What would that be?"

"Me." She drew in a deep breath for courage. "I was so focused on being what you needed me to be this week that I forgot something about myself."

The entire field waited for her next words. Words that would decide if she crawled away alone or took her place at Kieran's side.

"When I love someone, I fight for them. No matter the odds or the barriers. I don't run. But that's exactly what I did when you came to me in New York. I ran. Because I was afraid."

He took a step forward. "You've faced down far more fearsome opponents."

She nodded her agreement. "They didn't have the power to crush me." Drawing in a deep breath, she met his gaze. "I'll say it first. I'll say it a dozen times if you need me to. I love you, Kieran Clearwater. I don't care that you're a wolf or that you have a perfect woman waiting in the wings to make you happy. She can't do as good a job as I can." She reached out to touch him before thinking better of it. Her hand fell back to her side as she said, "I love you and I need you to tell me how you feel once and for all. Do you love me, Kieran? Can you ever? Or have I made yet another mistake?"

The entire forest seemed to freeze for the endless minute it took for him to respond. He opened his mouth but no sound came out. A frown crossed his face and a growl rumbled from his throat.

Her heart froze. She'd been wrong. He couldn't do it. He didn't love her.

Reaching out, he hauled her into his arms, pressing his mouth to hers.

Chloe clung to him for balance, reveling in the sensations she hadn't expected to feel again. When his lips left hers, the sweetest words she'd ever heard dropped from his mouth.

"I love you, witchling."

She blinked, sure she'd imagined the halting words. Though she'd practiced and planned, she'd hadn't really thought she'd succeed in this venture. But Kieran had said the words she needed to hear.

"Again," she breathed, her hands twining in his shirt.

"I love you." He shook his head. "I didn't think I'd ever be able to say that again. Didn't think I had it in me. But when I heard the words from you…" A surprised laugh escaped him. "Then you said them, and it didn't seem quite as hard."

"You mean it?" she said. "Can't take it back, you know."

"Never." He drew her close, leaning his forehead against hers. "Though you'd made it clear we were over in New York, I kept wracking my brain for a way to make it up to you. I've fought bloody battles and three little words stumped me." He tucked a strand of hair behind her ear.

"I know it's fast," she said.

He shook his head. "Mates always know each other, even if it takes them a little while to clue in."

"Mates?" she whispered.

"The first time I stepped into your office, my wolf knew you were different." He drew back to meet her gaze. "You're not a wolf, though. How do witches find their mates?"

She smiled, running her fingertips along his jaw. "I don't know how others do it," she said. "In my opinion, we sign up for ridiculous bargains and then fall for the last man we should ever want."

A smile split his face. "Is that so?"

"Yeah," she said. "One thing I do know, wolf. When I find my mate it will be forever. No more running."

He glanced at the priestess over his shoulder. "Then how about it, Chloe? We can make it official right here."

Her jaw dropped. "You're willing to sign up for eternity when a few days ago you couldn't even choke out a couple words?"

"And I've regretted it every since. My world shrinks without you in it. I never want to feel that way again." He cupped her face. "I know you are it for me, whether you want to take part in the ceremony now or fifty years from now. That reality will never change."

She opened her mouth to argue they should wait, but words failed her. Hadn't she believed he was it for her even when she'd thought there was no hope? The man of her dreams was standing before her offering her everything she'd ever wanted. A family. A home. A mate.

Mating wasn't an accident, and it wasn't temporary. If she believed he was it for her, there was no reason not to leap.

"Yes," she said. "Yes."

His triumphant laugh echoed through the field as he gripped her by the waist and swung her around.

"Thank you," he said as the priestess moved forward. "For coming back tonight."

"Thank you for trying to hire me," she replied.

He chuckled. "I told you back then, didn't I? I'd marry the woman who truly saw the man that I am."

And here he was, about to do the wolf version of that very thing. Chloe couldn't help thinking back over the twists and turns that had led her here. As Kieran leaned back down to claim another kiss, she knew Jessica had been right. Some things were worth fighting for and Kieran would always be one of those things.

"Ready for forever," he whispered to her.

"You did promise me time," she teased. "Now we have an eternity of it."

An eternity of happily ever afters, which she couldn't wait to start.

About the Author

Victoria Davies's love for writing started young. Luckily she had a family who encouraged believing in magic and embracing imagination. From stories quickly scribbled in bright pink diaries, her love of storytelling developed. Since then her characters may have evolved and her plots may have grown decidedly more steamy but she never lost her love of the written word. Writing is not only a way to silence the wonderful voices in her head, but it also allows her to share her passions with her readers.

Discover the **Fated Match** *series...*

LOVE AT STAKE

Abbey is the lone human working for Fated Match, a company that pairs members of the supernatural community with their eternal mates. To snag a young vampire socialite as their next client, Abbey agrees to find the perfect match for Lucian Redgrave, the most respected vampire on the East Coast. As Abbey coaches Lucian through his dates, she can't deny the chemistry between them. But humans are toys for vampires, and risking her heart isn't a part of the plan.

DYING TO DATE

Vampire socialite Melissa Redgrave needs is a little help finding love and enlists the help of New York's biggest supernatural dating agency. And her match is delicious enough to bite. Except that Tarian Drake is a necromancer with the ability to control the dead. When his family decides to make a stand—by kidnapping Melissa—Tarian finds himself caught between his family and unexpected feelings for Melissa. If he wants a future with his vampire, he'll have to stop a war–oh, and save her life.

Printed in the USA
CPSIA information can be obtained
at www.ICGtesting.com
LVHW040703030923
757068LV00028B/157

A FATED MATCH NOVEL

Good girls shouldn't date bad wolves...

Fated Match has spent centuries pairing supernatural
mates together. Witch and matchmaker, Chloe
Donovan, takes pride in helping her clients find their
happy endings. But when werewolf alpha and
millionaire playboy Kieran Clearwater stalks into
her office, she may have finally met the one
man she can't help.

Kieran has no intention of finding his mate. Love is a
weakness he can't afford. But with his pack growing
more concerned over his single status he needs to
assure them all is well. What better way to do so than
to hire a fake girlfriend he can parade around at the
annual pack retreat?

Chloe is coerced into becoming the wolf's temporary
mate, but she's determined to keep their agreement
professional. But her seductive partner in crime has
other ideas, and his considerable charm makes it
difficult for her to keep her eye on the prize. While
these two burn hot when they're together,
behind-the-scenes politics work to rip them apart.

Simply thrilling.   Entangled Publishing, LLC
www.entangledpublishing.com

www.entangledpublishing.com

ISBN 9781682810255

90000 >

9 781682 810255